Withdrawn

W9-BOL-454

TAKE ME HOME

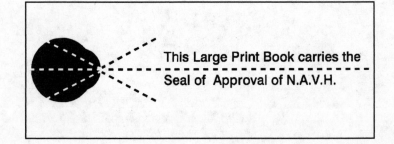

This Large Print Book carries the
Seal of Approval of N.A.V.H.

Take Me Home

Dorothy Garlock

THORNDIKE PRESS

A part of Gale, Cengage Learning

GALE
CENGAGE Learning®

Farmington Hills, Mich • San Francisco • New York • Waterville, Maine
Meriden, Conn • Mason, Ohio • Chicago

GALE
CENGAGE Learning®

Thorndike Press® Large Print Basic.
The text of this Large Print edition is unabridged.
Other aspects of the book may vary from the original edition.
Set in 16 pt. Plantin.

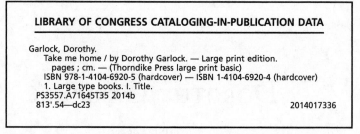

LIBRARY OF CONGRESS CATALOGING-IN-PUBLICATION DATA

Garlock, Dorothy.
    Take me home / by Dorothy Garlock. — Large print edition.
        pages ; cm. — (Thorndike Press large print basic)
    ISBN 978-1-4104-6920-5 (hardcover) — ISBN 1-4104-6920-4 (hardcover)
    1. Large type books. I. Title.
PS3557.A71645T35 2014b
813'.54—dc23   2014017336

Published in 2014 by arrangement with Grand Central Publishing, a division of Hachette Book Group, Inc.

For Larry and Claudette Mix
You deserved this a LONG time ago
I love you both

LIES AND LOVE

When I say "I love you,"
My dearest, it is true.
Yet I must lie to have you,
So what am I to do?

To live a lie for love's sake
Or tell the truth and go?
Whatever course I now take,
I'm still your friend — not foe.

We can overcome the enmity.
We can look beyond the war.
Someday declare the love we share
And be true forevermore.

— F.S.I.

PROLOGUE

Miller's Creek, Wisconsin
November 1939

Olivia Marsten sat in her seat in the Majestic Theater, her toes tapping the floor with excitement. For more than a week now, she'd been looking forward to watching the Sunday matinee of the latest Ann Sheridan movie, *The Angels Wash Their Faces.* Her mother liked to arrive early, so the theater had been empty when they'd entered, but it hadn't taken long for the seats to begin filling up. Outside, the weather was unseasonably warm, the late autumn wind scattering drifts of burnt red and brilliant orange leaves, so few people were wearing coats. Snippets of conversation and short guffaws of laughter echoed around the room. Sally, one of Olivia's friends from school, came in with her two younger brothers and waved from the aisle. Olivia had only just raised her hand when her mother spoke.

"Don't make a scene, Olivia," she scolded.

"But I was just going to —"

"That's not something that a proper young lady should do."

Meekly, Olivia lowered her hand and turned away from her friend. For as long as she could remember, her mother had been correcting her behavior. *Do this. Don't do that. For Heaven's sake, you know better than to act that way!* Elizabeth Marsten believed that even the smallest mistake, the most innocent of errors, could do irreparable damage to a young girl's reputation, to say nothing about sullying her mother's good name. Even now, Elizabeth sat stiffly in her seat, her eyes facing forward and her face showing no hint of emotion, as if everyone in the theater was watching and judging. To go against her wishes was a risky proposition. Though she had just turned seventeen years old, Olivia still found herself wilting in the face of her mother's displeasure.

Her sister, Grace, had no such troubles.

Sitting on the opposite side of their mother, Grace slumped in her chair, her feet pressed against the seat in front of her, absently twisting a long strand of blond hair around her finger. Eight years younger than Olivia at nine, Grace constantly antagonized Elizabeth, seemingly going out of her way to do things that would make her mother angry. Olivia would've felt sorry for her sister, but she suspected that Grace was enjoying herself.

"Sit up straight," Elizabeth admonished the girl.

Reluctantly, Grace did as she was told.

"And stop playing with your hair like that," her mother added. "I didn't spend all that time pinning it up to have you take it apart strand by strand."

"Yes, Mother," Grace grumbled, letting go of her hair, but only a few seconds later, she'd brought her thumb to her mouth and had begun nibbling on the nail; Olivia knew her mother wouldn't let that transgression go for long.

If only her father could have come with them. All week, they had planned on going to the movie together, a rare family outing, but at the last moment, he'd been called to work; as Miller's Creek's sheriff, there was no way of knowing when duty would call. His absence changed things. When John Marsten was around, it seemed to dull the sharpest of Elizabeth's critiques. Often, he would chuckle when his daughters got out of line, saying that it was only "girls being girls." Elizabeth always managed to smile, to agree with her husband, but Olivia knew that the moment her father was gone, they'd get a tongue-lashing for all they'd done wrong.

With only a few minutes left before the picture began, the theater was almost full. As carefully as she could, hoping her mother wouldn't notice, Olivia stole a quick glance at the crowd. Parents and their children mixed with young couples out on a date, everyone growing excited for the movie. Still, Olivia felt a pang of disappointment; she hadn't found who she was looking for. But then, just as she was about to give up hope, she saw him.

Billy!

Olivia couldn't have stopped the smile that spread across her face if she'd wanted to. Billy Tate had been her best friend since they were younger than Grace. She told him everything, about what made her laugh, cry, and even shout in anger. Olivia trusted him with the secrets she wouldn't dare share with anyone else. In turn, he did the same, slipping her letters in school and joining her for long walks beside the winding creek that gave the town its name. It was because Billy knew Olivia so well that he gave her only a quick wink before taking his seat a few rows ahead and across the aisle from her; the last thing he wanted was to get on Elizabeth

Marsten's bad side.

The curtain slowly parted and the projector whirred to life, its light flickering across the theater's screen. A few of the younger children clapped with joy. Olivia understood their excitement; she was ready to be entertained, too.

But it didn't take long for her good mood to sour. The first images to shine on the screen were the newsreels. Like all of the radio broadcasts Olivia had heard and the newspaper headlines she'd read, the subject was the same. War. Little more than two months earlier, fighting had broken out across Europe as Germany's armed forces invaded Poland. Since then, one declaration of war had followed another as England and France had been pulled into the conflict. Olivia listened intently as the news announcer's voice filled the theater.

"Headline Paris! The preparations for war continue as France and Britain mobilize, determined to come to the aid of a beleaguered Poland!" Images of airplanes roaring across a cloudless sky filled the screen. *"The defenders of democracy prepare themselves,"* the newsman continued, *"determined to become the rock upon which Hitler's army smashes itself to pieces!"* Suddenly, the allied forces disappeared from the screen,

replaced by row upon row of German soldiers, all marching in unison. There were so many men that they seemed endless. Interspersed into the newsreel were shots of Hitler screaming from his pulpit, his hand clenched in a fist, spittle flying from his lips.

Olivia shivered. The sight of all of those soldiers, their eyes dark beneath the shadowy brim of their steel helmets, a gun pressed tight against their chests, menacing as they lock-stepped for their Führer, unnerved her.

Ever since the war had started, Olivia had been fearful that the United States would become a part of the fighting. Everyone around her dismissed her worries, arguing that it was a European conflict and that America would remain neutral. Only her father, a veteran of the Great War, seemed concerned; she'd watched him listen to the radio after supper, his jaw clenched and his brow furrowed. Nervously, Olivia looked to where Billy sat; she didn't know what she expected to see, maybe some of the worry she felt, maybe a glance her way to show he sympathized, but he just stared up at the screen.

A feeling of dread filled Olivia. Watching the German soldiers frightened her. They looked like machines, unfeeling and monstrous, hell-bent on carrying out their master's bidding. The thought of confronting one, of being face-to-face with such a man, almost made her sick to her stomach. Fortunately, before her discomfort could get any worse, the newsreel ended and the Merrie Melodies cartoon began. Watching the animated pig chase after the dog, Olivia felt her fear slowly ebb until it was altogether forgotten, replaced with laughter.

Olivia woke with a gasp as her hand rushed to grab the collar of her nightshirt, the fabric soaked through with sweat. Her breathing was ragged, her heart pounded. Even though she was awake and aware of her surroundings, brilliant moonlight streaming through her window and falling across her bed, her nightmare still held her in its grip. Memories of her dream didn't float away, like a leaf caught in a swollen spring stream, rapidly disappearing from sight. She didn't just recall bits and pieces of it either, like a series of photographs.

She remembered every frightening moment.

In her dream, Olivia had been walking alone down a dark and deserted street. Suddenly, the sound of marching footsteps could be heard, growing increasingly louder, as if they were coming closer. Olivia had started to walk faster, but within seconds she was running as fast as she could. But no matter which direction she turned, the noise kept getting nearer and nearer, until she felt as if whoever was making it was right behind her. When a hand violently grabbed her arm, nearly pulling her off her feet, Olivia had tried to scream but the sound remained frozen in her throat. She'd struggled like a mouse caught in a trap, desperate to get away, but she was held fast. Frantically, she'd turned to find a lone German soldier, his fingers digging deep into the flesh of her arm, his eyes hidden beneath the brim of his steel helmet. It was then, just as the man opened his mouth to speak, causing Olivia to flinch, reacting as if the words would hit her like fists, that she mercifully woke.

Getting out of bed, Olivia hurried over and raised the window, letting in the November night. Outside it was quiet, the air cold and biting, the sky cloudless; the moon was thin, a few days short of vanishing. As goose bumps rose on Olivia's arms, she couldn't help but feel that a storm was gathering on the distant horizon, with dark clouds and deafening thunderclaps. As her teeth began to chatter, a feeling of dread still coursed through her; the dream had sunk teeth of its own into her and the fear refused to let go no matter how much she struggled.

"It was only a dream," she muttered.

Shutting the window, Olivia went back to bed and buried herself in her covers. Closing her eyes, she chided herself for her fears and tried to fall back to sleep, but it was hours later, almost dawn, before she finally succeeded.

CHAPTER ONE

Late April 1945

Olivia had just finished ringing up Martha Wolcott's purchase of a new set of laundry pins when she noticed Billy Tate pacing back and forth in front of Pickford Hardware's display window. Even through the dusty glass, he looked nervous, agitated, and more than a little out of sorts. As she watched, Olivia noticed that Billy was talking to himself, occasionally gesturing, his hands jabbing through the air. Every once in a while he paused to wipe his brow with a handkerchief.

"Thank you kindly, my dear," Martha said as she placed the pins in her purse. "I hated to have to buy them, what with the way I've always tried to make do with less for the war effort, but my old set plumb gave out!"

"Everything does eventually," Olivia mumbled, distracted; she was remembering how chilly it had been that morning on her way to work, the cold feeling more like winter than spring, and therefore couldn't understand why Billy was sweating so much.

"Wouldn't you agree?"

Startled, Olivia realized that by watching Billy, she hadn't been paying attention. "I'm sorry, Mrs. Wolcott," she admitted sheepishly, smiling in the hope that it might mask her embarrassment. "I didn't catch that."

"I was just saying that so much has changed in town since the war began that it's almost unrecognizable, especially to an old woman like me," she repeated with a smile that caused the wrinkles around her eyes to deepen. "Why, I doubt you would've ever imagined that you'd be here, working in the hardware store."

Martha was right; Olivia never would have thought that she would be working for Henry Pickford, selling nails, scrub brushes and buckets, light bulbs, and even the occasional set of laundry pins. But whatever direction her life had been going, it had never been the same after a cold Sunday morning back in December 1941. After the bombing of Pearl Harbor and the United States' entry in the war, fighting against both the Germans and the Japanese, Olivia's life, as well as the course of her country, had been changed forever. James Pickford,

Henry's son, along with most of the young men in Miller's Creek, had immediately enlisted in the armed services. Since Henry was a good friend of Olivia's father, she'd ended up taking James's place at the family business. Her days were spent behind the cash register, sweeping floors, and stocking the shelves with what few items weren't consumed by the war effort. Olivia had taken to the work right from the start; she especially liked talking with customers, and earning money of her own was both new and rewarding. Even though she still worried about the men fighting overseas, she knew she had to continue to do her part, whatever might be asked of her.

"I wonder what will happen when the men come home," Martha said.

Olivia had wondered the same thing herself.

Once Martha had started for the front door, Olivia turned her attention back to wondering what Billy was up to. But as she craned her neck, looking through the dusty glass, he suddenly entered the hardware store. Holding the door open for Martha, he smiled warmly at the older woman, sharing a kind word before purposefully striding toward the counter, his face no longer as friendly, but determined, even a bit grim.

Billy Tate had been clumsy as a child, all jutting elbows and knobby knees, and some of that awkwardness still remained; whenever he was in a hurry, as he was now, it looked as if he was about to trip over his own feet and fall flat on his face. He wasn't tall or muscular, but average in height and thin in build, his button-down shirt hanging a bit loosely on him. His black hair was pomaded flat above his prominent forehead. His dark eyes were as thin as his pursed lips. When he was nervous, his large Adam's apple bobbed up and down like a cork in the creek.

He was Olivia's oldest friend . . . Her *best* friend . . .

"I need to talk with you," Billy said when he reached her, his voice insistent. "It's important."

Olivia felt her stomach lurch. "What is it?" she asked, worried. "Did something happen?"

"Not here," he answered. "We need to go somewhere private."

Glancing at the clock that hung above the door to the storeroom, Olivia said, "I'm not supposed to go to lunch for another half an hour, but I guess I could ask if I could leave early."

Billy nodded urgently.

22

Henry Pickford told Olivia to go ahead. When she returned to Billy, she barely had time to take off her apron before he grabbed her hand and hurried them out into the spring afternoon. He moved so fast that it was a struggle for Olivia to keep up. Rounding the corner of the hardware store, he took off down the sidewalk.

"Where are we going?" Olivia asked.

For someone in such a rush, Billy seemed indecisive; he would take a long look one way before turning and staring in the opposite direction. "I don't really know," he admitted. "I just want to make sure we're alone."

"How about the old lumber barn?" she suggested.

"Good idea!"

Potter's Lumber maintained a large building across the street from Miller's Creek's library. Many years before, it had been used to store chunks of ice cut from the frozen waterway in the winter that were then packed in sawdust to be used over the rest of the year. But now, with refrigerators becoming more common, the building sat empty save for some old machinery and a few other odds and ends. When they arrived, the door creaking open on rusty hinges, there wasn't anyone else around, just as Olivia had expected.

"Now will you please tell me what's the matter?" Olivia asked. She stood in the sunlight that streamed through the open doorway, rubbing her arms for whatever warmth she could get, a chill still clinging to the air.

But all she got was more silence as he paced back and forth in the shadows, as agitated as he'd been outside the hardware store.

"Come on, Billy!" she insisted.

"I know, I know," he replied, flustered. "I just didn't think it'd be like this. I mean, I've said the words over and over again in my head so many times that I swear I could tell them to you backward. But now here we are and I'm tongue-tied." He pulled his handkerchief out and again wiped his brow. Glancing at her, he added, "It doesn't help that you're so darn beautiful."

"Don't say that," Olivia said, embarrassed.

"But it's true."

Olivia had never thought of herself as pretty, even if Billy wasn't the first person to tell her so. When she sat in front of her bedroom mirror at night, brushing countless strokes through her long blond hair, the young woman looking back at her didn't strike her as someone who would turn heads. Her dark blue eyes, small nose, and button mouth seemed well positioned enough, but she couldn't help but think that her skin was a touch too pale and the smattering of freckles across the bridge of her nose and along both cheeks was distracting, a blemish. To hear someone compliment her looks, as Billy had just done, always caused her to flush red with embarrassment.

"Is this about the Navy?" she asked.

"No . . . yes . . . both I reckon," Billy answered.

In a little more than a month, Billy was scheduled to report for boot camp at the Great Lakes Naval Training Center near Chicago. Twenty-two years old, the same age as Olivia, Billy had been trying to enlist for years, since just after he'd turned eighteen, but had always been rejected for medical reasons; an illness when he'd been a child had weakened his heart. But Billy hadn't been willing to take "no" for an answer. After countless attempts, and plenty of frustration, he'd finally found a doctor willing to look past his health problems and clear him to enter the service. Olivia had been the first person he'd told when he'd gotten the news.

"Well, which is it?" Olivia pressed.

"What I have to say to you isn't *about* the

Navy, but *because* of it," Billy explained. He'd finally stopped his pacing and had stepped nearer to Olivia; up close, she could see the beads of sweat dotting his forehead. "Ever since I found out that I'd be able to join up, to go off and fight for my country, I've been doing an awful lot of thinking about everything I'll be leaving behind."

"That's understandable," she answered.

Gently, Billy reached out and took Olivia by the hand; his touch was hot and sweaty, almost uncomfortable, although she had no inclination to pull away. "But what really got to me," he continued, his voice catching, "was that whenever I thought about not coming back . . ."

"Nothing's going to happen to you," Olivia insisted; she'd been telling him this for months, trying her best to convince them both.

Billy smiled. "*If* something happens to me," he said, "there's only one person I'd regret not being able to come back to." Pausing, he added, "You."

Olivia couldn't speak. She was both confused and growing nervous.

What happened next felt like something out of a romantic movie. Slowly, Billy lowered himself to the dusty floor, bending down on one knee in front of her. He fished around in his pocket for a moment before pulling his hand free; pinched between his thumb and finger was a simple gold band that shone brightly in the spring sunlight.

"Olivia Marsten," Billy said. "Will you marry me?"

The first time Olivia met Billy Tate, she had laughed in his face.

She'd been eight years old, walking along the bank of the creek, watching the swift spring waters race over rocks and around branches, carrying fallen leaves to some unknown destination. Suddenly, from around a bend in the waterway and beneath the shade of a budding oak tree, she heard a yelp of delight. Hurrying to the sound, she found a young boy pulling furiously on a fishing pole, his catch squirming desperately on the other end of the line. Just as he managed to reel in his prize, the fish clutched tightly in his hands, the boy noticed that Olivia was watching. Surprised and flustered, he'd inadvertently stepped backward, dropping off the bank and into the water. He'd landed on his rump in the shallows, completely soaked through from head to toe, the fish once again swimming freely in the creek.

Unable to help herself, Olivia had burst

out laughing; after a moment's hesitation, Billy had joined her. In that instant, a friendship had been born between them, one that Olivia would come to cherish with all her heart.

Billy had always been there for Olivia, listening when she complained about how overbearing her mother could be; nodding his head in agreement when she grumbled about how her younger sister, Grace, was always borrowing her things without asking; and holding her hand as they raced through the woods outside town, a summer storm coming, the booming thunder behind them, her heart pounding hard, as if they were being chased. In turn, Olivia had shared in Billy's triumphs and tragedies, holding him close after his mother had died of influenza, his head pressed tightly to her shoulder, his sobs shaking them both.

But other than the time when they'd shared a tentative kiss behind Ernie Peabody's barbershop, both of them curious to find out what all the fuss was about, there'd never been a hint of romance between them. When Olivia had pined for Clyde Barrow, a love that would forever remain unrequited, Billy had sympathized. When Billy had courted Meredith Armstrong, taking her to a couple of movies, Olivia had been jealous that she couldn't spend as much time with him as she would've liked, not because she'd wished she was the object of his affections.

She'd thought they'd been friends, pure and simple.

But somehow, Olivia had misunderstood.

Looking down at him on bended knee, her heart in her throat, Olivia would never have imagined that she'd find herself right here, right now, with Billy's words still hanging in the air between them, unanswered.

Olivia's mind raced. Even though she had been cold a few minutes before, rubbing her arms for warmth, she could now feel beads of sweat running down her face, tickling her neck. Never in her life had she ever been so confused, so completely unsure of what she should say or do. A part of her wanted to cry. Another wanted to run away. Yet another wanted to do nothing, to stay quiet, and to wait for Billy to fill the silence that slowly trickled on and on.

"I know this is a surprise," he finally said. "I can see it in your face as plain as day, but I just had to tell you the truth. I need you to know that I've been in love with you ever since the day we met."

Disbelief washed over Olivia. It felt as if she were caught in the web of a dream from which she couldn't wake.

"I've tried to tell you so many times," he continued. "But whenever I screwed up my courage, trying to convince myself that this time would be different, it failed me. I just couldn't go through with it. I was afraid that if I told you the truth, if I admitted to loving you and then you rejected me, it would ruin what we had. I just couldn't risk our friendship, so I kept it all bottled up inside.

"But things are different now that I'm going off to the war. There's no longer any reason for me to hold back." Giving Olivia's hand a gentle squeeze, he added, "That's why I asked you to marry me."

Struggling, Olivia thought about her own feelings for Billy. He was the best friend she could have ever hoped for. He was honest and dependable. He laughed easily, wasn't possessed of a temper, and listened with a caring ear. If his future was a star, it would have been the brightest in the sky. Billy's father was the president of the town bank; while the son had been handed his job, Billy had worked hard to live up to it, and had earned the respect and admiration of everyone he did business with. Because of his family's wealth, and the fact that Billy was sure to someday take over his father's position, whoever became his wife was sure to

newspaper with an amused smile on his face. For as long as Olivia could remember, Huck had been her father's deputy, working alongside John Marsten as he settled disputes, made the occasional arrest, and kept the town safe and sound as best he could. Just like his boss, Huck was fair but tough. Almost sixty now, the years had begun to show; his gray hair was thinning and his belly had grown plump enough to strain the buttons of his uniform. Everyone in Miller's Creek was familiar with the sound of his booming voice.

"One a my tires must've blown," Sylvester answered.

Huck's deep laugh echoed around the room. "Pert near everything on that truck got wrecked," he said. "The radiator's cracked, the windows are all busted out, and the fender's bent up sideways and back, but somehow not a one of them four tires got popped."

"Then it was a deer that done run out in front a me!" the drunk man declared, undeterred in his desire to provide an explanation that didn't involve a bottle of alcohol.

"I don't doubt that you saw *something* in the road," the deputy explained with a hearty chuckle, "but I bet it was a gremlin.

I hear those darn things are mighty common among folks who like tippin' back the whiskey."

Sylvester scowled. "I reckon you think you're funny! Probably fancy yourself a regular Bob Hope!"

Huck laughed so hard his belly shook; Olivia wondered if he wouldn't jiggle himself right out of his chair.

Olivia could only give their back-and-forth a quick smile before her thoughts once again returned to Billy. For the rest of her day at the hardware store, her mind had twisted and turned, unable to believe that she'd actually agreed to become his wife. Her work showed her distraction; she'd filled orders wrong, struggled to count back change, and Henry Pickford had caught her absently staring out the window. The ring that Billy had placed on her finger felt so strange, so out of place, that she'd tried to keep it hidden away from everyone she met, maybe even from herself. When it came time to close the store for the day, she'd hurried over to her father's office, hoping that he might be able to make her feel better. Unfortunately, he'd been out; since she'd decided to wait for him to return, she'd had to listen to Sylvester and Huck's banter.

"Psssst! Hey! Psst!"

Olivia looked up to find Sylvester staring at her. He'd pressed a finger to his lips, as if he wanted her to be quiet. "Olivia, darlin'," he said in what he thought was a whisper; he was still so drunk that he didn't realize that he was talking loud enough for Huck to hear every word. "You gotta get me outta here. How 'bout grabbin' them keys and openin' this here cell." Scratching his stubbled chin, Sylvester added, "In exchange, I'm willin' to give you my truck."

"That old piece of junk wasn't worth much *before* you smashed it up," Huck commented, turning the page of his newspaper.

Sylvester opened his mouth as if he wanted to protest, but then closed it; maybe deep down, drunk as he was, he knew that the deputy was right. With a sudden smile, still attempting to speak in a conspiratorial whisper, he said, "Then how 'bout we run off and get married instead?"

Olivia flinched; the man couldn't have known how close to home his words had come.

Sylvester's offer was enough to make Huck put down his paper. "Olivia ain't near ready to get married," he said. "And even if she was, it wouldn't be to no drunkard like you."

"I told you I ain't been drinkin', you damn fool!"

"That's it," Huck said, standing up from his desk, his voice growing deep, even a bit menacing. "You go sit down on that cot, Sylvester," the deputy ordered. "Only thing that's gonna get you right is sleep."

"How many times do I have to tell you that —"

"Now!" Huck thundered, grabbing hold of the cell bars. Reluctantly, Sylvester did as he was told, grumbling with every step, plopping down onto the cell's narrow bed, and turning to face the brick wall.

Satisfied that there wouldn't be any further disturbance, Huck sat down on the corner of Olivia's father's desk. "I'm right sorry about that," he said. "Sylvester's a good enough sort when he hasn't had too much to drink."

"He wasn't bothering me," she replied, trying to keep her new ring out of sight. "Not really."

"Well, he was about to fray my very last nerve," the deputy said with a weary smile. "Heck, you'd think that after all the years I been doin' this, I'd a learned by now not to talk back. It only encourages 'em. But I reckon I got too big a mouth of my own." When Olivia didn't respond, Huck frowned.

"You feeling all right?" he asked. "It's not like you to be so quiet."

Olivia tried to smile, but it faltered instantly. "I suppose I haven't had the best day," she admitted. "It's . . . complicated . . ."

"Anything you want to talk about?"

Olivia shook her head; even *if* she wanted to tell Huck about Billy Tate's proposal and her equally unexpected acceptance of it, she wouldn't have had the slightest idea of where to start. More than likely, she'd talk herself in circles until she burst into tears, something that she knew neither one of them wanted. Even with a long-time family friend like Huck, it was easier to just hold her tongue.

Huck nodded knowingly. "If you change your mind," he said, taking a step back toward his own desk, "you know just where to find me."

By the time the deputy had picked up his newspaper to resume his reading, Sylvester was already snoring noisily in his cell. Once again left to her thoughts, Olivia was more unsure than ever of what to do next.

Fifteen minutes after Huck had settled back down at his desk, the door to the sheriff's office flew open with a bang, and Olivia's father entered, dragging a large man with him, his hands in cuffs. The prisoner struggled against every step they took, one sleeve of his dirty shirt nearly torn from the shoulder, swearing a blue streak at the top of his lungs, kicking and clawing, fighting like an animal. Through it all, John Marsten's face remained determined.

"Finally caught him, huh?" Huck asked, quickly rising from his seat to grab one of the squirming man's arms.

"He made it easy on me," John explained. "It wasn't enough to steal gasoline out of Zeke Parker's drum once. He had to go back for seconds."

"Too greedy for his own good," the deputy said with a chuckle.

Olivia recognized the man in handcuffs the moment she saw him. Dale Keller had been a troublemaker around Miller's Creek for years. He'd been in and out of jail since he was a teenager for almost every offense under the sun, but he was a born thief. With rationing for the war effort, Dale had been suspected of a number of thefts, stealing whatever he could get his hands on in order to sell it on the black market. Up until today, he'd been able to avoid getting caught.

"You sons-a-bitches!" Dale shouted. "I

didn't do nothin'!"

"That's what I've been sayin'," Sylvester added; he'd been woken by all the commotion and was watching intently.

"Let's get him in there," John said, nodding toward the one remaining empty cell. "He'll calm down soon enough."

But then, just as they were a few feet from the open door, Dale suddenly lashed out with his foot and clipped Huck in the back of his leg. The deputy wobbled before eventually pitching over, letting go of the criminal's arm as he fell. Olivia gasped; she was sure that Dale was going to get free. But any hopes he might have had about freedom were short-lived. Calmly but firmly, the sheriff grabbed hold of the man's cuffed hands and lifted them up as he simultaneously pushed between Dale's shoulder blades, forcing him down. The strain he created on the man's joints was so painful that Dale cried out in agony. John walked him forward before giving him a shove, sending the thief sprawling onto the hard floor of the cell, his face landing with a thud. Before Dale could even turn around, Olivia's father had already pulled the door shut and locked it. Everything was over before it had really begun.

Sitting on his rump, Huck shook his head,

clearly discouraged, his pride more wounded than his rear end. "Sorry about that, boss," he grumbled, accepting John's hand and struggling back to his feet. "I feel like a fool letting that rat get the better of me."

The sheriff waved it off. "Dale's a handful," he said. "I know that all too well. He's been fighting me ever since I caught up with him. You should've seen me trying to wrestle him into handcuffs."

Still plenty intoxicated, Sylvester had started cackling at the sight of Dale's comeuppance; even the threatening way the thief was glaring at him wasn't enough to stop his laughter.

"You best knock that off," Huck cautioned. "Otherwise, I'll put you both in the same cell. I don't reckon it'll be so funny then."

The deputy must have sounded serious; the old drunk's guffaws dwindled into a series of coughs before he fell silent.

Olivia stared at her father. John Marsten was just shy of fifty, his sandy blond hair touched with silver at the temples, the skin around his piercing blue eyes starting to become marred by wrinkles. Though he was lean, he was strong in build as well as stature, the sort of man who commanded a room's attention just by entering it. Even in situations like the one that had just happened, he never appeared ruffled, but calm and collected. He'd been the law in Miller's Creek since just after Olivia had been born, a fixture in town as familiar as the red and white pole outside the barbershop or the clock high above the bank. Much like the rest of the townsfolk, he had always made Olivia feel safe.

Hanging up the cell keys, John finally noticed his daughter. "Olivia," he said, his face softening. "I didn't know you were here." Looking back at Dale, he added, "I'm sorry you had to see that."

"I'm fine," she reassured him.

Glancing down at his watch, her father said, "What brings you by? I would've thought you'd be home by now."

"Actually," Olivia replied, "I was wondering if we could talk."

"Of course."

Realizing that her father meant that they should have their conversation right *there,* she said, "I was hoping we might have some privacy."

John nodded. Looking over his shoulder at his deputy, he said, "Olivia and I are going to head outside for a bit, Huck. You think you can hold down the fort?"

Glancing over the top of his newspaper, Huck grinned. "Long as those troublemakers keep quiet, I reckon I can handle it."

The spring sun was beginning to set in the west when Olivia and her father stepped out behind the police station. The early evening still held a bit of the day's meager heat, but a light breeze carried with it the promise of a chilly night. John didn't seem at all uncomfortable, but Olivia shivered as she placed her hands in her armpits, both for the warmth and to keep her ring hidden.

"You want to go somewhere warmer?" her father asked, noticing her discomfort.

"This is fine," she answered.

John nodded as he pulled a pack of cigarettes from the breast pocket of his shirt. Once he'd wrangled one free, he struck a match and lit it, taking a drag and blowing a plume of smoke toward the sky. He looked over at his daughter a bit sheepishly and asked, "Can we keep this a secret?"

"My lips are sealed."

For years, Olivia's mother had scolded her husband about his smoking habit. Whenever he came home from work, his clothes smelling like tobacco, Elizabeth had turned up her nose and walked from the room. For his part, John had tried everything to cut back, but he still craved one from time to time.

"So what's on your mind?" he asked.

Olivia noticed how her father had phrased his question. Instead of asking what was wrong, about what had bothered her enough to come by the station to talk to him, he remained neutral; she knew that it was the lawman in him, not wanting to make any assumptions before he had the whole story.

All day, Olivia had tried to come up with a way to talk about the proposal that had changed her life. She'd considered just blurting it out, but her heart was pounding so hard that she settled on easing her way into it. "What do you think about Billy?" she finally asked, unable to meet her father's eyes.

"He's a good young man," John answered evenly. "Polite. Well-mannered. Comes from a good family."

"But do you *like* him?" Olivia pressed.

Her father's gaze narrowed inquisitively. "I do," he said. "I've always thought he's been a good friend to you."

"Well . . . now he wants to be much more than that . . ."

John had been bringing his cigarette up to take another drag, but listening to his daughter's words, he paused, the butt a few inches short of his mouth. "Did Billy ask you out on a date?" he asked.

"Yes . . . no . . ." Olivia stammered; she wondered if this was how Billy felt trying to find the words to ask for her hand.

"Which is it?"

Unable to hold the truth back any longer, she took a deep breath and answered, "He asked me to marry him . . ."

Even though Olivia knew that her father's success as a sheriff came from remaining unfazed by the most unexpected of occurrences, she saw that her revelation had stunned him, even if he didn't let it show for long. He nodded as he puffed on his cigarette, the drag undoubtedly deeper than he'd originally intended.

Now that Olivia had begun, the story tumbled quickly out of her. "He was so wound up, pacing out in front of the hardware store, that I started to worry," she explained. "I thought something bad must have happened, but the next thing I knew, Billy was down on one knee with a ring in his hand," she continued. "He proposed, and then . . . and then . . ."

"And then?" her father echoed.

"I said 'yes,' " Olivia answered, finally allowing her hand, and the ring on her finger, to show. At that moment, she finally felt the enormity of her decision, the weight of it;

maybe by admitting it to someone else, it had become real.

Olivia had expected her father to frown, to say that she wasn't ready, that she was too young to get married, the same sort of sentiments expressed by his deputy, but instead, he surprised her. John dropped his cigarette to the ground, crushed it beneath his boot, and smiled as he walked over and pulled his daughter close; Olivia was so shocked by his reaction that it took her a moment to return his embrace. After a moment, her father stepped back and said, "I suppose congratulations are in order."

Too dumbstruck to respond, Olivia could only stare.

Noticing, John said, "Usually when someone decides to get married, they're a bit more excited than this."

"I'm just . . . I'm just still in shock I guess . . ."

"That's understandable," her father replied. "After I asked for your mother's hand, I stumbled around in a daze for a week or so before things got back to normal. It'll eventually pass."

"Isn't it normal for a man to ask his prospective bride's father for permission?" Olivia prodded, asking another of the questions that had gnawed at her all afternoon.

"Didn't Billy say anything to you about it?"

"Not a word," John answered. "But what with him getting ready to leave for training, he might not have felt he had time." Pausing, he added, "If it makes any difference, if he *had* asked, I can't think of a reason why I wouldn't have given him my blessing."

How about the fact that I don't think I'm in love with him? Olivia thought.

"Have you told your mother?" John asked.

"Not yet," she answered with a shake of her blond hair.

"I'm sure she'll be excited."

Olivia had no reason to doubt her father. Elizabeth Marsten had always encouraged her daughter to better herself through marriage. To her, Billy couldn't have been more ideal; his family was one of the wealthiest in town. She could already hear the shriek of joy that would meet her announcement; just thinking about it made Olivia queasy.

"How much longer does Billy have left before training?" her father asked.

"Just about five weeks."

Tenderly, John took his daughter's hand in his own, his fingers rough against her skin. "It's not easy being married to a man who'll be heading off to war," he said. "Your mother might never admit to it, but she suffered plenty while I was gone."

In 1918, back during the first war in Europe in which the United States took part, Olivia's father had been an infantry-man. For months, he'd slogged across mud-strewn battlefields, marched through trenches, fighting against the kaiser's army. Decades later, he still didn't talk about those days, although one of the things he had acquired during that long year of war was an undying hatred of Germans. He enthusiastically supported the war against Hitler and his nation.

Olivia understood what her father was say-ing, but how could she admit that this was one of the reasons she'd accepted Billy's proposal? That she was afraid that if she had not agreed to marry him, he would go off to fight with a broken heart. That if he were killed in action, she would never be able to forgive herself. Holding her tongue seemed easier.

"I'll manage," she said simply.

Her father nodded solemnly; Olivia knew that she'd given him no reason to doubt her desire to marry, and it made her ashamed.

"Now run on home," John said. "Once I finish up with Dale I'll be along so we can celebrate as a family."

This time, when he took his daughter in his arms, it was Olivia who held him close, her eyes shut tight to hold back tears. Maybe it was because she'd begun to understand what accepting Billy's proposal meant. Or maybe it was because even though she didn't love him, at least not in a romantic way, Olivia couldn't imagine taking back what she'd done; it would kill him inside.

She was going to become Billy Tate's wife, and there was nothing that could change that fact now.

So when a lone tear finally did fall, Olivia wiped it away quickly.

CHAPTER THREE

Peter Becker rocked back and forth on his hardback seat as the train jostled its way down the tracks, the sound of its passing steady and rhythmic. Three dozen men shared the train car with him, yet it was oddly quiet; no one spoke, the silence occasionally broken by a cough or sneeze. Most heads were turned to stare out of the windows at the passing landscape. Brilliant sunlight shone down from a cloudless sky, bright on the endless fields as they rushed past, sparkling across the water of trickling rivers and streams, only to disappear when the train passed through a thick copse of trees. Once, a trio of deer had looked up from the tall grass they were eating. Peter would have liked to get up and move around, to take in all of these new yet strangely familiar sights, but that was impossible.

He could be shot just for getting out of

his seat.

Heavy iron handcuffs shackled both of Peter's wrists. A chain ran down through a bolt in the floor, connecting him to the man sitting to his right. An American soldier stood two seats in front, his back to the door that led between the train's cars, his gun held at the ready, and his eyes vigilant for the first sign of trouble.

Peter was a German soldier.

He was the enemy.

Nearly three months had passed since Peter's infantry unit had accidentally stumbled onto an American patrol in the forests of western Germany. He still remembered the bitter cold of that day, the way the wind burned the bare skin of his face, but nothing could compare to the icy fear that filled him when the Americans revealed themselves, the morning filled with their shouts demanding surrender. Two of his fellow soldiers had refused and raised their guns, only to be shot full of bullets, dead before their bodies even hit the frozen, snow-covered ground. Wisely, Peter and the rest had done as they were ordered.

After their capture, they had been treated well. For years, Peter and his fellow soldiers had been warned about what would happen to them if they were to fall into Allied hands; that the Americans would torture them mercilessly, shooting them like dogs when they'd had their fill. But that hadn't happened. Far from it, they had been given warm clothes and food, far better than they'd been receiving from Germany's beleaguered home front. Following weeks of endless questions aimed at determining what, if anything, they knew about German war plans, they had ridden trains to the Atlantic coast, boarded enormous transport ships, and then sailed west for the United States. After landing, it was more questions and more trains. Their final destination was to be a system of internment camps in Minnesota. For Peter, all sense of time had been lost; one day bled right into the next.

For all of those on the train, the war was mercifully over.

"When are we getting something to eat?!"

Peter stiffened as the man beside him, the soldier on the other end of his handcuffs' chain, shouted in German, his voice menacing; the suddenness of his voice in the silence of the train car made it sound much louder than it was.

Otto Speer was the rare soldier who relished the violence of war. He was squat and thick-necked, and his hands were so large that his rifle had always looked tiny in

53

them. With short-cropped black hair, dark eyes set a little too closely together, a nose bent awkwardly to one side, probably broken in a tavern brawl, and a jaw that looked as if it had been chiseled out of granite, Otto had been one of the most bloodthirsty members of Peter's unit. A passionate believer in Hitler and the Nazi cause, he constantly railed against the Jews, berated any of his fellow soldiers he felt were shirking their duties, and had once killed a French farmer in cold blood when the man had refused to part with a pair of rabbits, laughing while the man's wife screamed in sorrow. Otto claimed to be a distant relative of Albert Speer, the Nazi armaments minister, but no one believed him. Peter would have expected Otto to be one of the men the Americans had shot dead during their capture, but while Otto was undeniably dangerous, that didn't mean he was stupid. While most of their unit had been dispersed to who-knew-where, sent on different boats and trains to different places, Peter had unfortunately found himself with Otto every step of the way.

"I want something to eat!" he again demanded.

The American soldier was doing his best to ignore Otto, but Peter could see that he was becoming annoyed.

"It's been hours since we last stopped!"

"He doesn't understand a word you're saying," Peter hissed, trying to defuse the situation before it got worse.

"He might not know the words but he damn well knows the meaning!" Otto snapped, turning his fury on his fellow prisoner. "How many of these pathetic Amerikaner shitholes do we have to go through before we stop?"

Most of the towns they passed whizzed by so fast that there wasn't time for more than a glance: homes with gardens ready for planting; shopkeepers unfurling their awnings, ready to open their businesses; old men behind the wheel of their trucks, idling beside the tracks as they waited for the train to pass; a congregation leaving church, the ringing of bells filling the air. Once, some boys had pelted their car with rocks; Peter had wondered if it was because they knew the train was filled with German prisoners, or if it was just childish fun. It always seemed like it was simply another day in their lives; remembering the destruction of Germany's cities, Peter wondered if any of these Americans truly knew that their nation was at war.

The only time the train stopped was to

give the prisoners something to eat and allow them to use the restroom. The breaks were infrequent; it wasn't unusual for Peter's stomach to grumble or for his bladder to feel close to bursting. But instead of simply bearing it like everyone else, Otto had chosen to fight back. It was at moments like this that Peter wished he was sitting somewhere else, anywhere but beside the rabble-rouser who seemed hell-bent on causing a scene.

"How much longer are we going to put up with this?!" Otto roared, rattling the chain on his handcuffs, looking around the cabin as if he was trying to encourage the others to join his tirade.

"Shut up!" the American soldier snapped, his patience at an end.

"The driver of this train must be a Jew!"

"I said that's enough, you damn Nazi!" The soldier took a step closer; Peter saw the barrel of the man's gun lower, the knuckles on his hands white from gripping the rifle's stock so tightly.

"Let me out of these chains," Otto growled, "and I'll —"

"You keep your mouth shut or it'll be —"

"He's just tired and hungry," Peter said without thinking, forcing himself to be heard over the growing argument. But unlike Otto's shouted German, he immediately grabbed the soldier's attention. The man's head snapped to the side as he stared, his mouth slightly agape.

Peter had spoken in perfect, unaccented English.

"It's been a long journey for all of us, you included," he kept on. "We just want to get where we're going without any problems."

"How in the hell're you talkin' like that?" the soldier demanded, but before Peter could answer, he snapped, "Just shut up! Don't say a damn word!"

Angrily, the soldier lowered his gun so that the muzzle swiveled back and forth between Peter and Otto; the prisoners sitting in the seat in front of them ducked their heads to stay out of the line of fire. Just like that, Peter was considered as dangerous as Otto, all because he'd spoken English. All he could do was look helplessly at the gun barrel pointing at him; with his hands shackled, he couldn't even raise them to try to calm the situation.

"You two just sit there and be quiet!" the soldier snapped. "If I hear another word out of either of you, there's gonna be trouble!"

Otto chuckled, too low for anyone other than Peter to hear.

Peter did his best to calm himself, but his

heart thundered. Once again, the truth of who he was had nearly gotten him killed.

He was German.

He was a prisoner of war.

But Peter Becker was also an American.

Like millions of other young American men thirsting for adventure, Thomas Becker, Peter's father, had enlisted in the United States Army and gone to Europe to fight against the kaiser. He'd trudged through the rain and muck, had listened to thunderous volleys from cannons as large as a streetcar, and had seen far more men die than he would have ever thought possible. But unlike most, when the war finally ended in November 1918, Thomas had chosen to stay behind. Over a century earlier, his kin had left the Rhine River valley for America; now Thomas was making the journey in reverse.

A bricklayer by trade, Thomas had brought with him only the battered trunk he'd hauled from Pennsylvania and the smattering of German he remembered his grandmother teaching him as a boy. He'd settled in a village just to the north of Munich, rented an apartment from a kindly cobbler and soon found employment. In the months that followed, life was hard but rewarding. Thomas had trouble imagining he could be any happier.

Until the day he met Mareike Herrmann.

She was the daughter of the town's baker and the most beautiful woman Thomas had ever laid eyes on. As the weeks and months passed, he found more and more reasons to stop by the shop besides the freshly baked loaves of bread and sweet rolls. Mareike was patient with him; she waited as he tried to express himself in his halting German, laughed loudly at his most ridiculous mistakes, but she also became his teacher, helping his grasp of her language to grow. By the following spring, they were married.

A year later, Peter was born.

Thomas doted on his son, happy for the life the family lived in Bavaria, but he also wanted the boy to know where his father had come from. To that end, he taught Peter about baseball; that he should root for the Philadelphia Athletics and hate the New York Yankees, and also how to position his fingers on the ball's seams to make it curve. He told him stories about growing up on a dairy farm, taught him songs that would have made Mareike angry if she knew the true meaning behind the words, and encouraged him to read every book he managed to find about America.

And so, Peter grew up speaking both German *and* English.

But all was not perfect. Times in Germany were hard. The reparations that had been imposed on the defeated nation by the victors caused inflation so great that people paid for their food with wheelbarrows full of money. When the global depression hit, times got even harder. To make matters worse, Bavaria was a hotbed of nationalism, with racist groups using violence to express their mounting anger. Nearby Munich was the birthplace of Hitler's National Socialist, or Nazi party. Thomas hated what these groups stood for, but he knew enough to keep it to himself; some who dared speak out found their store windows smashed, their businesses burned, and in some cases, paid with their lives.

They talked about leaving, about going to America, but before they could do little more than dream, Thomas had fallen ill. No matter what they did, no matter what doctor they saw, nothing made him better. Peter's father grew thinner, weaker by the day, until one autumn morning he was gone. Only twelve, Peter had taken up his father's mantle and done his best to provide for his heartbroken mother. More years passed. Hitler became chancellor. Then came the war. Then the Army. And the next thing he knew . . .

Peter jolted awake as a deep rumble of thunder shook the train car. Outside, the weather had soured. Gone was the clear blue sky of the afternoon; in its place was an ominous darkness. A light rain fell, drumming across the roof and splattering the window, the water running in horizontal streaks because of the movement of the train. As Peter watched, a fork of lightning snaked from the heavens and crisscrossed the sky, brilliantly bright; a second later it was gone, everything plunged back into darkness, and then the thunder rumbled once again. Soon, the storm would come in earnest.

Peter sighed; the last dregs of his dream lingered. He'd been back in the forest just after his unit's capture. An American officer had walked up and offered a cigarette, all smiles, as if they were old friends. But when Peter had given his thanks in English, *unaccented* English, the smile had disappeared and he'd once again been the enemy . . .

Looking around the dark train car, Peter saw that most of his fellow prisoners were sleeping, even as the raging storm continued to grow; even the guard at the front of the train looked as if he was about to nod off. But then, just as Peter was about to try to get a bit more sleep of his own, someone spoke.

"He thinks you're dangerous."

As startled as Peter had been by the thunder, it was worse when he understood that it was Otto speaking to him. The man had been so quiet, so still, that Peter hadn't noticed he was awake when he'd first glanced out the window. Looking over at him in the gloom, he saw Otto nod toward the American soldier, his face twisted in a sneer.

"When you speak their language," the brutish man continued, "it unnerves them. It makes them afraid."

"I was only trying to calm him down."

Otto laughed; the sound made Peter think of the ogre who lived under the bridge in the fairy tales his father used to read to him. "And yet you ended up with the gun pointed at you, no different than me."

"He could have shot you," Peter insisted. "Shot us both."

"Not that one," Otto disagreed, again nodding at the drowsy soldier. "One look at him tells me he's never fired that gun, not for real, not to kill. If I'd kept shouting, you would have seen piss running down his leg."

Outside, another flash of lightning forked out of the night, punctuated by a booming rumble; it was so deep that Peter could feel it in his bones.

"My only regret is that the Amerikaner didn't come closer," Otto continued, jangling the steel that bound his hands. "A few more steps and I would have wrapped these around his neck and choked him to death."

Heavy raindrops began to pelt the train car, striking the roof so hard and fast that it sounded like gunfire. Strong winds suddenly rose up, swaying the branches of the trees, rocking them back and forth.

"That soldier's no different than either of us," Peter argued, sickened by the other man's bloodlust. "He's doing what he's been charged to do, no more, no less. Besides, the war's over for us. There's no more reason to fight."

"To hell with that!" Otto growled angrily. "I will not surrender! Just because those bastards managed to capture us doesn't mean that we are powerless to hurt them! Hitler demands that we fight until our last breath!"

Anger filled Peter's thoughts. Hearing someone praise Hitler, the same maniac who had led a whole nation toward a ruinous defeat, whose army had conscripted Peter into a war in which he'd wanted no part, was more than he could bear. He hated the Nazis, as his father and mother had, but it hadn't been enough to keep his own fate from intertwining with theirs. But he was done doing Hitler's bidding. At that moment, he didn't care how dangerous Otto Speer was; shackled, he'd have no choice but to sit there and listen as Peter told him exactly what he thought of his beloved Führer.

But he never got the chance.

Before Peter could say a word, he was suddenly, unexpectedly thrown forward into the back of the seat in front of him. The shrill, piercing sound of the train's brakes filled the stormy night. The American soldier, jolted awake by the sudden change, leaped to his feet, his rifle clutched against his chest, his eyes wide with both surprise and fear.

"What in the hell is going — ?!" was all he managed to shout.

The crunching sound of metal being twisted, the explosion of glass as it shattered, and the gasps and screams of men preceded Peter's being tossed up and out of his seat by only a second. He was lifted as effortlessly as a child's toy, thrown toward the roof, stopping short only because the metal of his handcuffs bit hard into the flesh of his wrists. Up became down, left turned into right; in the darkness of night, nothing made any sense. Peter saw the American soldier, unrestrained as he was, hurled upward, and then he was gone, swallowed by the chaos and the inky blackness. Peter's stomach roiled as uncomfortably as it had on the voyage across the Atlantic. When the train came crashing back to the ground, landing with a deafening thud on the left side of the car, the opposite from where Peter sat, it felt as if the world was exploding. Pieces of glass flew in every direction. Peter's head smashed into something hard, possibly the seat across the aisle, and the darkness grew deeper until everything was black.

What brought Peter back to consciousness was an insistent tugging at his hand. He blinked a couple of times, his head muddled; it felt as if he was swimming up out of deep water. Struggling to make sense of where he was and what had happened, he slowly opened his eyes. Until another fork of lightning flashed, everything was hidden in the darkness, but when the sky lit up, he saw the destruction that had been wrought. Shards of glass were littered around his feet, the wooden seats were snapped like kindling, and sharp jags of metal poked everywhere. Peter could smell the acrid odor of smoke. From all around him came the moans and cries of the wounded; when the lightning flashed again, he saw another German soldier staring at him, dead, his eyes never to see again.

"Get up!" a voice hissed. "Goddamn it, get up!"

This time, the pulling on Peter's still-manacled hand was so strong that it nearly yanked him all the way to his feet. He stumbled forward, his legs weak as he tried to steady himself in the debris of the crash. Strangely, he felt water stinging his face; looking up, Peter was amazed to find that a hole had been ripped out of the train car, allowing the rain to fall inside.

"Come on!"

Another tug and Peter was face-to-face with Otto. In the light of the storm, Peter saw that his fellow prisoner had suffered a cut across his forehead; blood trickled down one side of his face. Unlike Peter, who'd had one hand broken free of the handcuffs, both of Otto's were still restrained. The chain that linked the two of them together had come loose from the bolt on the floor.

"What . . . what happened . . . ?" Peter asked.

"We hit something," Otto answered. "It could've been another train or maybe a tree fell across the tracks. Either way, this is our chance."

"Our chance to what?"

"Escape, you fool!"

Still addled from the crash, Peter nodded. Around him, the smell of smoke grew steadily stronger; looking toward what he thought was the rear of the train car, he saw hungry flames flickering to life.

"The . . . the others are hurt . . ." he said.

The other man's answer was to again pull at the chain. As they picked their way toward another hole that had been torn in the car, broken and bloodied men moaned in the darkness. Someone must have grabbed Otto, pleading for help; he spat a curse and kicked himself free. Moments later, they were outside, the fury of the storm pounding down on them.

The train had come off the tracks and slid down an embankment. From farther up the line toward the engine, Peter heard the shouts of men and saw flashlight beams cutting through the darkness of the still-raging storm. Frozen in place, he could only watch them come closer.

"Move!" Otto barked, giving another pull on the chain that bound them together and heading for the tree line.

Rain fell into Peter's eyes, momentarily blinding him as they crashed through the underbrush, nettles tugging at his clothes and skin.

"They'll come after us," he argued.

"Don't worry about them," Otto answered, moving forward.

Peter kept thinking about the soldier in their car, the one who had pointed his rifle at him; he wondered what had happened to him.

"The Americans won't quit looking for us until we're caught."

Otto stopped, thunder rumbling all around them, and pulled Peter close. "They aren't even going to know we're gone," he growled. "If that fire spreads, it will be days before they know if anyone is missing, if ever. By the time they understand, we'll be a hundred kilometers away."

With that, Otto started to run again, pulling his fellow prisoner behind him.

Peter had no choice but to follow.

CHAPTER FOUR

"Billy Tate asked me to marry him . . ."

As soon as the words were out of her mouth, Olivia wished she could take them back. But it was too late for that. Now, no matter how hard she tried, Olivia couldn't look her mother in the eye. Elizabeth Marsten sat expectantly in her favorite chair in the sitting room, a smile teasing at the corners of her mouth, the knitting she'd been working on frozen in her hand, a stitch waiting to be finished. The seconds crawled slowly past. The only sound was the rhythmic tick-tock of the grandfather clock against the wall; its pendulum moved much slower than the fevered beating of Olivia's heart. Shifting her weight from one foot to the other, Olivia felt as if the words she'd spoken still hung in the air between them.

Ever since she'd left her father, Olivia had been dreading this moment. The thought of telling her mother that she had agreed to become Billy's wife terrified her. The whole way home had been agonizing; with every step, she thought of ways to avoid going through with it, had even considered pretending nothing had happened, but she knew that would only be postponing the inevitable. In the end, unlike with her father, she'd blurted it out.

Elizabeth stiffened in her seat, her long, dark hair pulled up tight, her hazel eyes narrowing as she stared at her daughter; there wasn't much of a resemblance between them other than the shape of their noses and the way they both chewed on their lips when they were deep in thought. Her mother was a proper woman, always trying to make a good impression; even now, at home without any visitors, her blouse's collar was buttoned all the way to the top. Elizabeth was trying to keep a straight face, but Olivia could see her emotions just below the surface.

"And what was your answer?" her mother asked.

Olivia swallowed slowly, her mouth dry. "I . . . I said 'yes' . . ."

Elizabeth smiled as brightly as the noontime sun as tears of joy filled her eyes. She shot out of her chair, dropped her knitting on the floor, grabbed her daughter, and pulled her close. For an awkward moment, Olivia stood frozen in her mother's embrace before slowly raising her hands and half-heartedly returning the affection.

"Oh, sweetheart!" Elizabeth gushed. "I'm so happy for you!"

Olivia struggled to find a response; failing that, she remained silent.

"My daughter's going to marry a banker!"

A spark of anger flared in Olivia's chest. It didn't really matter to her mother that Billy had always been her closest friend, that he was kind and courteous, the sort of man who went out of his way to help others. To Elizabeth, all that counted was that he came from an upstanding, successful family, that he made plenty of money, and that he was handsome enough that when he walked into Sunday church service, all of the young ladies' heads turned to look at him, jealously wishing that they were by his side.

Love had *nothing* to do with it.

"William will make a wonderful husband, don't you think?" Elizabeth asked; her mother had always refused to refer to Billy in any way other than with the formalized name he'd been born with; to do otherwise wasn't proper.

Olivia nodded, which caused her mother to frown.

"I would think you should be much more excited than *that*," she scolded. "What young woman wouldn't be ecstatic to marry a man like William? Think of all the wonderful dinner parties you'll get to host, the people you'll meet, the luxurious clothes you'll get to wear, and especially the home you'll get to live in!" As she spoke, Elizabeth looked around them, her nose turned up a bit; Olivia suspected that she was comparing her current surroundings to those she imagined her daughter would soon be entering, and found her own lacking.

"I am excited," Olivia lied.

"Let me see the ring!"

Olivia held out her finger for her mother's inspection. She saw Elizabeth's obvious confusion at the plain gold band; from a man with Billy's wealth, she expected something far gaudier. "It must be a family heirloom," she muttered. "Probably belonged to a great-grandmother."

Quickly, Olivia hid the ring from sight, self-conscious about it.

"When is the wedding going to be held?" her mother pressed. "It's sure to be before William heads off for the service, won't it?"

Olivia felt dizzy, as if the room was spinning around her. "We . . . we didn't set a date . . ." she explained.

Her mother's frown would have darkened the brightest of summer afternoons. "Why in Heaven's name not?" Elizabeth demanded, her hands on her hips. "How am I supposed to plan if I don't know when it will be? I have an engagement notice to write, family members to contact, menus to prepare, to say nothing about meeting with William's father. There's so much to do and little time to do it in."

"I'll talk to him about it . . ." Olivia managed, not for the first time wishing she'd kept her mouth shut.

"See that you do," her mother replied. "This has to be done right. Anything else would be a disappointment."

If there was one thing Olivia had gotten used to over the years, it was Elizabeth being disappointed in her. No matter what she did, no matter how hard she tried, it never seemed good enough for her mother. One winter morning when she'd been a little girl no more than seven, Olivia had lain on the floor beside the wood-burning stove, drawing her mother a picture of a much warmer day. She'd struggled to get the sun just right, had put in a couple of trees, and tried her best to make the house look just like theirs. Finally, beaming brightly with pride, Olivia had brought the drawing to Elizabeth.

"With all the time you've spent on this," her mother said, "I would've thought it would be better."

And that was the way it had always been between them.

In her mother's eyes, everything Olivia did had to be perfect; when it inevitably fell short, she wasn't shy about expressing her dissatisfaction. To Elizabeth, Olivia's singing voice was too shrill. Her cooking was either too salty or not seasoned enough. For a month, her mother had tried to teach Olivia how to knit but had finally given up in frustration when her daughter hadn't taken to it. Olivia's marks in school weren't high enough. Her friends weren't the sort a proper lady should consort with.

"Why are you never happy with me?" she'd once asked.

Her mother had answered with a question of her own. "Isn't that something you should be asking yourself?"

Because of the demands of his job as sheriff, Olivia's father wasn't around enough to act as a counterbalance to his wife. When Olivia complained, John would smile knowingly, as if he, too, knew what it was like to be held to Elizabeth's high standards. But nothing ever changed; if it was his responsibility to provide for the family, it was Olivia's mother's to raise the children. With Grace's birth, there had been a moment when Olivia had held out hope that her mother would ease up, but Elizabeth had instead doubled her efforts, becoming even more restrictive with two daughters than she had been with one.

But the one thing her mother had never interfered with was Olivia's friendship with Billy Tate. Ever since the day they had met by the creek, Elizabeth had welcomed the boy into the Marsten home with open arms, offering to bake cookies, giving Billy a gift at Christmas, and always asking about his father. Olivia knew that the only reason her mother did these things was that Wellington Tate was the president of the bank and she hoped that being associated with him would raise her own family's standing, but Olivia didn't mind; anything that kept her mother's displeasure at bay was fine by her.

Still, Olivia wondered if her mother hadn't been hoping for a romance between her and Billy all along.

The first time a boy had shown a romantic interest in Olivia, the summer she turned twelve, Elizabeth hadn't approved and had kept her daughter indoors for almost a month; by the time Olivia could go out, her suitor's attentions had wandered somewhere else. But there had never been any such restrictions with Billy. Had her mother seen a spark pass between them? Something that Olivia had missed? Had she known that someday Billy would ask her to be his wife?

Unfortunately, Olivia knew that now, when she desperately wanted to talk about her doubts about marrying Billy, her mother wasn't an option. Their relationship wouldn't allow for it. Elizabeth would think her crazy for even considering turning down his proposal, would take it as an affront to her parenting, and would excuse her worries as the normal jitters every soon-to-be bride faced. Regardless of how much Olivia might want to discuss it, she couldn't.

She was all alone.

Olivia sat at the window seat in her bedroom and stared out into the night sky. The moon hung high above the trees, half-illuminated. Thousands of stars dappled the darkness, twinkling brightly. A brisk wind blew the tops of the trees back and forth; even with the window shut, she had wrapped herself in a blanket to stay warm.

Downstairs, Olivia could still hear the

sounds of the dinner table being cleared. She knew that her mother would be upset with her for not helping, but after all that she had just endured she'd needed some time for herself.

Her mother had gone to great lengths to show how excited she was about her daughter's engagement, making telephone calls to relatives and starting preparations for the wedding by writing out a long list of things that would need to be done. Olivia had retreated to the kitchen, her mind twisting and turning as if it were caught in a storm. Checking the stove, tears had suddenly filled her eyes, but Olivia had stamped them down quickly. Her father had arrived just as she was taking out the roast, kissing the top of her head on his way to the dinner table; it had been a struggle for Olivia to smile in return, but somehow she'd managed.

Grace had wandered in just in time to eat. Fourteen years old, Olivia's sister was every bit a tomboy, the exact opposite of the prim and proper girl Elizabeth wanted her to be. She plopped down in her seat, her sandy-blond hair unkempt and plastered against her scalp with sweat. A streak of grime dirtied one of her cheeks, and her hands were so filthy that Olivia imagined that her sister had spent the afternoon rummaging around in the city dump. Her clothes were just as messy; her mother surely considered them the attire of a tramp or vagrant.

"Go clean yourself up this instant," Elizabeth ordered, aghast at her daughter's appearance. "You know better than to sit down looking like that."

Grace groaned before finally lurching to her feet and halfheartedly washing away the day's adventure.

After saying a blessing but before anyone could begin filling their plates, her father stood and raised his glass. Looking at Olivia, he said, "I do believe this occasion calls for a toast."

Elizabeth smiled brightly. For Olivia, it was a struggle just to look happy; as she raised her glass, she was relieved to see that it wasn't shaking. She hazarded a glance at Grace; her sister looked from one face to the next, clearly confused.

"To Olivia and Billy," her father announced. "May their marriage be filled with happiness."

"Marriage?" Grace blurted incredulously. "To Billy Tate?"

"He proposed today," John explained; Olivia was glad that he had answered, because she wasn't certain she would've been able.

"And you said 'yes'?" her sister asked.

This time, it was her mother who came to her aid. "I don't think your father would've proposed a toast if she'd turned him down."

Grace stared at Olivia from across the table, her expression one of bewilderment. She couldn't really blame her sister; sitting there at the table and listening as her family began to talk about her engagement, it seemed unbelievable to her, too. Between her mother's happiness, her father's warnings, and her sister's surprise, to say nothing of her own worries, Olivia had no idea what to think. But in her heart, Olivia knew that it was too late to change her mind. She couldn't break off the engagement now.

She was caught in a trap of her own making.

As her mother and father discussed how to announce her engagement, even details of the wedding itself, Olivia stared down at her untouched plate and kept quiet. She marveled at how much her life had changed with the uttering of a single word.

Olivia was still staring out her bedroom window, lost in thought, when she was startled by a short, insistent knock on the door. Her heart pounded; she was sure it was her mother, and the last thing she wanted was more of Elizabeth's enthusiasm. But just as Olivia was about to answer, the door swung open and Grace slipped inside. Her sister quickly hurried over to where she sat.

"You're marrying *Billy*?" she asked, her voice as full of disbelief as it had been at the dinner table.

All throughout the meal, as their parents talked, Olivia had felt Grace's eyes on her, imploring her to look up, to give an explanation for what she'd done. Frustrated, Grace had even kicked Olivia's shin beneath the table. Even then, Olivia hadn't given her sister the attention she'd wanted, but had kept looking down, absently pushing peas around her plate. But now she couldn't ignore Grace any longer.

Olivia nodded.

"What happened?" Grace demanded. "And don't you dare leave anything out!"

So Olivia recounted the whole story, beginning with Billy's arrival at the hardware store and ending when she watched him on his way back to work.

"And you had no idea it was coming?" Grace asked.

"Not a clue."

Olivia had spent the whole day asking herself the same question, searching back over the last couple of weeks for something that should have given away Billy's intentions, but she'd come up empty. There hadn't been any uncomfortable silences between them, no unexpected phone calls or awkward embraces, not even a stare that had lingered a little too long. Try as she might, she couldn't find anything to indicate that he had been about to propose.

"Do you love him?"

Grace's words shook Olivia because she had no answer. Oddly enough, neither of her parents had asked; she doubted that it mattered to her mother and figured that her father just assumed she did, otherwise, *why else would she have accepted?* But the truth was far more complicated than that.

"I do . . . and I don't . . ." she admitted.

"That doesn't make any sense," Grace said, shaking her head.

"Billy is the best friend I've ever had," Olivia explained, "and for that, I love him with all my heart." She paused, struggling to find the right words. "But when it comes to romance, to loving him like a woman should love a man, especially one who wants to be her husband, I . . . I . . ."

"You don't," her sister finished for her.

Once again, Olivia could only nod.

"Then why didn't you turn him down?"

81

Grace pressed.

"I couldn't break his heart," Olivia answered. "I just couldn't. Not now . . . not just before he leaves for the Navy."

"That's crazy!"

"If you could've seen the look in his eyes when I hesitated, you'd understand," she said, remembering the way Billy's smile had faltered, his hope fading. "If I'd turned him down, it would've killed him."

"But what about you?" Grace asked. "You're not supposed to marry someone you aren't in love with because of what it would do to him!"

"It's too late now."

"No, it isn't!"

"Yes, it is," Olivia insisted. "If I tell Billy that I've changed my mind, it'll be even worse than if I'd turned him down in the first place."

"So instead you'll just go along with it and hope that someday you fall in love with him?" Grace argued. "It doesn't work like that."

"What do you know about love?"

"Not much," her sister admitted, "but what you're describing sounds like something straight out of the movies."

Even as bad as she felt, Olivia couldn't help but laugh. Still, a part of her was

impressed by her sister's argument. She and
Grace, despite the very different ways in
which they dealt with their mother and her
demands, had remained close, defending
each other at every turn. In many of Olivia's earliest memories of her friendship with
Billy, Grace had been there, tagging along
as they splashed in the creek, laughing at
Billy's stupid jokes, and chasing fireflies
through the summer night. In some ways,
Grace's trouble in understanding her decision to marry Billy was the most damning
of all.

"What did Mom say when you told her?"
her sister asked.

Olivia sighed. "She was as happy as I've
ever seen her," she answered. "She thinks
Billy is the best husband I could ever find."

Grace didn't say a word, but Olivia knew
just what she was thinking; that her mother
was wrong and that if it were her, she
would, just as with most everything else the
two of them disagreed about, fight against it
with all of her might.

What she couldn't understand was why
her sister wasn't doing the same.

In a way, neither could Olivia.

CHAPTER FIVE

Peter felt uneasy being on a train again so soon after the crash. Even as the memories of darkness and the screams of men teased at the corners of his mind, the steady clickety-clack of the rails was trying to rock him back to sleep; he'd been dozing fitfully for hours. His feet were splayed out on the floor of the mostly empty freight car and his clothes were still damp and dirty from running through the thunderstorm.

His back rested against the rail car's wall. He sat beside the open door, chilled by the wind, his face turned to look outside. The spring morning was glorious; the sun was rising in a sky colored the blue of a robin's egg. Low-lying fog clung to the riverbeds and fields, slowly burning away as the sun continued to climb. Peter had no idea where they were, only that they were heading back the way they'd come, going east. Even as shaken as he was, he could still see the beauty of this land, the country of his father and therefore his own, if by nothing more than blood.

Otto sat silently beside him; the chain that still bound them together wouldn't let him get too far away. His fellow prisoner stared silently at the passing landscape. He looked wide awake; Peter hadn't seen him yawn once or close his eyes for longer than a blink. Occasionally, he leaned forward and peered out of the freight car in the direction the train was heading.

Neither of them had said a word for hours.

After leaving the wrecked prison train and escaping into the woods, they had run for hours, dodging fallen tree limbs and outcroppings of rock, forcing their way through sharp thorn bushes, all while getting drenched by the raging storm. With every step, Peter kept expecting to hear their pursuers bearing down on them, soldiers shouting for them to stop, followed by the crack of a rifle as it was fired. But all he ever heard was thunder and their heavy, weary breathing. Eventually, they came to a broad river, swollen from the storm.

"Are we going to cross?" Peter had asked.

"Not here," Otto answered. "The water's moving too fast. We'll follow it upstream and see if there's a bridge or some sort of

85

narrowing."

As they ran, Otto had Peter periodically step into the cold water, the river filling his boots in seconds.

"If they use dogs to track us," he explained, "it'll throw off the scent."

On and on they went.

The storm finally lessened, then fell away altogether; the clouds broke apart, allowing the moon to drift in and out of sight. Rain glistened from every surface. Peter was soaked to the bone, and the night chill made him so cold that his teeth chattered. Hours later, they came to an old rail trestle; in the faint moonlight, it resembled the skeleton of some wild beast. Climbing the rocky embankment, they carefully crossed the bridge and entered the forest beyond.

"How much farther are we going to go?" Peter asked.

"As far as it takes," Otto answered; in unspoken anger at having his decisions questioned, he pushed them harder, tugging on the chain whenever Peter lagged behind.

Then, just as Peter's exhaustion had gotten so bad that he thought he would collapse, the night was filled with a familiar sound. Hiding in the bushes, they watched as another train chugged down the tracks, its light cutting through the darkness.

"We have to get on it," Otto said.

Peter was too tired to answer.

Freight cars whizzed past. Watching down the line, Otto saw one whose door stood partially open; without hesitation, he was on his feet and running toward it. Peter followed, stumbling over the broken rock beside the track, struggling not to fall. The train was moving fast enough that he knew he would only get one try. Otto leaped first and scrabbled his way inside. Then it was Peter's turn, but even as he tried to time his jump, he knew it was too late; running from the wrecked train had sapped all of his strength. He was going to fail. Suddenly, he was pulled from his feet, the clasp of his remaining handcuff biting deep into his wrist. He looked up to find Otto pulling furiously on the chain that still bound them, reeling him to safety. With a loud grunt, Peter collapsed onto the train car floor. He knew Otto hadn't saved him out of compassion or friendship, but for self-preservation; because of the chain, if Peter wasn't in the train, Otto couldn't be either. He was thankful all the same.

Peter didn't know how long he'd slept, but now that he was awake, watching America race by outside, hunger had become a more pressing concern. His stomach grumbled, empty. It had been a long time since he'd last eaten; the prisoner train had stopped the previous afternoon, providing sandwiches and weak coffee. Running through the storm, he and Otto had drunk from the river, but there'd been nothing to eat. Though his hunger was uncomfortable, Peter tried his best to ignore it; after all, there was no telling how long it would be before something could be found.

Unexpectedly, Peter felt the train shudder; almost imperceptibly at first, they began to slow. Otto reacted quickly, sticking his head out to see what was happening; from the look that passed over his face, it wasn't good.

"We have to get off," he explained.

Surprise filled Peter. "Why?" he asked; after all that they'd done to get inside, he didn't like the idea of leaving.

"There's a town ahead."

"So?" he asked. "We've passed through others."

Otto shook his head. "That was during the night," he explained. "Chances are that no one was looking for us then. It'll be different during the day. Flashlights can't illuminate everything in the dark, but under this sun," he said, nodding toward the sky, "there'll be nowhere we can hide."

"Then how do we get off?"

"We jump."

Sticking his head out, Peter looked ahead. A town *was* quickly approaching; in the distance he saw a church steeple and a few houses. The depot might be in the center; if they waited, there'd be nowhere for them to run. They'd be found out.

They stood at the edge of the freight car, the chain hanging between them. Even though the train continued to slow, Peter knew that they were still going fast enough that their landing wouldn't be an easy one.

"Now," Otto hissed.

When they leaped from the train, Peter had the sensation that they were hanging in air, frozen in place, but it only lasted for an instant. Then they began rushing toward the slanted embankment of dirt and rock, hitting the ground hard before rolling. Something struck Peter's hip, causing it to burn with pain. They scrambled for cover in some bushes and then quickly turned back toward the train; they watched intently for a sign that they'd been spotted, but the cars just rolled by.

"What do we do now?" Peter asked.

"Scout around," Otto answered. "Look for something to eat or an automobile we can steal." Jingling the chain, he added, "Maybe we can find a way to cut this damned thing."

In that, Peter couldn't have agreed more.

Like a pair of foxes trying to sneak their way into a chicken coop, the two German soldiers moved carefully and quietly as they skirted the edge of town, looking for something to eat or a means to further their escape. The town wasn't much; there were a couple dozen buildings clumped together, with the depot in the center of it all, just as he had suspected. There weren't any outlying farms, either; the land was too hilly, the soil too rocky. But there were a few houses that were far enough away from the others to be worth checking; unfortunately, at each there were people at home or dogs that barked when they neared. After a couple of hours, they gave up and climbed to a small outcropping on a hillside that provided them with both cover and a view of town. They both plopped down, exhausted.

"We'll sneak onto another train once it's dark," Otto explained, "then move on to somewhere else."

"And then what?" Peter asked, fatigue loosening his tongue. "We're in the middle of the United States. What do you think we're going to do, keep hiding ourselves in freight cars until we reach the coast, slip onto a boat heading to Germany, and then go back to fighting again?"

This was the argument that Peter had thought about ever since he and Otto had escaped from the wrecked train. Even though they were no longer prisoners of the United States Army, they were far from free; the truth was that they were thousands of miles from home, without any food or shelter, still shackled together, and with no idea where they should go. Deep down, Peter knew that the best course of action was to turn themselves in. The war in Europe would soon be over; it didn't matter how hard Hitler's most fanatical supporters fought, they'd be overwhelmed soon enough. Peter wanted no part of their suicidal plans; for him, even if he spent his days locked up behind barbed wire, watched day and night, at least he'd be safe. Unfortunately for him, he doubted that Otto felt the same.

"What would you have us do, march back to the Amerikaners and surrender?" the brutish man snapped. "We will continue to serve the Fatherland and our Führer until we draw our last breath!"

"We won't be able to for long if we keep

running," Peter argued.

"That is why we will soon stop."

"What are you talking about?"

"You are right to say that we cannot hope to make it all the way to Germany," Otto admitted. "It would be pointless even to try. We would be captured for certain." He paused, his eyes boring holes at Peter. "That is why we will fight."

"With what?" Peter asked incredulously, holding up his still-cuffed hand so that the chain rattled between them. "We have no food, no weapons, and only the clothing on our backs, nothing more."

Otto nodded slowly. "For now," he answered. "But soon we will have everything we need to stay alive, all of the things you speak of. We can quit running. With only a rifle, we can hurt them. We will do what those damn Jews did in Mother Russia, fighting them from our hiding spots, picking them off one at a time, making their fear and frustration grow." Otto smiled cruelly. "Hitler will give us medals once the Amerikaners are defeated."

Listening to the hatred and venom that Otto was spewing, Peter knew without a shadow of a doubt that it had been a mistake to leave the prison train with him. But he had been rattled, shaken by the crash and the destruction it had wrought, unable to think straight. For Otto, death wasn't something to avoid, but rather to embrace; nothing would please the man more than to die for Hitler and his ridiculous cause, but not before he'd killed plenty of his enemies first. If he continued on his chosen path, he wouldn't survive; if Peter was still beside him, he, too, would perish.

He had to get away, and quickly. But until the chain that bound them was broken, he'd have to go along with Otto's nefarious plans.

Peter nodded, trying to act as if he saw the truth in the other man's words. "So we keep heading east?"

"Once it's dark, we'll make our way back down to the trains," he explained. "Until then, rest."

Leaning back against a tree's trunk, Otto folded his arms across his chest and closed his eyes. Even though Peter was tired, as much from a lack of food as from exhaustion, he found it hard to do as Otto had suggested. The man he was chained to was dangerous, the sort who had to be watched closely. Peter knew he had to be smart and to take a chance to get away only when the time was right.

His very life depended on his making the right decision.

■ ■ ■ ■

Once night fell, they made their way to the depot. There were lights on in some of the houses but they didn't see anyone. The locomotive hissed at the head of the tracks; it wouldn't be long before it departed. But then, just as Peter was taking his first step toward the open door of a freight car, he was grabbed hard from behind and hauled backward as a hand clamped down over his mouth. Shocked and surprised, he began to struggle; a sliver of fear raced through him that Otto had decided he was no longer worth the trouble and intended to kill him.

"Quiet!" Otto hissed in his ear.

Peter stopped struggling. A couple of moments later, he understood why Otto had taken hold of him. A lone guard made his way up the line of track, swinging his flashlight slowly up one side of the train and then back across the platform. Otto had pulled them between a couple of crates, out of sight. No more than ten feet away, the man stopped, fished out a pack of cigarettes, and lit one before inhaling a deep drag and blowing smoke into the sky. Behind him, Peter felt Otto's body tense; he knew that if the guard noticed them, Otto would attack

like a wild animal, trying to kill him before any alarm could be raised. But after a while, the man moved off, whistling a tuneless tune. Finally, once the guard was far enough away, they cautiously entered the dark freight car.

Eventually, the train began to roll. Under a blanket of stars, it traveled farther east. Peter tried to sleep, but found it too difficult, not because of his concern about Otto or what they were doing, but because of hunger. More than a day had passed since he'd last eaten and he felt as weak as a kitten. With every rumbling of his belly, pain filled him. By morning, the feeling had become unbearable. One look at Otto told Peter that the other man felt the same. It was decided that they had to get off the train and forage for food, no matter the risk.

As they had the day before, they jumped off the train just before they reached a town. Unlike then, they soon had better luck. In the hills north of the rail line was a cabin with a couple of outbuildings. They watched quietly for a long time, listening to the squirrels chatter and the wind gently rustle the boughs of the evergreen under which they hid. Nothing happened. Finally, they decided that they'd waited long enough. Breaking out one of the windowpanes, they forced their way inside.

The cabin looked to have been unoccupied for some time. Dust covered every surface and there was a musty smell in the air, as if it had been shut up for months. Immediately, they rushed to the cupboards in the small kitchen and rifled through them. They found a tin of sardines and a can of beans that they forced open and ate ravenously. Peter's stomach was so empty that it hurt to put something in it, but he ignored the ache and kept eating. Checking the rest of the cabin, they found some clothes in the bedroom and a couple of dollars in the back of a drawer.

"Too small for me," Otto said, holding up one of the shirts.

"I could wear it," Peter replied.

Otto nodded. "We've got to get out of these first," he said, rattling his cuffs.

"Let's look outside."

The first outbuilding they checked was empty, but the second had been used to store tools. A scarred workbench stood against one wall, littered with nails, a paintbrush missing half its bristles, and a bucket with a hole in the bottom. Tools hung between nails pounded into the wall. Most of them were covered in rust, untouched for far longer than the cabin; Peter hoped they were still solid enough to gain them their freedom.

From the wall, Otto snatched a weathered hatchet. Gauging its heft in his hand, he cleared a space, spread out the chain, and began to hack away at it. Over and over he swung, the clangs loud in the small space. Occasionally, sparks flew, but Peter couldn't see any damage being inflicted.

"Damn it all!" Otto barked, beads of sweat dotting his forehead.

"That won't work," Peter said. "It's not strong enough."

"The hell it isn't," the other man argued, doubling his efforts. After only a couple more blows, the handle suddenly snapped, worn through with rot, causing the hatchet's head to fall onto the ground.

Otto was just about to retrieve it when Peter stopped him.

"Let's try something else."

Peter grabbed a metal rod leaning against the wall. It was a couple of feet long and about as big around as his thumb.

"That won't fit though the chain links," Otto observed.

"It doesn't have to."

Peter slid the length of metal between his wrist and his one remaining cuff. The restraint had been damaged during the crash and he was able to squeeze it through. Fortunately, the rod wasn't rusty like the other tools; his wrist was still bloodied from the crash, so he was glad that he didn't have much risk of infection. Placing his wrist on the workbench, Peter grabbed the edge with his manacled hand, tightly gripped the metal rod with the other, and took a deep breath. Straining with all of the strength he had left, Peter began to push the bar to the side, prying against the broken clasp of the handcuff. The pain was tremendous. Soon, the wound reopened, staining his hand with blood, but he didn't let up, desperate to be free. Slowly, he felt the metal begin to bend. The tendons on his arms stood out, his muscles burned, and sweat beaded his brow. Finally, just as he began to fear that he would break before his bonds did, he yanked his hand out of the contorted steel. He'd done it.

"My turn," Otto growled.

Unfortunately, the same trick wasn't going to work twice. Because Peter's restraints had been loose, there was room to insert the bar; Otto's were clasped too tightly around his wrists. They'd have to find another way to get him out.

"Damn it!" Otto hissed angrily. "Let's make another handle for the hatchet," he suggested. "If we keep at it long enough, it'll give."

Peter shook his head. "Right now, we've got bigger worries. That little bit of food wasn't enough. We need more."

Otto reluctantly agreed, shaking the chain in frustration. Peter understood; if he was the one still bound to it, he imagined that he'd feel the same.

"So what do we do?" Otto asked.

"I'll put on those old clothes and take the money into town," Peter explained. "With my English, I can pass for an American. Hopefully we're far enough away from the crash that no one's looking for us. Once we have more to eat, we can figure out how to get you free."

"Make it fast!" Otto snapped. "The sooner I'm out of these damn chains, the sooner we can get about striking fear into these weak Amerikaners' hearts!" Flashing a sadistic smile, he added, "It won't take long to show them just how superior we Germans are!"

Peter nodded. The truth was that he had no intention of coming back for Otto, at least not in the way the other man expected. He was going to march to town, find the nearest lawman, and turn himself in. Peter knew that running from the train had been a mistake. He was done fighting. The last thing he wanted was for anyone else to get killed. If necessary, he would lead them to the cabin himself, anything to keep this murderous psychotic from causing any more harm.

Their war would soon be over. This time, for good.

CHAPTER SIX

"I can't believe you're getting married!"

Olivia only had time to smile weakly before Sally Albright embraced her tightly, jumping up and down in her arms. Standing on the street corner in front of her house beneath the bright morning sun, a dented wagon on the sidewalk behind her, Olivia could only imagine what the two of them must look like to anyone watching.

"And to Billy!" Sally continued, pulling back to look at Olivia but not letting her go. "I never would've imagined he would propose!"

That makes two of us . . .

Besides Billy and Grace, there was no one whom Olivia had ever been closer to than Sally. Since they were the same age, they'd been together for as long as she could remember, sharing a desk at school, singing in the church choir, and taking long walks beside the creek, whispering about boys.

They'd always confided in each other and that trust had never been broken.

Sally took Olivia by the hand and held her ring up to the light. Unlike her mother, her friend didn't see anything wrong with the simplicity of the golden band; instead, she saw it as romantic.

"I'm so happy that I'm going to start crying!" Sally gushed.

Watching her friend wipe a tear from the corner of her eye, Olivia understood why Sally had always been considered one of the prettiest girls in all of Miller's Creek. She was full figured and tall, and her curly red hair fell down across her shoulders. Her green eyes were wide with long lashes. When she smiled or pursed her lips, most men behaved as if they'd just met a movie starlet, either clamming up or talking so fast you couldn't understand a word they said. She was even more beautiful on the inside. But for all the attention she received, Sally had always had eyes for only one man; Chuck Albright. Four years ago, they'd been married; Olivia had never seen Sally happier than that day. But it was that love for Chuck, that desire to be forever by his side, that had aged her friend, causing many a sleepless night.

"Tell me everything!" Sally demanded, her

own problems forgotten because of Olivia's engagement.

"We can talk while we walk," Olivia answered, grabbing the handle of the wagon and starting down the sidewalk.

"Come on, Olivia! Stop holding out on me!"

"More working means more talking."

For more than a year now, Olivia and Sally had spent one day a week walking up and down the streets of Miller's Creek collecting anything that could be recycled for the war effort. They picked up newspapers, toothpaste tubes, tubs of cooking fat, and glass bottles. They scrounged up tinfoil and whatever pieces of scrap metal happened to be lying around. When they were doing their rubber drive, they'd taken everything from children's tire swings to women's girdles. With the men off fighting, they'd wanted to do their part, so they trudged all over town, dragging their wagon in the sun, rain, and even snow.

While they walked, Olivia told Sally about Billy's proposal. With every telling, it seemed to get a little easier, if no less believable. For her part, Sally peppered her with questions, trying to squeeze out every last detail.

"How do you feel about Billy going off to

the Navy?" Sally asked.

"I'm worried," Olivia admitted.

Sally took a deep breath. "You have good reason to be," she said.

Ever since Chuck headed off for basic training, Sally had been living with the fear that he would die in combat. He was a Navy Seabee, operating a bulldozer as his unit cleared jungles in the South Pacific, making roads and airstrips for the march to Japan. Each time there was a knock on her door, she was terrified, certain that it was someone from the military coming to tell her of her husband's death, to offer condolences that wouldn't begin to fill the void in her heart. Every night, she said her prayers for his safety. Every morning, she wrote him a letter, trying to stay positive, to not show her fear. In public, she maintained a smile, but Olivia knew her friend was hurting. Unfortunately, she'd soon know just how much.

"When does Billy leave for his training?" Sally asked.

"Five weeks."

Olivia's friend gave her an encouraging smile. "Maybe the war will be over by then," she said. "In his last letter, Chuck said it wouldn't be much longer."

"I hope not, for all of our sakes."

"So when's the big day?"

"I don't know," Olivia answered. "We didn't set a date."

"Well, you're going to have to hurry," Sally said. "There isn't much time if we're going to do this right." She then began to talk about engagement announcements, invitations, what type of decorations they could have, dresses, music, food, and even whether she and Billy should try to make time for a honeymoon; strangely, listening to Sally talk about such things wasn't as upsetting to Olivia as when her mother did so; still, there was so much said so fast that it made Olivia's head spin.

Because of Sally's excitement, Olivia didn't have the heart to tell her about her doubts. The night before, as she had stared at the ceiling above her bed, the hours slowly crawling past, Olivia had thought about everything she wanted to say to Sally; that she was afraid she'd committed a terrible mistake in accepting Billy's proposal, one she had no idea how to fix. She worried that admitting such things would make her look foolish, as if she didn't take the institution of marriage seriously, something that she feared would insult Sally, to whom it was her whole life.

So instead she held her tongue.

Besides, just as when she'd told her family, Olivia knew that it was too late to change anything. No one in all of Miller's Creek, friend or otherwise, would ever understand why she'd be reluctant to marry a man like Billy Tate.

So she would become his wife. Like Sally, she would just have to hope for the best. Her path had been chosen, and nothing, and no one, could change it now.

Peter made his way down the gently sloping hill and away from the cabin. Though there was still a chill in the early spring air, the sunlight on his skin was enough to keep him warm. The clothes that he'd put on, a blue button-down shirt and a pair of dark work pants, smelled just as musty as the place in which they'd been left, but he was happy to get out of his prisoner garb all the same.

He was also relieved to be away from Otto. Before leaving, Peter had listened to the man go on about what he should and shouldn't do in town; truthfully, he hadn't paid much attention, but just nodded his head. Ever since they'd been shackled together, Peter had been uncomfortable, listening to Otto's tirades against Americans and Jews, as well as his unwavering belief in Hitler and the Nazis. But it was all over now. Soon, both of them would be where they belonged, where they would have been had it not been for the crash.

So I might as well enjoy what little freedom I have left . . .

Soon, Peter found a road and began following it, staying along the shoulder. Towering trees rose on either side, the sun shining through their nearly bare branches, many of them only now showing the first buds of spring. Ahead, he could look down at a meandering stream of water winding its way toward the town he'd seen from the cabin. It was like most of the others he'd seen from the prison train; a clump of buildings with a church steeple towering highest of all. Homes spread out in every direction, many following the flow of the creek, eventually dwindling as they met the countryside. While it was certainly different from German towns, Peter was struck by its beauty, as well as the feelings of community it raised in him. He thought of his mother, as he often did. He doubted that Rothesburg, the town in which she lived, looked this lovely; it had probably been bombed into rubble by now. Worse yet, he had no idea if she was alive or dead.

Walking along, lost in thought, Peter was startled when a man suddenly stepped out into the road from behind a hedge. He was older, wearing a worn tweed coat and carrying a bundle of sticks, which he dropped into a larger pile. Noticing Peter, the man cheerfully said, "Good morning."

Momentarily stunned, fearful that he would do or say something to betray that he was German, it took Peter a second to recover. Somehow, he managed to find a friendly smile. "Morning," he replied.

"Out for a walk?" the man asked.

Peter noticed the man give him a subtle look-over. His eyes lingered for a moment on Peter's wrist; he'd tried to clean where the handcuff had dug into his flesh, wiping away all of the blood, but he knew that the cut looked red and angry.

"Actually, I was in a bit of an accident," Peter replied, the English coming to him surprisingly easily. Pointing back up the road behind him, he added, "Something darted out in front of my car a couple of miles back. I had to swerve to keep from hitting it and ran right into a tree. I've been walking ever since."

"Probably a deer," the man said with a compassionate nod. "This time a year they start to get a little frisky, if you know what I mean."

"Could've been," Peter replied with a chuckle. "There wasn't much light and it all happened so fast I'm afraid I didn't get too good of a look."

"You all right?" he asked, nodding at Peter's hand.

"I'm fine. Nothing broken, at least. It looks a lot worse than it feels."

"You should still head into town and get it looked at."

Running a hand through his hair, Peter said, "The truth is, I'm not exactly sure where I'm at."

"This here's Miller's Creek," the man explained. "It ain't much more than a spot on most folks' maps, but it's a fine place all the same."

Peter wasn't sure, but he thought he must be in Wisconsin. Still, he didn't ask; it would be far too suspicious. "Do you know where I might find a lawman?" he asked instead.

"You mean the sheriff?" the man asked, his eyes narrowing a bit.

"I thought I should let him know about my accident," Peter answered quickly. "The wreck is off the road, but come dark, someone driving along might not see it. There's already been one crash. I'd hate to be the cause of another."

The man nodded, accepting Peter's explanation as the truth. "The sheriff in these parts is a good man. Name's John Marsten.

The police station's across from the bank on Main Street. You get yourself turned around, I expect anyone you ask could point you in the right direction."

"Much obliged," Peter answered. The two men shook hands and he was again on his way.

Walking along, Peter smiled to himself. He'd learned where he was, as well as where he might find someone who could put an end to all of the madness he'd gotten into with Otto. But in talking with the older man, he was relieved that his English had betrayed no hint of his true identity. He'd grown up listening to his father, talking with him, thinking that he sounded like an American born and raised, but he'd always wondered if he spoke with an accent or some other tell that would give him away as a foreigner, but apparently, there wasn't one.

Eventually, Peter crossed a rickety bridge that spanned the waterway that must have given the town its name, and entered Miller's Creek. Using the tall church steeple as a landmark, he headed in that direction. A deliveryman drove past in his truck, giving a short tap on his horn and a friendly wave; Peter returned the gesture without thinking.

He walked down a street divided by a row of trees. Houses lined both sides of the road,

many with automobiles parked out front. From nearly every home, an American flag fluttered in the breeze; the sight felt very different from what Peter was used to in Germany, where the red, black, and white swastika was everywhere. Back home, while there were thousands of people who flew the Nazi symbol out of a love for what it represented, there were many who did so out of fear of what would happen if they didn't. He doubted that there was any such dilemma here.

Peter turned one corner and then another, the church steeple drawing steadily closer. He was trying to figure out what he was going to say to Sheriff Marsten when he saw something up ahead. Two young women were hauling boxes of newspapers toward a large wagon on the sidewalk. One of them stopped on the walk, clearly straining with the weight of her load, before dropping it down at her feet with a plop. She leaned back, stretched her aching muscles, wiped the sweat from her brow, and then looked up, catching Peter staring at her. He froze, his heart beating faster.

She was beautiful, almost breathtaking. In all of his life, he'd never seen a woman who could make him feel the way he did in that moment. And then she smiled at him, a gentle upturn of the corners of her mouth, her blue eyes narrowing as her blond hair swirled across her shoulders, and Peter's feelings for her intensified. In his head, he knew that he should just continue to the sheriff's office, turn himself in, and then assist in Otto's capture in any way he could. What he *shouldn't* do was go over and talk to that woman.

But he wasn't listening to his head.

What he wanted was coming from his heart: to know her name; to hear the sound of her voice; to look for a bit longer on her beauty; to say something, anything, that would make her smile a bit brighter. Afterward, he could keep walking, find the sheriff, and do just as he'd intended.

But only after . . .

The next thing Peter knew, he was walking toward her; he could no more have resisted her lure than a bee could a flower.

Olivia grimaced as she carried another load of old newspapers from Delores Wright's garage. Her muscles ached from the weight of the boxes. Sweat beaded her brow. But whatever discomfort she felt was well worth it. She and Sally had been coming to see the widow for more than a year, always asking if she would hand over her papers to be

112

recycled. Delores and her late husband, Frank, had owned Miller's Creek's mercantile for more than twenty years; for almost every one of those days, Delores had faithfully brought home a newspaper. Whenever they asked her about surrendering her trove, Delores had always turned them down, clinging to the belief that she might need them someday. Still, they'd never stopped asking; surprisingly, today the old woman had finally relented.

"If it'll really go to help with the war effort," Delores had sighed, "then I suppose you can have 'em."

That didn't mean that letting go of them was easy. Delores stood beside the garage, a pained expression on her face, watching Olivia and Sally hauling everything away; it was as if they were taking her jewels or some other family heirloom rather than yellowing newspapers.

By now, the wagon was piled high and they were far from finished. Olivia suspected that the only way to get all of them would be to either make multiple trips or arrange for a truck; regardless of which solution was chosen, Olivia wanted to make sure they got it all. She took her recycling responsibilities seriously; just as with her job at the hardware store, she wanted to do her part on the home front to defeat the Germans and the Japanese.

As she made her way down Delores's walk, the strain of Olivia's load finally became too much to bear and she let it drop heavily to the ground. Taking a deep breath and wiping the sweat from her brow, she glanced toward the street. Unexpectedly, she saw a man standing on the sidewalk, looking right at her. He was tall, with blond hair, and broad across the shoulders. He was also handsome; watching him stirred something in Olivia, a feeling that while unfamiliar, was far from unwelcome. Instead of feeling uncomfortable or embarrassed by his attention, Olivia returned his stare. Watching him, she felt her pulse quicken. Seconds passed, but she didn't look away. Then, surprisingly even to her, she smiled at him.

What do you think you're doing?

His reaction was immediate and unmistakable; a straightening of his torso, a hint of a returning smile, and a slight narrowing of his gaze; it was as if she'd touched him. From the wagon, she could feel Sally's eyes moving from one of them to the other, wondering what was happening, but Olivia paid her friend no mind.

Then he started walking toward her.

Olivia's heart beat faster. *Who is this man?* The only thing she could say for certain was that she'd never seen him before.

"You look like you could use some help," the stranger said once he had reached her, glancing down at the box of newspapers.

"They were heavier than I expected," she managed.

Up close, he was even better-looking than he'd been at a distance. With the sun high over his shoulder, the light caught his hair in such a way that it almost shined. His blue eyes, roaming over her features just as intently as she was regarding his, were flecked with a darker color. Even his voice appealed to her, deep yet pleasant. While Olivia noticed that his clothes were a bit out of fashion and wrinkled, that there was a smattering of whiskers on his cheeks, and that he appeared a little tired, that did nothing to dampen her interest. Just as she had with her father, Olivia kept her ring hidden, her hand at her side.

"May I?" he asked with a wisp of a smile, kneeling to take the box in his hands, holding its weight as easily as if it were filled with feathers.

Olivia nodded.

The man took the box over to the wagon, nodding to Sally on the way, and placed it on the pile. The newspapers shifted slightly, leaning awkwardly to one side; no matter how he tried to reposition it, the whole load seemed precarious.

"I don't think it'll hold any more," he said.

"We'll have to come back for the rest," Olivia replied.

"I'll go and tell Mrs. Wright," Sally added; before she walked away to talk to the widow, she gave Olivia an intense look, nodding toward the stranger.

Now that she was alone with the man, Olivia said, "Thank you for the help."

"It was nothing," he answered.

"I appreciate it all the same."

A momentary silence fell over them, but it wasn't awkward. Olivia wondered what the stranger was thinking, if he was enjoying her company as much as she was his. Eventually, her curiosity about him became too much.

"I'm Olivia," she said, extending her hand, wanting to be polite while hoping to learn his name in exchange. "Olivia Marsten."

The stranger had taken her hand in his own, enveloping it, his skin warm to the touch. He'd held it for a moment longer than might have been needed, although Olivia hadn't minded, but he let her go, his smile faltering, if only for an instant, at the mention of her name. It reappeared a second later, but Olivia had noticed all the same.

From somewhere in the distance, the sound of an automobile's horn being repeatedly honked came to her ears.

"Are you related to Sheriff Marsten?" the man asked.

Olivia's brow furrowed with curiosity. "He's my father," she answered.

The stranger brightened a bit. "That's one heck of a coincidence," he said. "He's just the man I was going to see."

Again, the sound of a horn's bleating filled the afternoon; this time, it sounded closer.

"And you are?" Olivia asked, cutting to the chase.

The man shook his head. "I'm sorry," he apologized. "Where are my manners? I'm Peter . . . Peter B—" he began, but then faltered; for the second time, his good cheer wavered; it was as if he had tripped on something, almost falling, but managed to right himself at the last instant. "Peter Baird," he finished.

"Why are you looking for my father?"

Peter lifted his elbow and placed his hand on the back of his head. Sheepishly, he said, "Well, that's sort of a —"

Before he could finish, they were once

again interrupted by the sound of honking. Both of them turned and looked up the street. An old, dented pickup truck rounded the corner, popped over the curb, and nearly collided with a telephone pole before it righted itself and headed down the street toward them, swerving every which way. The front end was all busted up, covered with dents, but it somehow kept running. Periodically, the horn sounded.

"What's going on?" Peter asked.

"Oh, no," Olivia answered, knowing just who it was. She would've recognized Sylvester Eddings's truck anywhere; there wasn't a person in all Miller's Creek who wouldn't have. He must have sobered up enough for her father to release him. The damage from the crash that had put him behind bars clearly hadn't been bad enough to keep his truck from running. Olivia imagined that Sylvester had left jail and headed for the tavern or, if it was closed, searched until he found a bottle hidden away and started drinking again. Now, he was behind the wheel, clearly driving drunk.

"If he's not careful, someone's going to get hurt," Peter warned.

Olivia cringed, thinking that Sylvester was about to sideswipe a car parked on the other side of the street, but he turned sharply at the last instant, the tires screeching, and gave the horn a quick beep. She could see him through the windshield, looking as if he was about to pass out. Suddenly, the car jerked violently from one side of the road to the other, and then back again.

She gasped.

It was heading right for them.

CHAPTER SEVEN

At first, Peter hadn't known why he had
lied. When he'd discovered that Olivia was
the sheriff's daughter, it had been a surprise;
seeing how her eyes had briefly narrowed
told him that he hadn't been able to keep
the shock from his face. Still, nothing had
changed between them, not really. But then
she'd asked him his name. He had started
to answer, to tell her the truth, but something stopped him, some reason he couldn't
completely understand, and he'd quickly
come up with Baird; it'd been the name of
one of the American soldiers on the long
boat trip across the Atlantic. As soon as he'd
said it, shame had filled him.

Even in the few minutes since they'd met,
Olivia Marsten had proven to be far more
than Peter could have ever imagined her to
be; not only was she truly beautiful on the
outside, but she was also charming, well-
spoken, someone around whom he felt

completely at ease. She was the last person he wanted to mislead.

But then the truth had hit him.

Looking into Olivia's eyes, Peter had suddenly understood that the reason he lied was that he wanted to spend more time with her, to get to know her better, and that could never happen if he turned himself in as an escaped German prisoner. So he'd invented a new identity in order to keep from being taken away from her. It was selfish and misguided, but the thought of never seeing her again was unbearable.

Peter was just about to come up with another lie to explain why he was looking for her father, when the truck had careened around the corner. His first thought was to be grateful for the distraction, but watching the vehicle weaving around the road, nearly smashing into a parked car, he began to grow worried. His concern turned to fear when the truck drove toward where he and Olivia stood.

"Move!" he shouted at Olivia

But she was frozen in place. He had seen this reaction before; on the battlefield, when a man's life was in danger, sometimes he could do nothing more than watch it happen.

Peter glanced back at the truck. It was

only a couple hundred feet away, its engine growling. This time, he knew it wouldn't turn.

Grabbing Olivia tightly by the wrist, he tried to pull her close but she resisted, her body rooted in place, her eyes wide with shock. Knowing he had only a matter of seconds to act, Peter did the only thing he could think of. With all his strength, he yanked Olivia's arm, sending her off her feet and tumbling across the grass, her face full of shock. As violent as it had been, at least now he knew she was safe. Unfortunately, he couldn't say the same for himself.

The runaway truck popped over the curb, its undercarriage scraping against the concrete, and smashed into the wagon, sending newspapers flying in every direction, scattered like frightened birds. Peter tried to get out of the way, but the truck's fender caught him flush on the hip and sent him hurtling through the air. The pain was instant and overwhelming. Just as when he and Otto had jumped from the freight train, Peter had the sensation of weightlessness, that he was hanging in the air, but this time the landing was even worse; he crashed with a thud, the air driven from his lungs, and cracked the back of his head hard on the ground. Struggling against the encroaching darkness, he had only the strength to raise his hand before it fell onto his chest and, for the second time in a matter of days, he tumbled down into unconsciousness.

Olivia screamed. Lying on her side, her shoulder aching, she watched helplessly as Sylvester Eddings's truck hit Peter and sent him flying through the air as if he was a rag doll. She gasped as he crashed back down to earth. Peter stirred, but an instant later fell still. Olivia scrambled to her feet and ran to him, struggling to control the sickening feeling that filled her.

Fortunately, Sylvester's truck had sputtered to a stop shortly after barreling into Peter. Olivia imagined that something had been seriously damaged when the undercarriage scraped against the curb; if it hadn't stopped, the truck could have kept going right into Delores Wright's front porch. Out of the corner of her eye, Olivia saw Sylvester stumble out of the truck's cab, but she paid him no mind, focusing instead on Peter.

He lay flat on his back, one arm draped limply across his chest and his eyes closed. A cut had been torn in his shirt sleeve, revealing a trickle of blood. His wrist also looked hurt, though it had yet to bleed.

"Peter," she said insistently, kneeling

beside him. "Can you hear me?" She gave his shoulder a gentle shake but there was no response. Panic inched its way into her thoughts. *Is he dead?* Pressing her head against his chest, she strained to hear or feel something that would tell her he was still alive. But before she could do more than touch him, a slurry voice spoke from behind her.

"What . . . what in tarnation happened . . . ?" Sylvester mumbled, weaving toward her. Just as in her father's jail cell, Olivia could smell him from a distance. His eyes were wet and bloodshot, and a stain ran down the front of his wrinkled shirt. "Did somethin' jump out in front a me again?" he asked.

Something inside Olivia snapped. This wasn't like before. Sylvester hadn't run off the road into a tree, hurting no one but himself.

"Don't you dare come any closer!" she shouted; the fury of her words was enough to cut through Sylvester's alcohol-induced haze, causing him to stumble to a stop. "Can't you see what you've done? You may have killed him!"

"Kill . . . killed what . . . ?" Sylvester muttered. "I was gettin' out a the way of some dog that come runnin' 'cross the road, s'all . . ."

"Go stand next to your truck and don't move an inch!" Olivia ordered. "When my father finds out what you've done this time, he's going to lock you up and throw away the key!"

For a moment, it looked as if Sylvester was going to argue further; his mouth opened and shut like he was a fish out of water, but no words came out. Finally, he did as Olivia told him, wobbling back in the direction he'd come, nearly falling over a time or two, before slumping against his truck's twisted front bumper.

Once again, Olivia pressed her head against Peter's chest and listened. Desperation knocked in her heart, hoping that he would be all right. At first, she heard nothing, but then, just as she was about to despair, she detected a slow, shallow beating.

He was still alive!

Uncertain what she should do next, Olivia was relieved when Sally came running around the corner of the house. Her wide eyes went from Olivia and Peter, to Sylvester and his truck, then back again.

"What happened?" Sally shouted.

"He hit Peter," Olivia explained, pointing at Sylvester; the still-drunk man waved back. "It's . . . it's my fault he . . . got hurt . . ." she continued, remembering the fateful moment. "I couldn't move . . . so Peter pulled me out of the way . . . that's why he got hit . . ."

Olivia knew it was the truth. *Peter saved me!* If it hadn't been for his quick thinking and sacrifice, *she* would've been the one struck. *She* would be lying on her back and possibly clinging to life. This man she had just met, who didn't know a thing about her, had protected her. For that, as well as the way he'd made her feel, an unexpected rush of emotion, she had to help him.

"Is he alive?" Sally asked nervously.

Olivia nodded. "But I don't know how badly he's been hurt."

"What do we do? Should we call the doctor?"

"We need to move him," Olivia answered with a conviction that surprised her. "I can't just let him lie here."

"But where are we going to take him?"

Both of them looked up at Delores Wright's house. The older woman stared back from inside; when the widow realized that they were looking at her, she quickly shut the curtains. Clearly, Delores didn't want the trouble and, given how hard it had been to talk her into handing over her news-

papers, Olivia knew it could take hours to convince her to open her door. There just wasn't time.

"We'll take him to my house," she said.

Olivia and her family lived across the street and around the nearest corner, five doors down. If they could get him there, then they could call Clem Hoskins, Miller's Creek's doctor.

"How are we supposed to get him that far?" Sally asked. "Even with both of us lifting, I doubt we could get him to the sidewalk."

"Let me give you ladies a ride," Sylvester offered before hiccupping.

Olivia ignored him. Instead, she looked around for something, anything that might solve their problem. Then she saw it. By some miracle, the wagon she and Sally had been piling old newspapers in hadn't been completely crushed by Sylvester's truck. It lay on its side, one end dented, empty of its former load.

Maybe, just maybe . . .

Olivia went to the wagon and righted it. Even with one wheel that wobbled a bit when it rolled, it looked sturdy enough. Bringing it back to where Peter lay motionless, she and Sally managed to get him up and into the wagon's bed; both of them had to strain with all their might. He lay there awkwardly, his head lolling to the side, but no part of him touched the ground. Giving the wagon a hard pull, Olivia was relieved to find that she could move it. Now, all she had to do was get Peter home.

"What's your mother going to say when she sees us?" Sally asked.

"We'll just have to see."

When they went past Sylvester and to the sidewalk, the old drunk was sound asleep against his truck, drool hanging from his lip, snoring like a hibernating bear.

Olivia's mother ended up surprising her. Elizabeth had seen them coming through the kitchen window and had run to meet them as they came up the drive. She didn't appear panicked by the sight of her daughter dragging an injured stranger along in a wagon, but rather calm-yet-concerned. Elizabeth didn't ask any questions about what had happened, at least not at first; instead, she focused on Peter's injuries.

"How badly is he hurt?" she asked.

"I don't know," Olivia answered.

With all three of them lifting, they managed to carry Peter from the wagon to the guest room on the first floor. There, Sally wiped the blood from his cuts while Olivia rounded up blankets and pillows to make him more comfortable. While she was busy running around the house, she heard her mother on the telephone.

"Dr. Hoskins will be here soon," Elizabeth said when she entered the room. Looking down at Peter, she asked, "Who is he?"

"His name is Peter Baird," Olivia answered. "He was helping me haul newspapers when he . . . when he got hit . . ."

"Hit by what?"

"It's more like, by whom." Olivia told her mother exactly what had happened, how Sylvester Eddings's truck had weaved down the street, how Peter had pulled her out of the way, and about how he'd been struck. Curiously, even to herself, there was one thing she didn't mention; that Peter had been looking for her father. She hadn't even told Sally. She supposed that it wasn't important, at least not now.

Clement Hoskins arrived five minutes later, looking harried, with tufts of his wispy white hair sticking out in every direction and his glasses slipping down his nose. He'd been the doctor in Miller's Creek for decades, long enough to have helped hundreds of people as they neared their deaths, and then delivered hundreds of babies to take their places. Examining Peter, he asked lots of questions about what had happened. He checked his patient's vital signs, raised the unconscious man's eyelids to shine a light in them, stitched up the deepest cut on Peter's arm, and wrapped his other injuries in bandages.

"I can't be certain something isn't broken," he remarked as he packed his instruments into his medical bag, "but I doubt it."

"Can he be moved?" Elizabeth asked; Olivia frowned, thinking that her mother was starting to show her true colors, unhappy at the thought of a strange man lying in her guest room.

To Olivia's great relief, the doctor shook his head. "I wouldn't advise it," he said. "Quite frankly, the best thing for him would be to get plenty of rest. That knock to the head he took was a good one. Unless it's too much of a bother, I'd recommend leaving him where he is."

"It's no trouble at all," Elizabeth answered, putting on her best smile.

By the time Olivia's father came home, Peter still hadn't awakened; he occasionally twitched or groaned, but never opened his eyes. Outside, the day was marching toward night, the shadows long and deep. John Marsten looked exhausted. He'd arrested

Sylvester at Delores's house, still asleep on the ground beside his trunk, still swearing his innocence. Olivia's father knew some of what had occurred, but he asked for her side of the story. Once again, she repeated everything up to Peter's getting hit, but still chose not to say anything about the stranger's reason for coming to Miller's Creek. All day, watching him, she had replayed their conversation, mulling over every word that he'd said, aware of the way he'd made her feel. When Sylvester's truck had first raced around the corner, he'd been about to tell her why he was looking for her father. Now, for her own selfish reasons, she decided to wait until she could hear the truth from Peter himself.

"Did he say where he was coming from?" her father asked; Olivia detected a hint of the inquisitive lawman in his question.

"No," she answered. Curious, she added, "Does he look familiar to you?"

John shook his head. "I've never seen him before," he said. He paused, and then added, "It's strange to see a young man his age traveling these days."

Olivia had wondered the same thing. Ever since the Japanese attacked Pearl Harbor and Germany declared war against the United States, men of service age had slowly left for the armed services. Almost overnight, recruiting posters and stations were everywhere and the lines to answer the call were long. Nowadays, in Miller's Creek, it was unusual to see a man between the age of eighteen and forty; when you did, they often went out of their way to explain why they weren't in uniform; usually, it was because of a medical issue that classified them as 4F, unfit for military duty. Billy had suffered under this burden for years until he'd finally managed to receive a doctor's permission to join the fight against the Axis. Peter might have a similar excuse; maybe he had a problem with his heart or lungs, or maybe he was just like Billy, about to leave for training.

"Whatever the reason, I'm glad he was there," John continued, placing his hand on his daughter's shoulder. "Some folks might say he was in the wrong place at the wrong time, but without him, only the Good Lord knows what might've happened to you."

"He may have saved my life," Olivia explained.

"For that, he will always have my thanks."

Just then, there was a familiar knock on the side door to the kitchen; one heavy rap followed by three quick ones. Olivia had heard it hundreds of times over the years, had always welcomed it, and had often run to answer. But today, the sound filled her with dread.

It was Billy.

CHAPTER EIGHT

When Olivia opened the kitchen door, Billy had his back to her, walking toward the far side of the drive; it looked to Olivia as if he was pacing, just as he'd done in front of the hardware store on the morning he had come to propose. At the first creak of the door's hinges, Billy looked back at her, his expression one of worry.

"I just heard about what happened," he said, hurrying back to her. "Are you all right? Have you been hurt?"

"I'm fine," she tried to reassure him.

"I don't think I've ever been so worried," Billy explained. "Marilyn Hargrove was telling everyone down at the bank how Sylvester's truck had come roaring down the street, went right over the curb, and —"

"I'll tell you all about it," Olivia interrupted, "but not here." Right then, the last thing she wanted was to have to worry about her family eavesdropping on their conversation, especially because she knew that she and Billy had plenty of other things to talk about, far more than just the accident. "Come with me."

The twilight sky was fast filling with stars. Above them, a pair of bats darted through the remaining light, searching for bugs to eat. Rounding the house, Olivia skirted her mother's victory garden; like most in Miller's Creek, Elizabeth had taken to growing her own food to supplement what had been sacrificed for the war effort. Though the garden was now barren, it would soon be spotted with new sprouts and thick with produce by summer. Her backyard had also been the sight of many memorable moments for her and Billy: playing hide-and-seek, chasing after fireflies on a hot summer night, and climbing trees as high as they dared. Whenever they'd been together here, it had been nothing but fun.

But this night was different. For the first time in their long friendship, Olivia felt uncomfortable being with Billy. They hadn't been together since he had proposed and things between them felt awkward, as if they were suddenly strangers. Part of the problem was that since she'd been blindsided by Billy's asking her to marry him, Olivia wondered what other things she might not know, what other surprises he might have in store for her. Chastising herself, Olivia tried to shake her worries. It wasn't as if she had planned on avoiding Billy forever.

Olivia led Billy to a familiar spot. A lone, towering evergreen rose at the rear of the property. Her father had always kept the lowest branches pruned back so that there was plenty of room to walk beneath the great tree. Pine cones and fallen needles littered the ground, and the air was full of the sharp scent of sap. John had built a rough bench; wiping away the odds and ends that had fallen onto it, Olivia sat. When Billy joined her, he took her hand in his own, his thumb rubbing over the ring he had given her, a much more intimate gesture than she was used to. She had to fight the urge to pull away.

"So what happened?" he asked.

Taking a deep breath to steady her nerves, Olivia once again recounted the horrible accident. Billy hung on her every word, only occasionally interrupting with questions. When she finished, Billy sat back on the bench, a look of astonishment on his face. "It's incredible," he said, "and a bit frightening, both at the same time. You could've been badly hurt."

"I could've been killed," Olivia corrected

him. "I don't even want to think of what would have happened if I hadn't been pulled out of the way. Instead, all I have are bruises."

"Let me see," Billy asked curiously.

Gently, Olivia rolled up the right sleeve of her blouse until it was just past her elbow. Her wounds were ugly. Even in the last of the daylight, the discoloration was obvious; a dark mottling of purple, blue, and brown bruises that ran roughshod up her forearm, around her elbow, reaching even higher. Just after it had happened, it had been little more than a dull throbbing, but now it ached. When Billy reached out and touched her, Olivia winced and pulled away.

"Sorry," he apologized.

"It's all right. It just stings."

"Did Dr. Hoskins take a look at it?"

Olivia shook her head. "I'm fine. It's just a bad bruise," she said. "Besides, he had more important things to worry about."

"That guy that came along and pulled you out of the way . . ." he muttered. "What did you say his name was?"

"Peter. Peter Baird."

Billy nodded, his jaw set tight, his lips pursed as if he was deep in thought. "So this guy . . ." he began, "Peter . . . who you've never seen before, just happens to be walking by and offers to help you carry boxes of old newspapers . . . sort of unusual, isn't it?"

"Not really," Olivia answered. "They were heavy and I'd dropped one. He saw it and came to help. I thought it was nice of him."

Instead of agreeing, Billy fell silent. "How old is this guy?" he finally asked. "What does he look like?"

"Why does it matter?" she asked, surprised by his odd request.

"I want to know, that's all."

"He's . . . he's the same age as us . . ." she answered. "Maybe a little older . . ."

"Is he tall or short? Does he have blond or dark hair?" he kept on, the questions coming fast. "Is he *handsome*?"

Olivia gasped; she couldn't believe what Billy was saying.

"I just find it odd that this guy was showing such an interest in you," he kept on. "For all you know, he could be some kind of degenerate."

"He's not like that! He might very well have saved my life today!"

"And I'll thank him for that," Billy shot back, clearly growing upset at her refusal to answer him. "I just want to know who this man is," he added. "Especially since he put his hands on my fiancée."

It was then that Olivia understood; Billy was jealous. He was jealous of a man he had never met, simply because he'd spoken with her. He felt threatened that Peter had been by her side, regardless of the fact that he'd protected her from Sylvester and his runaway truck. His fears were so irrational, so emotional, that they were enough to make it evident that he clearly didn't trust *her*. He was so insecure, so worried about their relationship, that he saw dangers everywhere he looked.

But while there was a part of Olivia that pitied Billy for his concerns, there was another that knew his worries weren't entirely without cause. She still remembered the way she'd felt talking to Peter, how just seeing him on the sidewalk, watching her, had brought a smile to her face. One of the questions Billy had asked was whether she found Peter handsome; she doubted that her fiancé would have liked her answer. Peter was unlike any man she'd ever met. Though she'd only spent a couple of minutes with him, she definitely wanted to know him better.

Olivia's thoughts must have shown in her face. Billy had been watching her intently, waiting for the answers he so desperately wanted, but suddenly his features softened and his eyes looked quickly away, as if he was ashamed of how he'd been behaving. For a moment, neither of them spoke, the only sound beneath the evergreen coming from the early-spring crickets, chirping in the darkness.

It was Billy who finally spoke. "I'm sorry," he said. "I didn't mean to upset you, especially after all you've been through."

Olivia remained silent.

"It's . . . it's just that ever since I heard about what happened," Billy continued, "I've been worried sick. I couldn't bear to lose you . . . just the thought of it makes me crazy. But instead of being happy that you weren't hurt, I jumped to conclusions and made a fool out of myself." He paused. "Can you forgive me?"

"Yes," she answered truthfully.

"So . . . will he . . . will Peter . . . be all right?"

Olivia remembered the way Peter's head had hit the ground and how still he'd been when they'd loaded him into the wagon. "I hope so," she said. "The doctor said that the only thing we could do was let him rest."

"Well," Billy said with a slightly forced smile, "when he does wake up, I want to be the first person who thanks him for what he did." It was the same sentiment that her father had expressed, but Olivia didn't find it nearly as convincing coming from Billy. Though he was doing his best to hide his true feelings, she could see that he was ill at ease.

Ever since Billy had dropped to one knee and proposed, Olivia had felt lost, as anchorless as a teacup in a tempest. When she'd surprised even herself and agreed to become his wife, it hadn't taken long for her to begin doubting her decision. More difficult questions had followed from family and friends. For too long, Olivia had been on the defensive. Maybe it was time for her to be the one doing the asking . . .

"Why didn't I know?"

"Know what?"

"That you were in love with me," Olivia answered. "When you proposed, you said that you've loved me ever since the day we met along the creek, but whenever I think back, looking for some sign that might've given away how you felt, there's nothing. How did you keep it from me? How could I have mistaken your love for friendship for so long?"

Billy turned to look at her, but didn't answer.

"Tell me," she insisted.

He sighed. "The reason you didn't know,

why I did whatever it took to keep it from you, was because I was scared that if I was honest, if I just told that I was in love with you, there was a chance you would've rejected me. The truth could have destroyed our friendship, and that was a risk I wasn't willing to take."

Olivia wondered if he was right; if Billy *had* told her years ago, would she have turned him down?

Probably . . .

To Olivia, Billy had never been more than her friend, her *best* friend. She hadn't once considered him as a potential boyfriend or husband.

"Our friendship would never have ended," she said.

"But I didn't know that," he answered. "The problem with reaching for the stars is that you have that much farther to fall."

"Is that what I was to you? A star?"

"The brightest in the sky. You still are."

Billy's words made Olivia blush. Unable to think of what to say, she sat back on the rough bench and looked into the darkness.

Inside her home, lights shone brightly in the kitchen. Even from so far away, Olivia could see her mother finishing her preparations for dinner. Suddenly, her father appeared, sliding up behind his wife, trying to steal a bite of something, and then getting his hand playfully swatted away. It was a tender moment between them, something Olivia rarely saw; her mother's hardness rarely allowed for shows of affection. But right before her eyes, even with an injured stranger sleeping in the guest room, it was clear her parents were still in love.

"They look happy."

Olivia looked at Billy; he smiled, then turned back toward the house.

"Yes, they do," she answered.

As they watched, her mother suddenly began to laugh heartily, the sound trapped behind the glass, her eyes shut and her head tilted back, her shoulders shaking slightly. Olivia could only imagine what had caused it; probably one of her father's infamous jokes.

"Do you think we could ever be like that?" Billy asked. "After we've been married for twenty years, had a couple of kids, maybe a grandchild or three, and are happy in our home, that we'll be the ones standing in front of the kitchen window, laughing together?"

Olivia didn't respond; she didn't know how. This was the very question she had been unable to answer, no matter how hard she tried. That was because something important was missing from her relationship with Billy.

Love.

Having a family, growing old together, sharing moments both good and bad, needed love. She saw it in her parents, even if her mother could be difficult, and Olivia had always wanted the same for herself. She wondered if she'd ever love Billy as passionately as he did her, if at all. She just didn't *feel* it. He didn't make her heart flutter. She didn't count the time until she could see him again. He hadn't filled her with a desire to kiss him. To make matters worse, meeting Peter Baird had troubled the already muddy waters; he had stirred unfamiliar feelings inside her, some of them the same emotions she'd never felt with Billy.

Questions filled her. Could things between them change? Would it take months, maybe even years, for the love to come? Without it, how could they hope to get to where her mother and father were? What if she gave in and married him? Would she spend the rest of her life regretting her decision? Would she be giving up her dreams of love? Would everything between them, especially their friendship, be ruined, just as Billy had feared? In her desire not to hurt Billy, would

she only end up hurting them both?

"Billy, we need to —" she began, determined to find a way to talk about what she was feeling, to give voice to her worries. But when she turned toward him, Olivia found that Billy had already come closer, his face mere inches away. His eyes roamed across her face, so imploring that it felt as if he were asking her something. "What?" she asked, as if that was precisely what he'd done.

Instead of answering with words, Billy reached over and tenderly placed his fingers against the curve of her cheek. Ever so slightly, so softly that Olivia wondered if she was imagining it, he turned her head toward him and moved forward. Time felt as if it was standing still, her pounding heart marking the countless seconds that should have passed, as Billy drew closer. At the last moment, Olivia closed her eyes. When his lips touched hers, Olivia reached out and grabbed Billy's shoulder, squeezing tightly. It was all so sudden, so unexpected, that she became swept up in the moment. Hope filled her; maybe there was a chance, maybe there was a fire waiting to be kindled . . . But then, as their kiss lengthened, Billy's passion steadily growing, Olivia's waned; to her it felt forced, unnatural, and lacking in the romance she knew it needed. Still, she didn't stop it; unwilling to hurt him, she made no move to push him away.

Olivia felt like a fool.

Somehow, she had managed to make her situation even worse . . .

Billy Tate walked quickly down the darkened streets of Miller's Creek; he moved as if he had someplace he needed to be, but the look on his face seemed to say that he had no idea where he was going. Absently, he glanced up at the thousands of pinprick stars and the slyly winking moon. He didn't know what time it was, but wouldn't have cared if he had. He could only think of one thing.

I kissed Olivia!

He could still remember the moment their lips had touched, the taste of her, the feel of her fingers digging into his arm. It was as if he'd been floating above them, watching from the branches. It hadn't lasted long, but the truth was that even if it had gone on for hours, it still wouldn't have been long enough.

After all the long years that he had loved Olivia from a distance, had kept his true feelings hidden, Billy couldn't believe how things had worked out. Proposing to Olivia had been the hardest thing he'd ever done. He'd talked himself out of it more than a dozen times; even that fateful morning, standing in front of the hardware store, he'd been wishy-washy, ready to go in the door one moment, wanting to run back to the bank the next. Somehow, he'd managed to go through with it. Kneeling on the floor of the warehouse, listening as Olivia agreed to become his wife, was undoubtedly the greatest moment of his life. Somehow, it had been even better than the countless times he'd fantasized about it. It was like a fairy tale; now all he had to do was worry about whether they would live happily ever after.

And there had already been problems . . .

The first had come while Billy had been down on bended knee. He had noticed Olivia wavering, about to either reject his proposal or ask for more time to consider, neither of which were outcomes he wanted. Before she could say anything, he'd tried to backtrack, to apologize and say that he was at fault for surprising her, that he'd been wrong to ask; for Billy, it would have been better to take the offer away, anything to avoid being turned down. But then, shockingly, surprisingly, she'd accepted, proving his worries to be unfounded.

The second problem had come tonight.

Ever since he'd heard about the accident, Billy had been half-sick, playing out all sorts of scenarios in his head. Olivia was the love of his life, as well as his best friend. If she'd been hurt . . . But his relief at finding out that she was safe was soon replaced by a different emotion, something he never would have expected.

Jealousy.

When Olivia told him that she'd been talking with a man, with a *stranger,* and that that same man was responsible for saving her from being run over by Sylvester Eddings, it felt as if he'd been slugged in the gut. He had tried to ignore those jealous feelings, to hide them just as he'd hidden his love for Olivia, but he had failed miserably. His words had surprised even him. Billy supposed that it was because he knew how tenuous, how fragile his engagement to Olivia actually was; he might have been a dreamer, but he wasn't a fool. One good knock from any direction, and the whole house of cards he'd carefully built would come tumbling down. Once again, he would be alone.

But now, after he and Olivia had kissed, Billy no longer felt so worried. He found himself relieved, even excited for what lay ahead of them. They would be married, he would go off to the Navy for as long as the war lasted, and then he'd come home and their life together could begin at last.

Finally, Olivia was all his.

CHAPTER NINE

Ever so slowly, Peter began to wake. As his head cleared, he started to wonder when he'd fallen asleep and which of his fellow soldiers had taken first watch. Surprisingly, he didn't feel cold, even though it had been months since they'd had adequate blankets or coats. He hoped that someone had put on some coffee.

But then, as Peter tentatively opened his eyes, the brightness of the morning sun made his head hurt so badly that he saw stars.

"Verdammte Scheiße," he mumbled.

"What was that?" a woman's voice answered.

Instantly, Peter shot wide awake. Even though his temples throbbed so badly that he felt sick to his stomach, he opened his eyes and took in his surroundings. He was in a bedroom. Beside him, the curtain had been raised a couple of inches to allow for a little sunlight. A clock ticked steadily on the nightstand, keeping time far more slowly than his pounding heart. At the foot of the bed in which he lay was a dresser; a mirror hung above it, facing him. Staring at his reflection, Peter was shocked; he looked exhausted, his hair matted to his scalp with sweat, dark circles beneath his eyes, his pallor as pale as a ghost. And there, sitting in a chair beside the dresser, looking at him with concern, was Olivia.

"I didn't understand what you said," she told him, setting aside the book she had been reading and rising to stand by his bedside.

It was then that Peter understood he'd made a terrible mistake.

He'd spoken in German.

"It . . . it was nothing . . ." he hastily explained, searching for his English like a drowning man searching for a floating log. "I must've been . . . dreaming . . ."

Olivia smiled at him. Looking at her, Peter's heart started to pound, just like when he'd first seen her. Coming to stand beside his bed, the sunlight catching her hair, she looked like an angel, even more beautiful to him than before. But as spellbound as he was, he was still panicked. Desperately, he tried to get his bearings, to understand exactly what had happened to him.

"Where . . . where am I . . . ?" he asked.

"You're in my home," she explained. "It was the closest place I could think to bring you."

Peter tried to sit up on his elbows, but moving caused another wave of pain and nausea to wash over him. Wincing, he fell back against the bed, his agony even worse.

"Easy," Olivia soothed. "The doctor said that it's going to take time for you to get better. There's no need to try to do too much. You need your rest."

"The . . . the doctor . . ." Peter repeated. "What . . . what happened . . . ?"

"Don't you remember?" she asked. "The truck was heading right for us. You pulled me out of the way and then it hit you."

Slowly, it all began to come back to Peter: the truck, his fear for Olivia's safety, getting hit, the whole story. He reached up and felt the huge bump on the back of his head. Bandages ran the length of his right arm, all the way down to the wrist, even covering the cuts that had been made by his hand-cuffs when the train had crashed.

"How . . . long have I been asleep . . . ?" he asked.

"A little more than a full day. It's late in

the afternoon on Wednesday."

Peter nodded as if he understood; ever since he'd been captured back in the forest in France, he'd had no idea what day of the week it was.

"And you've been watching me sleep?"

Olivia looked away for a moment, as if she might have been a bit embarrassed. "I haven't been in here for long," she explained. "When I came back from work, I decided to sit and read. I thought that if you woke, it would be better for you to see a familiar face." She paused before adding, "Besides, you may have saved my life yesterday. It's the least that I could do."

"You took care of me," he answered. "That was more than enough."

Olivia smiled. "Is there anyone you'd like me to call?" she asked.

Peter's first thought was that she was asking him whether he had a wife or a girlfriend, but he quickly put it aside as foolish wishful thinking; that he was smitten with her didn't mean the attraction was mutual, not necessarily. He shook his head. "No, there isn't."

"What about your family?" she pressed.

Unable to hold her eye, Peter looked away. He thought about his mother. If she was still alive, she was surely suffering, but as

153

hard as it was to accept, neither of them could do anything for each other, not now. "My parents . . . neither of them . . . they're not in my life anymore . . ." he explained.

"I'm sorry," Olivia replied.

"Don't be. It all happened a long time ago and far from here."

"Where are you from?"

Peter hesitated, thinking of his father. "Pennsylvania."

"That's an awfully long way from here," Olivia said. "What with the war and the restrictions on travel, it's not often that you see a man your age just wandering about." As she spoke, Peter thought she looked a little sheepish, as if she was uncomfortable prying. "It got me to thinking that you must be a soldier."

Olivia wasn't asking him a direct question, but Peter understood that it was one all the same. "You're right," he began, trying to think ahead through his lie, fearful that he would stumble badly enough to give himself away. "But not in the way you might think. I have a deferment, because of my job." With every word he spoke, his confidence grew, the made-up tale getting easier to tell. "I probably won't ever wear a uniform, but I'm doing my part, like everyone else."

"It sounds exciting."

"Some days, I suppose."

Deep down, Peter knew that lying to Olivia was wrong, but there was another part of him, an insistent voice, that kept telling him that speaking the truth meant being hauled away, never to see her again. He'd come into town to turn himself in to the sheriff, Olivia's father, and to lead the law to where Otto hid. It had all seemed so simple. But meeting Olivia, feeling the way he did when he was around her, made him want to be by her side as long as he could. Her beauty, the sound of her voice, the way that she smiled all drove him to stay by her side. Peter was filled with a sense of hope that somehow, some way, he could have her. He couldn't let it end, not yet, even if it meant that he had to lie through his teeth.

"So this job of yours," she said. "What is it exactly?"

Peter paused. "I can't tell you that," he answered. "All I can say is that it's important to the war effort."

Instead of cutting off Olivia's curiosity, Peter's response seemed to inflame it further. "It's a secret?" she prodded, her eyes sparkling with interest.

"One of national security," he lied, digging his hole deeper.

"What branch of the service do you work with?"

"Olivia, I told you . . ."

"Okay, okay," she replied. "I won't keep trying. As long as what you do is put to use against those terrible Germans, it's all right with me."

Peter's heart felt like it stopped beating.

"When the war started," she continued, "I used to go to the movies and watch the newsreels and be so afraid. I couldn't believe all of those people cheering Hitler, waving those horrible flags, shouting for the soldiers as they marched by, bloodthirsty for war. It made me sick." Olivia frowned, shaking her head a little at the unwelcome memory. "I know I shouldn't say it, but all of those people are getting exactly what's coming to them."

Though Peter was surprised, he knew that he shouldn't have been. Germany's blitzkrieg through Europe had brought the world to war and taken countless lives. Hitler deserved to swing from the tallest tree that could be found. But to assume that every German believed in their Führer and his murderous cause was a terrible mistake. Peter thought about those he'd known back in Bavaria who, soon after Hitler was declared chancellor, had dared to speak out against him. One after the other, sometimes in the dead of night, all of them had disappeared. In particular, he remembered Holger Robben, the kindly old man who had run the drugstore and who, one fateful afternoon, had made an off-color joke about Hitler within earshot of someone who didn't find any humor in it. That night, the drugstore's windows had been shattered into pieces, and the inside put to the torch. Just like that, the man's life was ruined. Peter's own fortunes had been little different. He hated everything the Nazis stood for, but in order to protect his mother, to ensure that she would be safe and to keep her from receiving some of the same punishment as their neighbors, he'd gone off to fight, an unwilling soldier from the very beginning.

But to hear Olivia's hatred for Germans nearly broke his spirit. Without revealing his true identity, that he was one of the very people she felt such disgust for, how could he hope to convince her that she was wrong?

Misinterpreting the cloud that passed over his face, Olivia said, "You look like you might be hungry. Would you like something to eat?"

Managing a weak smile, Peter nodded. He *was* hungry. His stomach hadn't stopped growling since he'd woken; other than the meager scraps he and Otto had wolfed down at the cabin, it had been several days since he'd eaten anything.

"Let me go see what I can find."

Olivia headed toward the door but, just as she was about to leave the room, she stopped, turning back to him.

"I just . . . there's one thing that keeps nagging at me," she said.

"What is it?" he asked, feeling a bit nervous.

"When we met, you said that the reason you'd come to town was to talk to my father, the sheriff," Olivia explained. "But before you could say any more, Sylvester's truck turned the corner. Does it have something to do with this secretive job of yours?"

Peter froze. He remembered every word of their conversation. Desperately, he tried to come up with some plausible answer, something that was believable. Stumbling, he raised his hand, wanting to run his fingers through his hair, a tic that often showed when he was nervous, but the moment he touched his scalp, he set off another terrible tremor of pain. Gnashing his teeth and pinching shut his eyes, inspiration struck him and he grabbed for the only straw available to him.

"Maybe . . . maybe the doctor was right . . ." he began. "That crack on my head must've been a doozy . . . I just can't remember . . ."

Olivia nodded, frowning at the same time. "Don't worry about it now," she said. "Just get your rest. I'm sure it'll all come back with time."

With that she went, leaving Peter to his worries. He was in serious trouble. If he really wanted to spend more time with this woman who'd enthralled him so completely, whom he, as unbelievable as it seemed, was falling in love with, he was going to have to come up with a better excuse.

And quick.

CRACK. CRACK. CRACK.

Over and over, Otto brought down his still-cuffed hands as hard as he could onto the dulled blade of the broken axe. Sweat stood out on his forehead. Moments of dizziness weakened him. Dark blood wet his restraints, dripped onto the worn workbench, and splattered onto the ground at his feet. Regardless, he kept going, hard but steady, desperate to be free.

CRACK. CRACK.

Watching Becker make his way toward town, Otto had tried to resign himself to

159

the fact that there was nothing more he could do. The only option that remained was to wait. He'd impatiently paced around the cabin, tried to lie down and get some sleep, anything to take his mind off the situation he found himself in. When his hunger got the better of him, he once again ransacked the cabin, reopening every cabinet and drawer, growing so frustrated at not finding anything that he smashed a nightstand into kindling. In the end, he'd only managed to make his hunger worse.

CRACK. CRACK.

Somehow, he'd made it through the night. At every creak of the cabin or whisper of the wind through the trees, he'd startled awake, sure that Becker had returned. But every time, Otto had still been alone. When the sun had begun to shine in the east, he'd begun to have his first doubts. Maybe the damn Amerikaners had gotten on their trail faster than he'd expected. Maybe his fellow soldier was a useless fool and had gotten captured thanks to his own stupidity. Either way, he had to assume he was now on his own. That meant he had to get free.

CRACK. CRACK.

Rooting around on his hands and knees in the faint dawn light, Otto had finally found the axe head that had broken off after only a few whacks. On the workbench, there was a gap between two of the boards; whether because of rot or shoddy craftsmanship, Otto couldn't have cared less, but he was thankful all the same. Wedging the piece of steel into the space, pushing until he was sure it was secure, he'd begun slamming the chain down onto the blade.

CRACK. CRACK.

He didn't know how many times he'd struck the axe head. Fifty? A hundred? More? Occasionally, sparks flew from the steel, but the cuffs' chain held. It didn't take long for the metal that still bound his wrists to pierce his flesh, drawing blood. But Otto didn't slow, didn't even consider a different plan to gain his freedom. Until his last ounce of strength ebbed, he'd keep trying. For himself. For Hitler. For Germany. For the revenge he would take on these people the moment he was no longer their prisoner.

CRACK. CRACK. *CLINK* . . .

Otto looked down at his trembling, bloody fingers. The chain that had bound his hands was finally broken, a snapped link lying on the workbench. Taking a deep breath, he stretched his muscles, sticking out both of his sore arms, a movement he'd been unable to make for far too long. It hadn't been easy, but finally, he was free.

The only question left was what to do next.

The first thing was to get something to eat; just thinking about food made his stomach grumble loudly. Otto knew that if he wanted to eat, he would need to steal his food. Right then, he would've killed for it. Once it grew dark, he'd pick his way along the edge of town in search of someplace like this cabin, unoccupied and isolated, break in, and take what he needed. If he was lucky, he'd find some clothes to replace his prison uniform; ideally, a long-sleeve shirt to hide the cuffs that still circled his wrists.

Wherever he went, whatever he did, Otto knew he'd have to be cautious. If the authorities in town had captured Becker, they'd be on high alert. It'd be dangerous, risky. But he couldn't get caught. Not now. There was still far too much that needed to be done. Once he got his bearings, some food in his belly, and then somewhere safe to sleep, his real work could begin.

Otto held no illusions of returning to Germany or, for that matter, living much longer. He was deep in enemy territory, a fugitive in the American heartland. But maybe this was a blessing in disguise. Maybe here, he could do far more good than he ever could've done on the battlefield. Before he died, he would sow the seeds of terror in Hitler's name.

Looking down on the unsuspecting town, Otto couldn't help but smile.

CHAPTER TEN

"Just follow my finger."

Peter did as Dr. Hoskins instructed, tracking his hand as he moved it from left to right, then up and down, and finally in a circle. Whenever the doctor's finger neared the window, Peter winced slightly, his eyes narrowing as he tried to block out the pain from the light, but he never broke his gaze. When the doctor finished, he sat and studied his patient for a moment, humming a bit under his breath.

Three days had passed since Peter had been hit by the truck. Over that time, his apprehension about being in the Marstens' home had grown. Whenever there was a knock on the guest room's door, he jumped, expecting it to be the United States Army, sending soldiers to come and collect their runaway prisoner.

But so far, it had yet to happen.

Olivia's family was almost as nice and

charming as she was. Her mother rarely stayed in his room for long, bringing him meals and books to read. Elizabeth was always smiling and polite, though Peter still had the feeling she considered him an intrusion on their lives. Grace, Olivia's younger sister, reminded him of a cat he'd had back in Germany, overflowing with curiosity but not bold enough to do anything about it. He'd noticed her sneaking glances when the door was opened, but she'd never spoken a word to him.

Then there was the sheriff, Olivia's father. When they'd first met, John Marsten had shaken Peter's hand vigorously, thanking him for what he'd done for his daughter. John had told Peter to consider their home his, to stay and rest for however long he needed. But no matter how kindly the lawman was, his presence still unnerved Peter; it was hard for him to relax when John stood beside the bed with a holstered pistol. Still, there was one detail that Peter couldn't help notice; John never asked about why he'd come to Miller's Creek, particularly about why it had been to see *him.* From that, Peter had to assume that Olivia hadn't told her father. But why not?

Another question that kept nagging at Peter was what had happened to Otto. Days had passed since he'd left him at the cabin. The more he thought about it, the more it seemed there were only a couple choices his fellow prisoner could make. If Otto had chosen to follow Peter into town, there was little doubt in his mind that Otto would have been noticed by now; with his hands still chained together, he would have stuck out like a sore thumb. If he'd been found out, Peter was certain he would have overheard John Marsten talking about it with his family. Otto's capture would have also led the authorities to Peter; after all, the brute hadn't escaped alone. Of course the other possibility was that Otto had gotten on another train and headed elsewhere. With Otto gone, there wouldn't be any real danger in Peter's pretending to be someone he wasn't. Things might change with time, but for now, he could remain Peter Baird from Pennsylvania. A part of Peter felt relieved; wherever he was, Otto wasn't his problem anymore.

Dr. Hoskins sat on the edge of the bed and began to remove the bandages on Peter's arm. Bruises still colored his flesh, but they were slowly beginning to fade. Peter couldn't help but stare at the scabs around his wrist, cuts that had been made by his handcuffs; he knew that everyone assumed he had sustained them when he'd been hit by the truck, but he felt nervous seeing them. The doctor turned his arm one way and then the other, inspecting the stitches that he'd made when patching him up.

"This is healing nicely," he commented. "No signs of any infections." Turning Peter's head, he gently touched the knot at the rear. "This isn't as swollen, either. How does it feel?"

"I get headaches now and again," Peter answered. "And I'm still kind of sensitive to light, but not as bad as before."

"Good, good," the doctor mumbled. Rewrapping his patient's arm, he added, "Well, my boy, I can safely say you're on the road to recovery."

"How long until he's up and about?"

Olivia stood beside the door; she'd been there since the doctor had entered, watching everything. As a matter of fact, to Peter it felt as if she was always somewhere close by, keeping an eye on him, not that he didn't like the attention. Since he'd first woken, Olivia had visited him often, telling him about her day at the hardware store; the night before, she had dragged in the radio so that they could listen to a serial program. Twice, he'd woken from a nap to

167

find her sitting quietly beside the dresser, reading. Fortunately, she hadn't asked any more uncomfortable questions; the anticipation of hearing them set him on edge. But that didn't mean Peter wished she would go away. Quite the contrary. By now, he would have expected to not have his breath taken away every time he saw her, but her beauty still felt like a kick in the gut. Each time he heard her voice, each time she laughed at some joke she'd heard, or laid her hand upon his, even if for just a second, he became more smitten than ever.

"I reckon he could get out of bed any time now," Dr. Hoskins explained. "As a matter of fact, I'd recommend getting some fresh air."

Peter nodded. Other than making trips across the hall to the toilet, a short distance that nevertheless made him feel woozy, he'd been bedridden since the accident. Getting out of the Marstens' guest room meant that his health was improving, but it also meant that he was closer to having to make a decision about what to do next; stay or run.

"Good," Peter agreed, although he wasn't sure if he meant it.

"When do you suppose he's going to leave?"

Olivia gasped, unable to believe what her

mother was asking. They stood in the kitchen, cutting vegetables for dinner, a breeze rustling the curtains of the open window. Neither one of them had been speaking, happy to listen to music on the radio, so the question had been as unexpected as it was unseemly. Olivia was so rattled that she nearly dropped her knife into the sink.

"Keep your voice down!" she hissed. "He might hear you!"

Even though they were far from the guest room, the thought of Peter listening to what her mother had said made Olivia flush with embarrassment. Several hours had passed since the doctor had left, so she hoped that he would be sleeping, but . . .

"I wasn't against you bringing him here," Elizabeth kept on, ignoring her daughter's concerns. "The house was close and you had to take him *somewhere.* But it doesn't take someone long to overstay their welcome."

"He may very well have saved my life!" Olivia argued.

"I didn't say I wasn't grateful, but I can only imagine how tongues are wagging in town. Why, I bet we're the biggest tidbit of gossip in Miller's Creek!"

In a way, Olivia's mother was right. Every

day since the accident, someone had come into Pickford Hardware and asked her about what had happened, wanting her to recount it moment by terrifying moment. In a way, Peter had become a hero, the stranger with a heart of gold, like something out of Hollywood, willing to risk his life in order to protect a beautiful young woman. People were talking, but not in the way Elizabeth imagined.

"Besides," her mother explained, "the sooner he's out of the house, the sooner we can start planning for your wedding."

Cringing, Olivia quickly turned her attention back to the cucumbers she had been cutting up. Every single day since she'd told her mother about her engagement to Billy, Elizabeth had been pestering her with questions.

What should we write in the announcements?

What music do you want to play when the two of you leave the altar?

I don't want to invite your Aunt Audrey. What do you think?

No matter how hard Olivia worked to avoid answering, she never managed to change the subject for very long.

"Have you and William set the date yet?" *This* was the question her mother asked more than any other.

"Not yet," Olivia grumbled.

"I swear," Elizabeth replied with a frown. "If I didn't know better, I'd wonder if you really wanted to marry William at all!"

Surprised, Olivia's breath caught in her throat. Maybe this was the opportunity she'd been hoping for. After her ill-advised kiss with Billy beneath the evergreen, Olivia had more doubts than ever about marrying him; there'd been nothing, no spark, no passion on her part. In the end, she'd made things worse.

And then there was Peter.

Olivia liked spending time with him. Peter Baird was easy to talk to; he listened attentively to her, even when she talked about the boring, everyday goings-on at the hardware store. When he laughed, sometimes wincing in pain from his injuries, she couldn't help but join in. Even if it was the result of unfortunate circumstances, she enjoyed his company. It also didn't hurt that, even as banged up and tired as he was from the accident, she found him extremely handsome. There was something about him that made her hurry home from work. When she first knocked on the door to his room, her heart began to beat a little faster. She knew that what she was doing and feeling was wrong or, at the very least, inappropriate. Even if he'd saved her life, Peter was a stranger, someone she'd known for only a matter of days. Besides, she was engaged to another man. What would Billy think if he knew how much time she was spending with Peter? How upset would he be if he knew what feelings another man was stirring in her?

For all of these reasons, Olivia decided that she needed to be honest with her mother, to admit her doubts and fears and maybe, just maybe, receive a little understanding in return. But then, just as she opened her mouth, struggling to find the right words, her mother continued her thought, dashing her wishes.

"Of course, who wouldn't want to marry a man like William Tate? If you turned him down, you'd be the laughing-stock of the whole town!" Elizabeth explained, punctuating her words with nervous laughter. "Why, I doubt that I'd ever be able to live down the embarrassment!"

This time, Olivia dropped her knife.

Surprisingly, her mother noticed. "What's wrong?"

Slowly, incredulously, Olivia shook her head. Anger, frustration, and sadness pounded in her chest. She was a fool for thinking that her mother would ever understand how she felt. The only thing that mattered to Elizabeth was herself. It didn't matter that Peter had kept her daughter from harm; she was worried about what people would think about a strange man staying in her home. It didn't matter that Olivia feared she was making a mistake by marrying someone she wasn't in love with, not the way that she should be; her mother was concerned by how embarrassed she'd be if her daughter didn't accept.

"It's nothing," Olivia managed, struggling to hold back her fevered emotions, to keep from letting out all she kept locked inside.

Elizabeth stared at her for a long moment. When she finally spoke, her voice was low and serious. "You need to stop dreaming, get your head out of the clouds, and put your priorities in order," she said; Olivia wondered if she was talking about Peter. "Opportunities like this don't come around as often as you might think. If you keep dillydallying, William might start thinking that you aren't serious about him. If he walks away, I promise that you will spend the rest of your life regretting it." Picking the knife up out of the sink, Elizabeth pressed it into Olivia's hand. "The next time the two of you are together, you set a date. You can't keep putting this off."

As Elizabeth went back to preparing dinner, silence once again descended between them. Olivia's heart raced; she knew that her mother was right.

She needed to make a decision.

"Have you ever done something because you felt like you had no choice?"

Peter glanced up at Olivia. From the blank look on his face, she knew that he'd been surprised by her question. She understood why. She'd just switched off the radio show they'd been listening to; the Shadow had finished administering his brand of justice to the criminal underworld. Outside, darkness had fallen on another day.

Ever since her conversation with her mother, Olivia had been consumed with what had been said between them. All through dinner, she'd been silent, speaking only when spoken to. Elizabeth had stared at her from across the table; Olivia had done her best to ignore the unwanted attention. No matter what, she resolved not to give in and do as her mother asked. Even if the end result was the same and she married Billy, she would come to that decision in her own way and her own time.

But that didn't mean she wasn't still confused.

From that confusion had come the decision to talk to Peter. Even though he was part of her problem, Olivia felt that if she didn't speak in specifics, maybe there was a way in which he could help. All through the radio program, she'd gone over the words, waiting for the right time. Now, it had arrived.

"I don't know if I follow you," he said.

"Well," Olivia began, coming over to sit on the edge of Peter's bed. "What if there was something you didn't want to do," she explained, "but if you went through with it, you were pretty sure it would make the people you cared about happy. Have you ever had to make a choice like that?"

Peter's gaze drifted from her, but he didn't respond.

"I'm not making any sense," Olivia said, frustrated.

"Actually," he replied, still looking away, as if he was searching for something. "I know exactly what you mean."

"You do?"

Peter nodded. Slowly, he looked back at her, their eyes meeting; Olivia was struck by the strength in his gaze, as if he were trying to tell her something without speaking.

"Not all that long ago, I had to make a difficult decision . . ." he said; his words were chosen carefully, as if he was concerned that if even one was out of place, his whole story would be ruined. "If I made one choice, then I was the one who would suffer," he continued. "But if I made the other . . ." Here, Peter paused, staring at her; Olivia's heart pounded hard as she waited. Finally, he said, "If I chose differently, it would have hurt my mother."

What could force you to have to make such a choice?

Olivia caught herself just before she blurted out her thought. She so desperately wanted to know what had happened to him that it was a struggle to hold back her curiosity. Somehow, she managed. It was a welcome surprise when Peter spoke, answering as if she had asked.

"It's . . . it's still hard to talk about . . ." he explained with a faraway look in his eye, almost pained, as if he was reliving the memory. "I suppose it's still too recent. But I can say that when I made my decision, it was the most difficult thing I've ever done."

"What did you choose?" Olivia asked.

Peter paused. "My mother."

"Over your own happiness?"

He nodded.

"In the end, do you feel like you made the right choice?"

"I don't have any regrets."

"None?" Olivia asked. "How can that be?"

Peter smiled knowingly. "Because whenever I think about what my mother would have had to endure if I'd chosen differently, I know that I couldn't have burdened her with that much suffering. Even if I could go back, do it all again, I wouldn't change a thing."

Olivia believed him. The strength of his conviction was admirable. Whatever she finally decided to do about Billy's proposal, whether she chose to marry him or changed her mind and broke his heart, Olivia hoped she would be as resolute about it as Peter was.

For a while, they both fell silent, a state that Olivia found harder and harder to maintain. Every day that Peter had been in her home, Olivia had thought of more questions she wanted to ask him. Over and over, she had to bite her tongue, swallowing down her curiosity. Though she enjoyed Peter's company, he still remained something of a mystery to her. He'd come out of nowhere, a complete stranger, and had sacrificed himself to keep her from harm. But here they were, days later, and she still knew next to nothing about him. He was from Pennsylvania. He had a deferment from the military, though he couldn't talk about why. Truthfully, what he'd just said about his mother was the most intimate detail he'd ever provided. Olivia wanted to know more. Now that she had begun to ask questions, she found that she was standing on a slippery slope.

"So what were you doing here in Wisconsin?" she asked.

Peter looked momentarily startled. "Excuse me?"

"You said that you were from Pennsylvania, but that's hundreds of miles from here. It made me wonder what had brought you here."

He paused, his tongue darting out to wet his lips. "My job," he finally answered, but added no details.

His response intrigued her. "Strange then that when we met," Olivia said, "the only things you had with you were the clothes on your back."

Peter stiffened slightly, then looked away. Olivia watched his expression closely, but had trouble reading it. This was something that had been troubling her for days. When she had first met Peter, he'd had no suitcase, no baggage, no possessions at all. The clothes he'd been wearing were worn and hadn't fit him particularly well. When Olivia washed them, the only thing she'd found in his pockets were a couple of ratty dollars and a handful of coins. When she'd put them on the clothesline to dry, she half-expected them to fall to pieces. In order to dress him after the doctor's initial visit, they'd had to borrow from her father.

"It's . . . it's kind of embarrassing . . ." Peter answered. "Everything I had was taken from me against my will."

Olivia gasped. "Stolen?"

Peter nodded. "I was on a train coming back from Minnesota when two guys entered my cabin. I woke up and found them rifling through my bag. I tried to fight, but they were too much for me. I'm not sure what happened, whether one of them had a blackjack or just landed a punch, but I was knocked cold. The next thing I know, I'm being thrown off a moving train. When I landed, I must have hit my head because when I came to it was morning. I got up, dusted myself off, and started walking toward the nearest town."

Olivia had been listening raptly; it sounded just like the serials she liked to listen to on the radio. "Which was Miller's Creek," she finished for him.

"When I was jumped, all I'd been wearing was my nightshirt. I hate to admit it, but the clothes I was wearing I took from a cabin up in the hills."

"And that's why you were going to see my father?"

Peter nodded. "A man I met on the way told me where I could find the sheriff," he said. "I thought I should tell him what had happened."

"Why didn't you tell me this when I first asked?" Olivia prodded.

"I couldn't remember at first," he explained. "I was still so groggy from the accident that I had trouble thinking straight. Eventually, it all came back. I suppose that I was too ashamed to say anything."

"You were robbed. That's no reason to cling to your pride."

"Maybe you're right."

A sudden, terrifying thought struck her. "Those men didn't jump you because of what you do for the war effort, did they?" she exclaimed. "You . . . you're not involved with fifth column spies, are you?"

But Olivia's worries were dashed when Peter started laughing. "My goodness, no," he said. "I think one of the reasons I woke up when they entered my cabin was how terrible they smelled. They were vagrants, hobos searching for money, nothing more. I was just unlucky."

"Then it just got worse when Sylvester hit you with his truck."

"I wouldn't say *all* of my luck is bad."

Unexpectedly, Peter reached out and took Olivia's hand. She had to suppress a gasp; he held the one on which she wore Billy's engagement ring. Every time she was with him, she'd taken great pains to keep it out of sight. But she'd been enthralled by his story and had forgotten.

"This is pretty," he commented, rubbing his thumb over the band.

"It's nothing," she lied.

"Compared to *your* beauty, you're right."

Olivia's heart began to race. As time crawled slowly past, their touch lingered. She remembered what had happened with Billy beneath the evergreen tree, how things had quickly spiraled out of her control. Olivia suddenly realized how it would look to be seen like this, alone with a man who wasn't her fiancé, their hands entwined, so she tried to move away, but Peter held her fast, unwilling to let what they shared end. She looked up to find his eyes searching her face.

"Thank you for all you've done," he said.

"You may have saved my life," she replied.

"I don't know if I can ever repay what I owe you."

He smiled. "In the end, I think that *I'm* the one in *your* debt."

Without warning, Peter leaned forward and kissed her. As with Billy, Olivia was caught completely unaware; but *unlike* then, this time, she felt her heart leap so hard that it felt as if it was going to burst out of her chest. Her thoughts raced; she was unable to fully believe what was happening, but thankful for it all the same. Emotions she'd been struggling to grasp, to understand, refused to remain unheard. Their kiss was tender, a soft touch that felt almost fragile, as if it was precious, but it was undeniably powerful, a sudden storm that shook the ground she walked on. Olivia held her breath and closed her eyes, giving herself over to the moment. Her hand, still in his, squeezed tightly. But then, just as quickly as it had begun, it was over. Her eyes fluttered open to find him smiling at her.

Feeling a bit rattled, Olivia stood up and went to the door, wondering if her face was as red as she imagined. Peter made no move to stop her, but she was certain that his eyes never left her. At the door, Olivia stopped and looked back; as when they'd held hands, their gaze lingered. Neither of them spoke; she wondered what she could possibly say. To Olivia, there was much about Peter that remained a mystery, but there was no doubt that he had kindled a fire inside her, something completely unexpected.

But maybe the greatest mystery of all was what she was going to do next.

CHAPTER ELEVEN

Peter stood in the yard behind the Marstens' house and stared into the sky. Brilliant, warm sunlight washed over him as the breeze pushed a couple of clouds across a mostly clear sky. Birds chirped as the squirrels scurried around, digging up the nuts they'd buried back in the fall. Somewhere nearby, a dog barked. Closing his eyes, Peter breathed deeply, inhaling the sweet scent of pine.

Absently, Peter ran his fingers over the cuff of his shirt. True to her word, Olivia had gone through her father's closet and found him a couple of outfits. Though everything smelled of mothballs, he was happy to have them all the same. Other than the musty clothes he'd taken from the cabin, it had been a long time since he had worn something other than the garb of a soldier or the prisoner he'd become. Years, by his count. Even though he was still a fugitive, he felt somewhat normal. He supposed that, by outward appearances, he looked American.

Slowly, a smile spread across his face. Never in his wildest imagination would he have thought he'd be here. As confusing a turn as his life had taken, Peter knew it could have been much worse; he could be dead, crushed in the train wreck or killed on the battlefield. A different twist of fate and he never would have seen this beautiful day. He was glad that he'd listened to Olivia's advice and gone outside; it was the first time he'd done so since the accident.

It was also the first time he'd been by himself.

Olivia and her father had gotten up early and headed into town for work. Peter had no idea where Grace had gone; he'd heard her holler to her mother, followed by the kitchen door slamming shut, and then her girlish shout as she almost certainly leaped from the porch on her way to whatever mischief awaited. Elizabeth had worked around the house for a couple of hours before she'd knocked on his door to tell him she was going to run some errands.

So now what . . . ?

Not for the first time, Peter considered running away. It would be easy to go back inside, grab some food, scrounge around for whatever money he could find, and head for the train tracks. With luck, he'd be gone before anyone even realized he was missing.

But that meant leaving Olivia behind.

Guilt gnawed at him. It felt to Peter that, ever since he'd met Olivia, everything he'd told her was a lie; the only truth had been what he'd said about his mother, something he'd never shared with anyone before her. But whenever she asked him a question about who he was, where he'd come from, or why he'd been traveling with nothing more than the clothes on his back, there was nothing for him to do but make something up. He wished that he didn't have to lie to her, but what other choice did he have? He *couldn't* tell her the truth. How would she react to discovering that he was an escaped German soldier, a prisoner of her nation? He remembered what she'd said about his mother's people, *his* countrymen, about how they deserved whatever punishment they got. How could he hope to convince her that he hated Hitler and the Nazis as much as she did, and that the only reason he'd joined the army was out of a fear of what might happen to his mother if he refused?

If Olivia knew the truth, she'd hate him.

Then run! Or do as you'd intended and tell her father who you are!

But he couldn't. Not now, not after kissing her.

Spending time with Olivia made his heart race. Every time he saw her, she seemed more beautiful than before. When she smiled at him, he was dumbstruck, staring at her so hard that he worried she would feel uncomfortable. Yesterday, when he'd taken her hand in his own, the desire to kiss her had been intoxicating, overpowering. His heart had urged him forward, wanting, needing their lips to touch; when they had, her skin hot and moist against his, all of Peter's many worries had vanished, replaced by a longing for that moment to go on forever. His head counseled caution, warned him about the mess he was making, about all of the lies he had spun, but he ignored it, embracing his heart and its desires, damn the consequences. Later, he wondered if Olivia had secretly wanted the same thing, to kiss him; from the look on her face when their kiss finally ended, a shocked, faraway depth in her eyes, he imagined that she had.

But what was he to do now? What kind of future did he think he could have with Olivia? No amount of hoping could change who he was, *what* he was. Eventually, his haphazardly constructed charade would crumble, and then what?

Off in the distance, Peter heard the shrill whistle of a train; the sound made him think of how he'd arrived in Miller's Creek, which in turn caused him to wonder about Otto. Even though the man was cruel and heartless, embodying everything Olivia feared and detested about the Nazis, Peter still wished he knew what had happened to him. Where was he? Had he been recaptured? Was he still alive? Just then, as if in answer, a gust of cold air washed over him, sending a shiver racing across his skin.

It left him with the feeling he was being watched.

Glancing around, Peter was shocked to discover that his suspicion was right. Someone *was* watching him. An elderly woman stood on the wraparound porch of a neighboring house, looking toward him. She was short, with a thick head of curly white hair, her body wrapped in an overcoat that was too long for her, the tails bunched around her feet.

Tentatively, Peter raised his hand and waved, but the woman gave him no reply in return, no acknowledgment, and just kept staring.

Feeling uncomfortable with the attention,

Peter decided to go back inside. But as he began walking across the yard, he noticed the woman's gaze following him intently. Nervously, he stopped. He'd come closer to where she stood and was surprised to see that she wasn't looking right at him, but rather just behind him. As he watched, her head turned one direction and then another; he had the impression that she was *listening* for something.

"Hello?" Peter called out. "Are you all right?"

The woman turned to look straight at him. "Of course I am," she answered. "Who wouldn't be on a beautiful day like this?"

"No one, I suppose," he said, ever so slightly taken aback. "The sun's a little bright but I can't complain about how warm it feels."

At that, the older woman let out a hearty laugh. "I reckon I'll have to take your word on the first half of that."

Immediately, Peter understood what was different about her. She was blind. That explained the absent, faraway look she'd given him in the yard. It also told him why she hadn't reacted when he'd waved. When he'd started back toward the house, she hadn't been watching him, but rather listening to his footfalls, reacting when he stepped on fallen sticks and leaves.

"I'm Ruth Pollack," she said, introducing herself.

"Peter. Peter Baird," he answered, his fictitious last name still sounding uncomfortably foreign to his ear.

"I heard you when you first came outside," Ruth explained. "I might not be able to see, but I reckon that even if I was deaf, I'd still be able to hear the Marstens' kitchen door slam shut. That thing's loud as thunder!"

"I'm sorry if I made too much noise. I didn't mean to disturb you."

"Don't you worry none. I've been living next door to that family for going on twenty years now. I know each and every noise they make," she said. "Hearing you didn't bother me. Rather, it made me curious."

"Is that right?" Peter asked cautiously.

Ruth nodded. "The Marstens all make different sounds, some noisier than others, especially Grace. That girl hollers like the devil himself was chasing her," she explained with a laugh. "But they all greet me each morning without fail. It might be nothing more than a quick hello, a comment on the weather, or an offer to come sit awhile and gossip, but they do it all the same. Then today, you came outside," Ruth said, pointing her wrinkled finger right at him. "You didn't say a word, which made me interested."

Peter didn't answer.

"You're the one who kept Olivia from being run over by that old drunk Sylvester, aren't you?" she kept on.

"You heard about that?"

"There isn't a person in town who hasn't by now," Ruth answered. "Maybe even a couple of towns over, too. I think half the company I've had lately has really come by in the hopes that they'd get a glimpse of you. Delores said you were a handsome one, but whatever good looks you have are lost on me," she said with a smile. "With the way everyone's carrying on, I suppose that for these parts, you're what passes for famous."

Peter was glad the blind woman couldn't see him frown; the last thing he wanted was to attract attention.

"I did what I had to," he replied. "I didn't want anyone to get hurt."

Ruth turned her head a bit, just as she'd done when he'd been walking across the yard. "Where are you from?" she asked.

"Pennsylvania," Peter answered nervously. "Why do you ask?"

"You have any German blood in you?"

The blind woman's question made Peter's

blood run cold. He was sure that all the color had drained from his face. "My . . . my mother's family came to Pennsylvania from Bavaria . . . originally . . ." he managed.

"That would explain it," Ruth said with a nod.

"Explain what?"

"Your accent," she explained. "I've been blind since I was five so I never had a chance to get good at studying people's faces. I've learned to pay attention to their voices instead. You can tell an awful lot about someone just by listening to them talk. If they're happy, nervous, or angry. Whether they're young or old, even if they're too heavy because of how hard they breathe. If I listen close, I can tell where someone's from. Even though my friend Rita DePasqua has lived here most all her life, she still sounds as Italian to me as she surely did the day she stepped off the boat. With you, I hear German."

Peter didn't know what to say. To his own ear, his English sounded perfect, the same as his father's. "My grandmother used to speak it around the house," he finally spat out.

"That explains it," Ruth said. "Although it must be hard for you, what with the war and all, one family fighting against another. You should hear all the terrible things Rita has to say about Mussolini."

Desperately, Peter tried to think of a way out of their conversation. It amazed him that in all the time since he'd left Otto at the cabin, the person who had come the closest to divining his true identity was a blind woman. But as he considered which excuse he'd use to get back to the safety of the Marstens' home, he was rescued by an unlikely source.

From the street, a car horn honked. Peter turned to see a police car pull into the Marstens' drive. For a moment, he thought he'd been discovered, that the law was coming to get him; his heart raced and he chastised himself for not running when he had the chance. But then he saw John behind the wheel, waving out the open window, and his anxiety subsided a bit.

"Afternoon, Ruth," the sheriff said once he'd joined them, unnecessarily tipping his hat in the blind woman's direction, surely out of habit. Peter tried to stay calm, but the sight of the badge pinned to John's shirt unnerved him just as much as the gun strapped to the man's waist, maybe even more so. "I see you've met Peter."

"I have," she answered. "We were having a

nice conversation. He was telling me about where his family originally comes from."

Peter's heart thundered, but he didn't say a word.

"Then I'm sorry to interrupt," John replied. "I hope you don't mind if I take him off your hands."

"Not at all."

"Much obliged." Turning to Peter, he said, "Olivia mentioned that you might be up and about today, so I thought that I'd come by and offer to take you to lunch. Goslee's Diner isn't fancy but they make a darn good plate of food. Besides, I'm sure you're sick of being cooped up," he added, nodding toward his own home. "This will give us a chance to talk and maybe I can show you around town a bit."

Peter stumbled for an instant, leery. The sheriff's offer might very well be genuine, another way of offering his gratitude for keeping his daughter from harm, but Peter couldn't help but wonder if there wasn't more to it; maybe he saw a chance to dig a little deeper into the life of the stranger staying in his home. Either way, Peter knew that turning down the invitation would only make the lawman more suspicious than he might already be.

"I'd like that," he answered.

John must have noticed his hesitation. "You sure you're feeling up to it?"

"Really, I'm fine."

"All right, then."

They said their good-byes to Ruth and headed for John's police car. Just before he got inside, Peter looked back toward the blind woman.

She was staring right at him.

"What do you recommend?" Peter asked.

"I'm partial to the hash and eggs," John answered. "But there isn't a bad choice to be made."

With the number of people crowded into Goslee's Diner, Peter figured that the sheriff was probably right. Just a little past noon and almost every seat was filled, including all those running the length of the diner's long countertop, people wedged in elbow to elbow. When they'd arrived, most everyone they met had greeted them; Peter assumed they did it to be friendly or out of respect for John's position in town. Bits of conversation and the clinking of silverware mixed with the faint sound of music coming from the kitchen. The smell of grease was everywhere.

"Here we are, fellas."

Denise Goslee set down a couple cups of

coffee, pulled a worn notebook out of her short apron, and tugged out a pencil that had been wedged behind her ear. According to John, Denise and her husband, Sam, had been fixtures in Miller's Creek for decades. Many a belly had been filled with their food; from the roundness of Denise's waist, it was clear that she wasn't above sampling the dishes, either. She quickly scribbled down their orders. Just as the waitress was about to leave, she nodded at the open newspaper John had begun to peruse.

"You reckon the Cubs will have much of a team this year?"

"I'm hoping to win the pennant," the sheriff replied.

"I've got my fingers crossed." Turning to Peter, she asked, "How about you? Are you much of a baseball fan?"

"I've always rooted for the Athletics," he answered proudly, remembering his father's passion for the game and the Philadelphia team he'd grown up cheering, a love he'd taken great pains to instill in his son.

"I never much liked that Connie Mack," the waitress said with a frown. "Those bushy eyebrows he's got look like they belong on a mule."

While Denise went to start their order, John unfolded the newspaper and quickly scanned through the pages. From his side of the table, Peter stared at the headlines on the front.

GERMANS SURRENDER IN ITALY! ALLIES PRESS TOWARD BERLIN! VICTORY MAY BE JUST DAYS AWAY!

Peter couldn't believe what he was seeing. Even when he'd been fighting in Germany, freezing in the snow, his belly and rifle both nearly empty, he'd known that it was only a matter of time before Hitler and his cursed Third Reich fell. From the moment of his capture, he'd only heard snippets about the war, usually about gains that Allied forces had made; he'd wondered whether it was the truth or just propaganda to help further demoralize the Germans. But now, reading and rereading the headlines, he knew which it had been. Emotions, some of them contradictory, raced through him; elation, fear, shock, and hope, all at the same time. In that moment, Peter was filled with questions.

What does all of this mean for me?

If the war ends, would I still be considered the enemy? A prisoner?

Could I . . . could I stay here . . . ?

To all, he had no answers.

When John folded up the newspaper, Peter tentatively said, "Looks like the war in Europe isn't going to last much longer."

"It's a shame it's gone on this long," the sheriff replied, shaking his head. "But then, even when I was on the boat back from France in '19, I just knew those damn Germans were going to drag us over there again someday."

"You fought in the Great War?"

"The 'War to End All Wars,' " John spat. "The worst year of my life is more like it. I hadn't but just turned eighteen when I signed up. Thought I was going on an adventure. Instead, I ended up slogging through rain and mud up to my knees. I've hated the Germans ever since."

Peter nodded. While John's honesty wasn't easy for him to hear, it at least helped explain where some of his daughter's fear and disdain for his country came from; Hitler had surely done the rest, and deservedly so. Though Peter knew it'd be best to hold his tongue and agree with everything the sheriff said, he felt something in him stir.

"My father fought in France, too, but after the fighting ended, he decided to stay . . . for a while . . ." he began, catching himself. "Eventually, he traveled to Germany and lived among the very people who'd been trying to kill him months earlier. When I was a boy, he told me that it hadn't taken long for him to understand that while there were many who loved the kaiser, who'd wanted the war as bad as they'd wanted anything in their lives, not everyone agreed. He cautioned me not to blame them all for the mistakes of their nation."

John's eyes narrowed. "Are you telling me that you don't blame the Germans for all this?"

"I'd gladly give my life to be the one who put a bullet between Hitler's eyes," Peter explained. "But I cannot bring myself to believe that every German is as evil and sadistic as him. Not all of them are guilty. Some have to be innocent."

For a long moment, John sat silent, watching him. Peter thought he was weighing whether to argue further, to defend his hatred of Germans, but instead he said, "Olivia mentioned that you have a military deferment."

"Yes, sir."

John glanced down at the newspaper headline. "I know most folks stare sideways at a young man your age who isn't in uniform, but I don't judge. I've been there. I know what hell war is like, and as long as you're doing your part, you'll get no grief from me." The sheriff smiled. "Take it from an old soldier," he said. "It's an honor to fight for your country, but let's hope that you never have to."

Peter didn't answer. How could he possibly admit to John that he knew exactly what it was like to fight on the battlefield? That it was because of that service that he was right here, sitting across the table from him at a diner, thousands of miles from home?

"I look at you and can't imagine I was ever that young," the sheriff continued, flashing a wry smile. "Men like you and Billy don't seem near old enough to be going off to fight."

Confused, Peter asked, "Who's Billy?"

"Olivia didn't mention him?" John replied. "Billy Tate? My daughter's fiancé?"

Peter was stunned speechless. All he could do was stare blankly at Olivia's father. He would have sworn that his heart had stopped beating. Time stood still. *Fiancé?* She'd never mentioned anything of the sort, he was sure of it, but he had no doubt of the truth of John's words. "I . . . I don't remember . . ." he mumbled.

Now it was the sheriff's turn to look puzzled. "Huh," he said, absently scratching at his arm. "I reckon that she must've, but that maybe you were still too addled to take it in."

"That must be it . . ."

But Peter was sure that it wasn't. Over and over, he pored over the moments he'd spent with Olivia, replaying their conversations, searching for something, any clue that she might have dropped to the fact that she was promised to another man. *She kissed me!*

There was only one thing that gave him pause; her ring. She'd kept it hidden out of sight, and when he had finally noticed it and asked, she had given him an evasive answer, but he'd known that it wasn't the truth. Now, he understood.

It had been her engagement ring.

Just like that, Peter knew that there was no reason to keep up the charade he'd been playing. In his heart, he knew it had been a fool's errand, anyway. No matter how much he wished otherwise, there was no changing who he really was: a German prisoner, a fugitive of the law. There was only one thing left for him to do.

He'd tell the sheriff the truth, right here and now.

"There's something I need to tell you," Peter began, looking right at the sheriff; if he was going to admit to lying to John and his family, he'd do so as a man, eye-to-eye. "I'm not —"

But that was as far as he got before the front door to the diner flew open and a large, sweaty man came rushing over to their table.

"Sheriff!" he shouted. "We got a problem!"

John had already risen out of his seat. "What is it, Huck?"

"Carl Hendrickson called in and said Roy Lafferty's barn is on fire! He seen Roy tryin' to get his horses out, but the flames was growin' fast! You can see the smoke from here!"

"Did you call Mike?"

The other man nodded. "He said the truck's comin'."

As if on cue, the sound of a siren rose in the distance.

John looked down at Peter. "We don't have much of a fire department here," he said. "More than likely, we're going to need every hand we can get. You up for it?"

Even though he'd been about to turn himself in, Peter stood without hesitation. Revealing his true identity and taking whatever punishment he had coming to him could wait until after the fire had been put

202

out. He owed that much to Olivia and her family.

"Let's go," he said, and they did.

CHAPTER TWELVE

Peter sat beside John in his squad car, racing south of town. They whipped across a wide, wooden bridge, the tires slapping hard and fast across the boards, before speeding alongside the gurgling creek, heading toward the fire. In the distance, black smoke rose into the sky. Behind them, Huck and another volunteer followed in the deputy's vehicle. The road followed the route Peter had used to enter Miller's Creek; when they passed near the cabin, he strained to get a look at it, still wondering what had become of Otto, but it shot by so fast that it was gone in a blink.

"Roy's place is a couple miles out of town," John explained as the car dropped down onto a long straightaway; the lawman pressed his foot down hard on the accelerator, making them go so fast that the scrum in the ditch blurred past Peter's open window. "Because of the way the roads are around here, we'll have to cross back over the river to get there."

"Any idea what might have started it?"

"I got a hunch," the sheriff answered. "Back during the days of Prohibition, Roy's old man had a still set back a mile or so from the barn. Used to sell his moonshine liquor to everyone within a ten-mile radius. Every couple months, I'd come along and make sure things hadn't grown bigger than I was comfortable with, but I never arrested him. What would've been the point? I hadn't had the job long and the last thing I wanted was the whole damn county mad at me. I'd have been voted out on my rump."

John paused his story as he turned the car into a sharp curve, the wheels skidding slightly, before the car righted itself and again shot forward.

"Old Theodore passed away about seven years back and since Roy was raised up with it, I figure he'd know every trick in the book. Problem is, he's always been lazy as a summer afternoon. It's been a few years since I trudged out into the woods to look at the family operation. Maybe Roy moved it into the barn to keep from having to make the walk himself. If everything's on fire, it might mean that the still blew."

"What was that about horses?"

"I've never understood how he's done it, but Roy's managed to keep at breeding horses. That's a job that requires more gumption than I'd expect to find in a man cut from Roy's cloth. But he's been lucky to have had a couple of sons who aren't as worthless as he is. This time, the apple fell far from the tree. They're big boys, strong as the animals they tend. Problem is, they're all off fighting overseas and Roy's been left to do it all himself. Maybe he started falling behind on his bills and thought he'd fire up the still to make the money back. We'll find out."

Just as John had explained, they had to drive back over the creek in order to reach the Laffertys' farm. But unlike the bridge leaving town, this one was narrower; when they raced over it, Peter leaned inward as the car's mirrors came within inches of the bridge's railing.

They passed through a thick stand of trees, majestic elms and oaks, their branches sprouting the first leaves of spring, rounded a bend bordered by a weathered length of fence, and drove down a short hill. From the open window, the acrid smell of smoke reached them. Seconds later, John pointed ahead.

"There it is," he said.

The barn was set off a bit from a two-story home up a gravel drive from the main road. The house had seen better days; one of the upstairs windows was boarded up and the whole thing leaned to one side. A mangy dog sat on the porch, watching as its owners ran around like chickens with their heads cut off, frantic.

The barn's front doors stood open; black smoke poured out of them and up toward the sky. The fire raged a brilliant array of colors — crimson reds, deep oranges, and even a smattering of yellows and blues. Most of the windows had shattered from the heat. A couple of men and an elderly woman raced back and forth sloshing buckets of water at the blaze, a futile gesture. Another man struggled to hold the reins of a panicked horse as its nostrils flared wide and its eyes rolled white with fear; several others whinnied in a corral safely away from the fire's fury.

The squad car skidded to a stop in the gravel and both of them were out of the car before the dust began to settle. A man near the barn doors spotted them and came running. He was short, balding, with a pot belly that pushed against his overalls. Sweat slicked his skin and grime caked his clothing. His face was beet red from the heat.

One of his eyebrows looked to have been singed off.

"That's Roy," John said before the man got too close.

"It's all burnin' to the ground, sheriff!" Roy shouted, distraught. "Everythin' I got in the world is goin' up in smoke!"

"The fire truck should be right behind us," John answered calmly, looking over the chaotic scene. Peter could see that Olivia's father was a natural leader; not rattled, even in the face of danger, he was the type who'd look for a solution as others complained about the problem. Peter also noticed that John wasn't concerned with why the fire had started, at least not yet; there'd be plenty of time for that once it was extinguished.

"Ain't gonna be nothin' left by the time it does!" the man wailed.

Ignoring Roy, the sheriff directed Huck and the man who'd accompanied them from town to take control of the bucket line; maybe if they focused the water they might be able to save something. Turning to Peter, he said, "We'll rescue the horses still inside."

But then, just as they started toward the barn, they heard the shrill sound of sirens behind them. Turning around, they saw the fire engine make its way down the drive, bouncing along the rough road. John frowned. "I'll need to coordinate things with the chief first," he said. "Give me a minute to get them set up and then we'll go in."

"I'll start without you," Peter said.

"Are you sure?"

Peter nodded.

"It'll be dangerous on your own." Peter thought that he saw a flicker of concern pass across the lawman's face. "If something happens . . ."

"There isn't time to wait."

In many ways, Peter was a lot like Olivia's father; whenever he saw a problem that needed solving, he wanted to confront it sooner rather than later. Waiting meant that fewer horses would make it out of the barn alive. He'd witnessed too much death over the last few years; now he wanted to save something.

"Be careful," John told him before hurrying toward the engine.

Peter took a deep breath and ran for the barn.

Peter slammed into the wall of heat radiating from the burning building; it was so hot that it forced him to narrow his eyes and momentarily turn away. Through the smoke, he made out Huck pointing and shouting as he directed the line of buckets throwing water against the barn's side. One after another, they went back and forth to a nearby duck pond, slipping in the mud they made, dredging up loads of the murky water.

Shielding his face, Peter hurried to the pond. When the next man approached, he took the bucket from his hand, filled it, and then poured it on himself. It wasn't much, but if he was going to enter that inferno, he'd need whatever protection he could get.

Back at the barn doors, he hesitated. Even over the sounds of the fire, he could hear the horses whinny in fear. A few feet away, a man was on his knees, spent, coughing up smoke; he was the one Peter had seen when they had arrived, the one who'd been tasked with rescuing the horses. Peter was on his own. He knew that the longer he waited, the worse things were going to be, and the greater the chance that he wouldn't make it out alive.

Then stop standing here! Go!

Pulling in a deep breath, Peter dashed into the barn. Past the doors, the flames were everywhere at once; the heat was so intense that the water he'd doused himself with began to steam from his clothes and skin. Covering his eyes and mouth with his arm, he kept going forward, making his way toward the horse stalls.

Several of the stalls stood empty; they'd either been unoccupied or belonged to those the Laffertys and their hands had managed to get outside. But it didn't take long for Peter to come to one that still held a horse. It was tawny with black spots, huge in size, deeply muscled across its back and down its flanks. The poor animal was so terrified by the fire that it was kicking, desperate to get free; its powerful hooves slammed into the planks of its pen.

Without thinking, Peter reached out and grabbed the latch that held the gate shut, but the moment he touched it, he drew his hand back in pain; the metal had gotten so hot from the fire that it burned. Silently cursing, he yanked out the hem of his shirt. Wrapping it around his hand, he punched at the latch until it finally came loose. A second later, the horse came charging out of its pen as fast as a bullet. Peter had only an instant to dive out of the way to keep from being trampled. He gave thanks that at least the horse headed straight for the open doors and safety.

Peter did the same at the next two stalls, remembering to stay well clear when the animals rushed out, but when he opened yet another gate, the horse remained inside.

It was younger than the others, smaller, a white pony with a black smear down the middle of its forehead. It snorted fearfully, watching him with wide eyes, its ears back. Already backed into the far corner of the stall, it kicked up loose straw with its hooves, trying to get farther away. While hoping that the animal would come to its senses, Peter heard the unmistakable snap of a beam somewhere overhead. There wasn't much time left for the frightened horse to change its mind.

He was going to have to go in after it.

"Easy now, boy," Peter said, inching his way into the stall, doing his best to ignore the fire all around them.

The horse whinnied loudly in answer.

With the gloom momentarily thinning, Peter was relieved to see a bit in the animal's mouth and a leather lead dangling beneath its muzzle. Until then, he'd had no idea how he might entice the horse out of its stall; grabbing for its mane or slapping its flank might have resulted in his own leg being broken.

Inch by patient inch, he moved closer, one hand across his nose, the other held out in front of him, reaching toward the lead.

"I'm not going to hurt you," he said, but when he spoke, the horse suddenly rose up on its back legs, kicking the air with its front hooves. Peter stopped, unsure what to do now.

Without thinking about it, he began to speak to the terrified animal in German, saying things his mother had once uttered to soothe him. *"Das wird schon wieder,"* he said, telling the horse that everything would soon be all right. For whatever reason, and to Peter's great relief, it worked. Though still clearly terrified, the horse stayed still long enough for him to grab the lead. Tentatively, he placed his hand against the animal's face, which seemed to calm it further.

"Let's get out of here," he said, leading the horse out of its stall.

In the few moments he'd been inside the barn, the fire had worsened. Flames were everywhere. The heat seared the air in his lungs. Black smoke tried to smother him. One loud crack was followed by a crash as another part of the structure gave way. The water that he'd doused himself with had long since evaporated, leaving his skin to burn.

Once he and the horse were within sight of the door, he peered through the inferno, looking outside. John stood there, frantically waving his arms, shouting something that Peter couldn't hear. Behind the sheriff, firemen stood and watched; clearly, they'd decided that the blaze was too far along to try putting it out.

"Go on!" Peter shouted, swatting the animal on its rump.

The horse did as he insisted, bolting for its freedom. But it was so traumatized by the fire that it careened to one side, slamming into the barn door before making its way outside.

Peter had been just behind the horse, but when it hit the door, he'd stopped. He watched in horror as part of the barn's front crumbled, sending burning beams and planks crashing to the ground at his feet. The noise was deafening. By the time everything had settled, there was a gaping hole high above where the hay loft should have been, but where the open doors had beckoned moments before, it was now blocked with burning debris. He was trapped.

Just like on the battlefield, Peter was once again faced with the prospect of his own death. But unlike then, when he'd thought of his parents, of the peaceful life they'd lived together in Bavaria before the Nazis had come to power, of his dreams for the future, he now thought of Olivia. When John had told him that his daughter had a fiancé, his first inclination had been to surrender, to come clean about who he was and never see her again.

But now he wanted to fight.

Too many things remained unanswered. Peter wanted to know why Olivia had never told him about her engagement. He wanted to know who this other man was and why she'd chosen him. He wanted to know if he had only imagined the attraction he'd felt between them. Most intensely, he wanted to know why, if she was promised to another, she had kissed him the way she had . . .

The only way to know these things was to live.

Peter looked at the burning rubble in front of the barn doors. Splintered wood mixed with broken glass and nails, all of the things that had once held the building together. Now it all burned. To get out, he had to find a way past it. Turning around, he considered trying the opposite direction, to see if there was a rear exit, but he couldn't see through the smoke and flame. Heading that direction could mean succumbing to the fire or, if it was also blocked, not having enough time to get back. He couldn't take the risk.

Doing his best to ignore the heat, Peter

began looking for a way out. He was about to give up, to go against his better judgment and try the rear of the barn, when he saw it. A thick beam had gotten wedged sideways; plenty of wreckage lay on top of it, but there was a small gap beneath. From where Peter stood, he wondered if he wouldn't have to force himself through, but it was the only option he had left.

Don't think! Just do it!

Taking a couple of quick steps, Peter leaped over the burning debris, aiming for the hole. Hanging in the air, it felt as if the fire was reaching for him. He landed in the gap a little to the left of where he'd intended, his bare skin scraping against the burning wood, and had to grab hold of the braced beam with his hand to keep from tipping backward. The pain was instantaneous and agonizing. Fighting down panic, he forced his way through.

When he crashed down the other side, skidding across the flaming debris, Peter's shirt caught fire; before he'd come to a complete stop, he was trying to pull himself free, wriggling and tugging it off his chest. Within seconds, another pair of hands began helping him. Finally, the shirt came off and he flung it away, the flicker of flame still devouring it.

"Give me your hand."

John stood above him. Peter took the offered help and together they brought him to his feet. They hurried away from the barn just in time; before they reached the police car, there was a tremendous crack and they turned to watch the barn's roof cave in, shooting sparks and clouds of smoke high into the afternoon sky. Peter knew that if he'd still been inside, he would be dead.

"Are you all right?" the sheriff asked.

With his top half bare, his broad chest heaving, Peter tenderly touched his arm. Blisters had already begun to form where he'd touched the burning beam. There was a similar swath running across his shoulder and down to his collarbone; he had no idea when that had happened, but thought that it must have been when his shirt caught fire.

"I'll be fine," he answered.

"I was yelling at you to get out of there," John said. "It was already so far gone that the fire chief didn't want to get out of his truck."

"I couldn't hear you. All I wanted was to get those horses out."

"Roy's going to be mighty happy that you did."

"Any idea yet what started the fire?"

"Nope," the sheriff replied; Peter saw the

217

man's eyes lock on Roy Lafferty, following him as the man paced back and forth in front of his destroyed barn, tears and sweat running down his face. "But I'll keep asking questions until I get the answers I need."

Peter nodded.

It was time for him to do the same with Olivia.

Otto picked his way through the budding trees and thick bushes as he climbed toward the top of the ridge. He stopped just short of the summit and wiped the sweat from his brow with his hand. He looked back behind him at the black smoke that continued to billow into the blue sky and smiled, knowing that it was *his* handiwork.

Ever since Otto had left the cabin, he'd constantly been on the move. He'd broken into a home and stolen some clothes. He had looted an unlocked garage for a bit of food, a tattered blanket, and a few other odds and ends. He'd scrounged up enough to feel confident that it was time to strike, to begin terrorizing the Amerikaners in Hitler's name.

Soon after, he had set his sights on the barn. There'd been a small container of kerosene on a workbench near the rear. After splashing it around, he'd lit a match he'd taken from the garage and, within minutes, the barn had been engulfed in flames. He was well on his way back into the woods by the time he heard the first shouts of alarm.

While Otto knew that it would have been safer to start the blaze at night, there were still risks, particularly that it would've been much harder to get away in the dark. Still, there was a part of him that had wanted to stick around and watch, to see who came to put out the fire. He'd learned during the war how valuable it was to know the enemy's leaders; after all, these were the men who'd captured Becker. But in the end, he understood that the reward wouldn't have been worth the risk.

All that mattered now was that he would live to fight again. One day, he might grow too bold or too careless and would pay for it with his life. Until then, he'd continue to fight his enemy deep within their nation.

This was only the beginning.

CHAPTER THIRTEEN

"Honest to Betsy, that was one of the craziest things I've ever seen," Huck exclaimed, slapping one meaty hand against his knee as he reclined in his chair at the police station. "I can't figure how you done it! I'd have been fried to a crisp for even tryin'!"

Olivia waited for Peter's answer, but he didn't give one. The more she thought about it, she realized that he hadn't said much since she'd arrived, breathless from running after word had spread around town about the fire.

Peter sat shirtless in his seat, another borrowed item of clothing lying on the table next to them. With a cloth and a bottle of alcohol, Olivia gently dabbed at the raw, blistered flesh of his arm. She tried to be as careful as she could, but every time she touched him she felt him flinch; he struggled to remain impassive, to keep from showing the pain he obviously felt. Olivia didn't know what shocked her more, the ugliness of his burns or the amazing story of how he'd gotten them. Still, to intimately touch him in such a way, to see his muscular body, sent a ripple of excitement racing through her.

"That hole you jumped through didn't look much bigger'n a knot in a tree," Huck continued. "I ain't sure how you made it!"

"Just lucky, I guess," Peter muttered.

"You best hope not," the deputy said with a laugh, his ample belly jiggling, " 'cause I think you done used up 'bout ten years' worth this afternoon."

Peter frowned. When Olivia had first arrived, he'd looked straight at her, glanced down, and then turned away. She'd assumed that it was due to fatigue or the shock of almost dying in the burning barn, but the more time passed, the more withdrawn he became, until she began to wonder if it wasn't *her* that was making him behave this way.

"I'm wonderin' when someone's gonna thank me for all this."

Sylvester Eddings slumped on his cot, his head resting against the wall of his jail cell. He looked miserable, with a couple days' worth of whiskers on his sagging cheeks, his eyes bloodshot and narrow; since he hadn't said a word or moved an inch since she'd arrived, Olivia had thought he was asleep.

"What in the hell'd make you think you deserve any thanks for what Peter done?" Huck asked, chortling but curious.

The jailed man took a deep breath before he spoke, his lungs wheezing. " 'Cause if I hadn't hit him with my truck," he explained, "he woulda already done left town. Who woulda saved them horses, then?" The old drunk chuckled at his own joke before he even told it. "Even if both them barn doors had been thrown wide open, I bet your fat ass woulda had to squeeze to get inside."

The smile on Huck's face deflated so fast it was as if it had been popped. "Funny talk from a man who can't keep himself outta that jail cell."

"I done told you I shouldn't be in here," the jailed man grumbled bitterly.

The last time Olivia had listened to Sylvester as he sat inside a jail cell there'd been more playfulness in his voice, due in large part to his still having been drunk at the time. Now, after being locked up for nearly a week, he was stone sober, a condition that clearly didn't suit him. But Olivia didn't pay his grumpiness much mind; she was more concerned with Peter's surliness.

"If half of what Huck said is true, what

you did was incredibly brave," she told him as she finished cleaning his burns.

Peter glanced at her, the first time he'd looked at her in quite a while, but once again turned away. "I did what I had to," he said simply.

Setting down her cloth, Olivia began to unroll a strip of gauze. As she started wrapping it around his arm, her heart and thoughts raced. It bothered her that something wasn't right between them. By now, she'd become convinced that he was upset with her; otherwise, she was certain that he would have told her what was bothering him or, at the least, given her a smile to set her mind at ease. But he hadn't. The problem was that she hadn't the slightest idea what she had done.

Olivia knew she shouldn't let it bother her as much as it did, that she hadn't known Peter long enough to feel so out of sorts, but there was no point in denying the spark between them, one that both excited and perplexed her. It was much more than the fact that he'd kept her from harm. It was talking with him, the way he smiled, even watching him sleep. It was their kiss . . . When she'd heard that he'd been hurt in the fire, her fear surprised her. Even though she was engaged to Billy, there was nowhere

223

she wanted to be other than by Peter's side.

She had to know what it was that she'd done.

"What's bothering you?" she asked him.

But Peter didn't respond, which made her a little angry.

"Tell me," Olivia insisted; when she spoke, she was so worked up that she accidentally squeezed his arm, causing him to pull away in pain. "I'm sorry," she apologized quickly, shocked by what she'd done. "I just want to know what's got you so upset."

Slowly, Peter raised his eyes to hers; the way he looked at her made Olivia feel as if he was accusing her of something. "Not here," he said, his voice low and weary. "Not now."

Olivia was about to say more, to argue that that wasn't good enough, when the argument between Huck and Sylvester interrupted.

"I've 'bout had enough of this," the deputy barked.

Sylvester stood at the bars of his cell, feebly rattling them with what strength he had left, beads of sweat standing out on his pale forehead. "And *I'm* tellin' *you* that I shouldn't be in this jail no more! I oughta be gettin' a medal pinned to my chest!"

"Keep it down in here!"

Every head in the room turned toward John. He had a hand cupped over the telephone he was using, staring hard at Sylvester; even as ornery as the old drunk was, he held his tongue, unwilling to anger the sheriff further. No one said another word until John hung up the receiver.

"What's the good word, boss?" Huck asked.

"The fire's finally out," he answered. "By Roy's count, looks like only two horses were lost."

Olivia thought Peter would have been happy to hear the good news, but from the frown that creased his face, he reacted as if he hadn't saved a single one.

"Any idea 'bout what caused it?" the deputy inquired.

"We won't know for certain until things cool off a bit. Once we get a chance to sift through the ruins, my hunch is we'll find what's left of a still. I'll go out and question Roy in the morning. If we're lucky, maybe he'll give it up without much fuss."

"His old man sure could brew a drink," Sylvester commented, a faraway look in his bloodshot eyes.

"You been out that way lately?" John asked him.

The old drunk shook his head. "With the

way I've been treated 'round here, I wouldn't tell you even if I had," he huffed.

The sheriff shook his head. "We'll find out in due time." He walked over and sat on the edge of the desk opposite Peter. "How're you feeling?"

"I've been worse."

"Like when Sylvester hit him with his truck," Huck said with a chuckle.

"I don't much like the looks of those," John said, nodding at Peter's burns. "It's going to take me a while to tie up all these loose ends. Why don't I have Huck drive you back to the house so you can get some rest?"

"If it's all the same, I think I'd rather walk," Peter replied. "I reckon the fresh air might do me some good."

"I'll go with him," Olivia offered quickly; since they were sure to be alone, she thought it would be the perfect opportunity to finally find out what was bothering him. "I can see that he gets home safe."

Instead of protesting, Peter said, "All right with me."

With as quickly as he had answered, Olivia began to wonder if she shouldn't have been more careful about what she'd asked for.

The sun was setting in the west when Peter

and Olivia set off from the police station for home. There was something about the early evening that reminded Peter of springtime back in Germany; it might have been the color of the sky, the way the sun burnt the bottoms of the low clouds, or the pleasant nip in the air. But for as much as things were similar, he was constantly reminded that he was a stranger in a strange land.

While the buildings had been constructed differently and the cars weren't exactly the same, there was still something about Miller's Creek that was comforting to Peter. Even the American flag, so strikingly different from the swastika, spoke to him; in it, he saw a people who had come together, sacrificing for the greater good to fight against an evil so that others might be free. When he'd been on the prison train, he had wondered whether Americans truly knew that their country was at war; it hadn't taken him long to see how wrong he had been. Watching the stars and stripes flutter in the breeze filled him with hope.

But there were other things that filled him with dread.

Peter glanced at the front of the hardware store. There, taped to the inside of the display window, was a poster. It depicted Hitler with a pistol in his hand rearing up over a globe turned toward the United States, a Japanese soldier beside him, holding a bloodstained knife. In large print, it read, WARNING! OUR HOMES ARE IN DANGER NOW! Immediately, Peter thought of Otto and the acts of violence he'd promised against the town and its people. For a while at least, the poster had been telling the truth.

"How do you feel?" Olivia asked shortly after they'd resumed walking.

"I'm fine," he answered curtly.

"I was worried I might have wrapped your bandages too tight."

From the quick smile Olivia flashed him Peter understood that she was trying to break the ice between them. She wanted to get him talking so that they could discuss what was bothering him. But regardless of his earlier intentions, he wasn't yet ready, so he stayed silent.

All of your big talk has gone up in smoke!

Back in the burning barn, all Peter had wanted was a chance to confront Olivia about her engagement, to learn why she'd never mentioned her fiancé, to see if the attraction he'd felt growing between them was real or a figment of his imagination. But now, he struggled just to look at her.

How could he ask Olivia to explain why

she'd been keeping secrets from him when almost everything he'd told her was a lie? The answer was that he couldn't. It would make him a hypocrite. If he wasn't willing to come clean about his own past, it was hardly fair to expect the same of her.

But then, a sudden, unexpected thought struck him, something that he'd never considered. Maybe Olivia hadn't told him about her relationship with another man for a reason other than what he'd assumed. Maybe she had avoided talk about her engagement because she had begun to be attracted to him! Sure, Peter had been the one to initiate their kiss, but it was more than that. Thinking back on their time together, there were hints that he was right; it was in the way she looked at him, her eyes lingering a moment longer than might have been considered appropriate, in the way she laughed, her eyes shining brightly, the fact that she had kept her ring hidden from sight. Earlier that afternoon, Peter had stood in the Marstens' backyard, wondering whether there was a chance for him and Olivia . . .

Deep in his gut, Peter knew he had to *take* a chance.

Odds were that he was wrong, that he was going to make a fool out of himself and embarrass Olivia, both at the same time. Just like when he'd walked away from the wrecked train with Otto, he knew that once he'd taken that first step, there would be no going back. Still, it was worth the risk. Silently, he swore a vow. If he was wrong, if Olivia had no romantic feelings for him, if she had no interest in finding where those feelings might take them, he would tell her the truth and the two of them would turn around and march right back to her father's jail.

Peter took a deep breath.

Walking home, Olivia became more and more frustrated with every step she took. When she and Peter left the jail, she had assumed that he would finally tell her what was bothering him. But so far, he'd hardly said a word. While she had tried reminding herself that he was surely exhausted from all he'd been through, her patience was fast running out. He was keeping something from her, some offense that she'd committed. She'd tried everything she could think of short of throwing a fit to get him to come clean, and that option was under serious consideration. But then, just as she was about to give in to her temper, he spoke.

"There's something that I want you to

know . . ."

Olivia's heart began to beat faster. *Finally!* "What is it?"

He paused. "I don't have anyone back home."

"You told me. Both of your parents . . ."

"That's not what I'm saying," Peter explained. Though they were only a couple of blocks from home, he suddenly stopped walking; he turned his face toward the sun, his expression serious. "What I need you to understand is that there isn't someone special writing me letters or waiting for me to walk back through her door."

Olivia's breath caught; he was telling her that he didn't have a sweetheart. It was as surprising as it was exciting. Looking at the way the sunlight danced across Peter's face, his blue eyes sparkling, it seemed impossible to her that a man so handsome, so kind and strong, wouldn't have a woman to share his life with. An unexpected tremor of happiness raced through her.

Was it relief that she was feeling?

Neither of them spoke. Peter watched her intently; she felt as if he was waiting for something. Olivia could guess what it was; he wanted to know if there was a man in her life. But even though she knew she should tell him about Billy, about their

231

engagement, she couldn't bring herself to do it.

But why not? What am I afraid of?

Finally, it was Peter who spoke. "This afternoon, before the fire, I had lunch with your father," he said. "He told me that you're promised to another man."

Olivia gasped; it felt as if she'd been slapped. Peter had already known; his admission had rendered her speechless.

He reached out and grabbed her left hand and raised it between them. Peter held her engagement ring up to the sun, the gold catching the light. Before, she had lied to cover what that band meant, but now she remained silent. She'd been caught.

"Is it true?" he prodded.

Slowly, Olivia nodded. "It is," she told him, her voice small.

Peter frowned; his face looked pained. He let go of her hand. "Why didn't you tell me?"

"I don't . . . I don't know . . ." she answered.

"Olivia . . ." he said.

"I've . . . I've been so busy . . . what with the accident and worrying about whether you would recover . . . it must have slipped my mind . . ."

He shook his head. "Agreeing to marry

someone isn't the sort of thing you forget about."

Shame flushed Olivia's cheeks. He was right. Her excuse was a hastily constructed lie, and not a very good one. But what was the real reason? Deep down, she knew; it was that she'd been charmed by the handsome stranger who had suddenly appeared one morning on the sidewalk, the man who had allowed himself to be hurt to keep her from harm. Still, there was no way she could tell him that . . .

Or maybe I can . . .

Ever since she had accepted Billy's proposal, all in order to keep from hurting her dearest friend, Olivia had kept the truth locked tightly away. Other than Grace, she had told no one of her reservations. She allowed herself to go along with what others wanted, even if it ran against her own wishes. She had put her growing feelings for Peter to the side, afraid of what would happen were she to acknowledge them, to let them into her heart. But for what? Maybe her sister had been right; if she wasn't careful, she'd live her whole life worrying about the happiness of others, at the cost of her own.

Maybe if, just once, she was honest, if she told someone how she truly felt, things might be different . . .

"The man I agreed to marry . . . Billy . . . is my best friend," Olivia began. "He has been since we were kids. He knows everything about me, and I about him, but I've never had feelings of love for him," she admitted. "Not romantic ones, at least."

Olivia expected Peter to say something, to ask her why, if that was true, she had agreed to marry the man, but he waited for her to continue.

"The morning before you and I met, Billy showed up at the hardware store and said that he had to talk to me about something, that it was urgent," she explained. "I went with him, worried that something was wrong . . . but then . . . he dropped down on one knee and asked me to be his wife . . .

"I had no idea it was coming. None. He'd never told me he had any feelings for me, not those kinds. No matter how hard I look back, there was nothing that would have clued me in to what he was planning to do. I was so shocked that I swear you could've knocked me over with a feather!"

"But you still accepted," Peter said, breaking his silence.

Olivia nodded. "I did, but there's a reason why," she said. "In little more than a month, Billy leaves for the Navy. If he sees fighting . . . it means that he might not come back . . . I couldn't let him leave with a broken heart. If something happened to him . . . knowing that I'd hurt him so badly . . . I couldn't live with that. So, I agreed to become his wife . . ."

Waiting for Peter's reaction, Olivia had no regrets about telling him the truth. By admitting to what she'd done, it felt as if a heavy burden had been lifted off her. Still, that didn't mean she wasn't nervous about what came next.

"Do you love him?" Peter asked.

"No. Not the way he does me," Olivia answered.

"Then you need to tell him what you just told me. You have to be honest."

"I've tried," she said. "I really have. He came by the house just after your accident and I wanted to tell him, to explain how I felt, but . . ." Olivia paused, remembering the awkward kiss she'd shared with Billy. "I couldn't find the words . . ."

"You have to," Peter said. Slowly, he reached out and again took her hand; this time his touch was tender, exhilarating.

"But it will ruin him."

"If you don't, you'll be the one who suffers," he replied, looking at her intensely. "It's too late to change what's already been done, but there's still time to make things right. If you're as good a friend to him as you say, then you owe it to him to tell him the truth, no matter the consequences."

Olivia knew he was right. Her doubts about marrying Billy had never lessened. If she continued to ignore them, everyone would suffer. No matter how much changing her mind might hurt Billy, regardless of how angry her mother would be, she owed it to them all, herself included, to do what was right.

"Is this why you were so out of sorts?" she asked Peter.

He nodded. "Yes."

"Tell me why," Olivia insisted. For a moment, she thought he might be as reluctant to talk as he'd been back at the jail. But she was wrong.

"It bothered me because of the way I feel about you," he said. "From the first moment I saw you, I knew there was something between us. All this time, watching you as you read at the foot of my bed, waiting for you to come back home from work, I've been wanting to ask you something . . ."

"What is it?" she managed.

"Are you as attracted to me as I am to you?"

Olivia gasped; Peter's boldness had surprised her. Though he hadn't said anything that she hadn't already suspected, the strength of his request had managed to catch her off guard. When Billy had admitted his feelings for her, Olivia's shock had been mixed with disbelief; immediately, she had wanted to turn him down, to run away. Now, with Peter, she experienced the opposite; knowing that he was interested in her romantically, she wanted to embrace what she was feeling, to embrace the man who had caused those emotions.

"I . . . I am . . ." she admitted. "Those feelings you described . . . I felt them, too . . . When I first saw you standing there on the sidewalk, I . . . I can't explain it . . . all I wanted was to know your name . . . to hear the sound of your voice . . ."

Without warning, Peter stepped forward and kissed her. As his lips touched hers, one of his hands found her waist and the other wrapped around her side, tickling her ribs. Olivia's eyes went wide with surprise. Ever since she and Peter had met, something had been building up inside her, yearning for release. With Billy, there was a bond between them that had been built out of years of friendship, but between her and Peter, there was something else, something different, whispers of a passion that had proven to be too intoxicating to resist. It beckoned to her, called for her to match his boldness, to give in. And so, in the last sunlight left to the day, Olivia surrendered to her desire.

Peter did the same.

He pulled her close, their bodies pressing together. Their first kiss had been tentative, cautious, but this time it was much more; within seconds, her mouth opened and she felt his tongue, warm and wet against her own. Olivia shut her eyes, allowing herself to be swept away. Time no longer mattered. It was as if she was floating. Her kiss with Billy beneath the evergreen couldn't hope to compare; *this* one made her forget everything around her, made her breath catch and her heart race. It was what she'd waited her whole life for.

She never wanted it to end.

But even as Olivia continued to kiss Peter, as she fell deeper into the passion enveloping them, she knew it would.

Someday soon, there would be consequences for her actions. Eventually, she'd have to come clean. Lives would be forever changed, including her own. Imagining Billy's reaction was the worst of all; once again, she would hurt him. Still, for the first time in a long time, she was being true to herself.

But that was later. Right now was a different story . . .

CHAPTER FOURTEEN

"I saw what you did."

Olivia stopped, her sandwich raised to her open mouth, and stared at her sister. Grace sat beside her on the hardware store's rear steps, the girl's feet dangling over the side, a half-empty bottle of Coca-Cola in her hand. Every so often, Grace would come to share lunch with her, the two of them trading the latest in town gossip, listing their complaints about their mother, and wondering when the war might end. Today, Olivia had noticed that her sister wasn't as talkative as usual, that she was more subdued. Now, she had a clue why.

Deep down in the pit of Olivia's stomach, she knew what Grace was talking about, but she asked anyway. "Saw me do what?"

"Kissing the guy who saved you," she replied, the words not accusatory, but almost matter-of-fact. "Peter . . ."

Olivia's heart pounded. Ever since she and

Peter had kissed, her mind had been topsy-turvy. It had been a struggle not to stare at him across the dinner table. Purposely, she'd avoided going to his room, fearful that she wouldn't be able to control her urges. Instead, she'd lain in bed, staring up at the ceiling as the hours crawled slowly by, thinking about what she'd done, as well as what she had to do. By morning, she was no closer to a decision.

"I was coming back from the creek," Grace continued. "Me and Joe Griffin had been down there lookin' for frogs and I knew I had to get home quick 'fore Mother started yellin' to beat the band. I came 'round the corner by the Kilmeades' place and there the two of you were."

While Olivia had enjoyed kissing Peter, it had been brazen to do so out in the open. She'd tried to comfort herself with the fact that it had been late in the day, a time when most folks were just home from work and getting ready to sit at the dinner table. Still, it had been risky. If one person with loose lips had seen them, the whole town would soon know, including Billy. But Olivia had never imagined that it would be *her sister* who discovered them.

Olivia didn't know what to say. Lying wasn't an option; not only had Grace seen them as plain as day, her sister already knew of her doubts about marrying Billy. As different as they may have been, Grace was still one of her closest friends.

"There's somethin' I just gotta know," her sister began, smiling mischievously. "Who kissed who? Was it you who made the first move or did he come over and take you in his arms like they do in the movies?"

"He did," Olivia said. "When it started, I was a little surprised."

"Didn't look that way when I come along."

"How long did you watch us?"

Grace shrugged. "All the way back to the house," she answered. "I wasn't gonna let a show like that go without gettin' my money's worth."

Olivia flushed with embarrassment. "Did you tell anyone?"

Her sister turned to glare at her. "Of course not," she said, looking more than a little put out that Olivia would worry she had. "Who would I blab to, anyway? If it doesn't involve mud or dead animals, Joe doesn't care, and it's not as if I'd say anything to our folks." She paused. " 'Course, when they find out, the fireworks are gonna fly."

"I know," Olivia answered; all night, she'd

thought the same thing.

"So what does this mean for you and Billy?"

Olivia felt queasy. "It means we have to have a long talk."

"Yeah, you do," her sister said, echoing Peter's sentiments. "I wouldn't wait too long, neither. Waitin' will only make it worse, especially 'cause you've been friends forever!"

"Which is what makes telling him so hard," Olivia said with a pained smile.

Grace lifted her soda bottle and took a long swig. "So is it serious?"

"Between me and Peter?"

Her sister nodded.

"Yes, it is," Olivia admitted; to her it was and, when she recalled how out of sorts Peter had been to learn that she was engaged to another man, she believed he felt the same. "Whenever I'm around him, I don't want our time together to end. When we're apart, I count the hours until I see him again. Sometimes, I find myself staring at him, my heart beating faster. And when we kissed, I couldn't help but think that we were the only two people in the whole world."

"Well, I suppose he's handsome enough, although I still have trouble believin' that boys grow up to be men you'd want to do that sort of thing with," Grace said. "Whenever I look at Joe, I can't imagine that the day would *ever* come where I'd want to get within' kissin' range of his lips."

Olivia couldn't help but laugh.

But then, just as she was about to ask Grace for advice on how to talk to Billy, the shrill sound of a siren unexpectedly rose, growing louder by the second. Moments later, the two sisters watched as their father's police car roared past, kicking up dust as it headed out of town.

"I wonder what that's all about," Grace said.

"An emergency, I suppose," Olivia answered, thinking about what had happened the day before with the fire that had burned Peter.

"People here have it good," her sister said, pausing to drain the last inch of her Coke. "Whenever they need help, Dad comes runnin'."

Olivia nodded.

Unfortunately, *her* problem wasn't one for which she could call the sheriff. For the most part, she was on her own.

Peter placed the last of the dirty dishes on the kitchen counter, pausing to linger beside

Olivia. She stood next to him, her hands submerged in the soapy water that filled the sink, scrubbing away what was left of their meal. Careful not to stare right at her, Peter instead looked at her reflection in the window, at the stray strand of hair that dangled across her face, the thin smile on her lips.

What I wouldn't give to kiss them, right here, right now . . .

He had surprised even himself by kissing her. It hadn't been his intention; what he had wanted was to know how she felt about him, and to then consider revealing his true identity. But when Olivia had admitted to being attracted to him, Peter had been overwhelmed. It had been bold, maybe even brazen, but when she had returned his passion, her body pressed against his, their lips touching, everything had changed. He hadn't slept well last night; between the dull ache of his burns and the memory of Olivia's kiss, he'd tossed and turned until dawn. Even now, thoughts of her consumed him.

"When can I see you again?" he whispered.

"How about right now?" she teased.

"That's not what I mean."

"I know. I'm just trying to be careful," Olivia said. "Someone saw us yesterday . . ."

"Who?" he asked, his heart pounding.

"Grace," she answered. "She told me she saw the whole thing."

Peter didn't dare look at himself in the window; he was sure the embarrassment he felt would be written across his face. Suddenly, the way that Olivia's sister had been stealing glances at him during dinner made a lot more sense. Fear filled him that the Marstens would find out what had gone on between them. He'd heard bits and pieces of Olivia's conversations with her mother and had little doubt Elizabeth wanted him out of her house sooner rather than later.

"Did she tell anyone?" he asked nervously.

"She told me that she didn't."

"Do you believe her?"

Olivia turned to look at him. "I do."

Her certainty made him feel more at ease, but he wasn't free from worry.

"I need to talk to you," he said. "Soon."

Olivia glanced up at him. "I bet you do."

Peter knew what she was thinking; that he wanted to kiss her again, which he indeed did. But she could never have guessed his actual reason; that he needed to tell her the truth about himself.

When she finds out, I doubt she'll be as happy as she expects to be . . .

But before Peter could say more, the

kitchen door opened and Olivia's father entered. John looked out on his feet. His eyes were underlined by dark circles. His clothes were filthy; there was even a streak of grime across his badge. Without a word, he dropped wearily into a chair.

Olivia was shocked. "What happened?"

"Another fire," he answered. Nodding to Peter, he managed a smile. "I thought we'd used up a year's worth of excitement yesterday, but then I got a call that Carter Fredette's place was burning and we were off. and running again."

"Grace and I saw you drive by around noon," Olivia said.

Her father nodded. "Been there ever since." Again, he looked toward Peter. "Be glad you got to sit this one out."

"That bad?" Peter asked.

"The Fredettes' place isn't like out at Roy's. It's right up against its neighbors. We spent hours just trying to keep the blaze from spreading. Somehow, we managed, although I reckon Carter doesn't feel as good as I do about it, what with his place no more than a pile of burnt wood and ashes."

"Two days of fires in a row?" Olivia observed.

"Here's to a better tomorrow," John said

with a chuckle.

"But doesn't that seem strange? What are the odds of that happening in Miller's Creek?"

"I've seen some mighty bizarre things over the years," the sheriff answered. "I'm not much surprised by anything anymore."

Peter could see that the fires were worrying John more than he wanted to let on. Olivia was right; what *were* the chances of fires on consecutive days? Of course, it could be a coincidence and the blazes were unrelated, but Peter's gut said otherwise. In fact, his worrying even had a name.

Could it be Otto . . . ?

Up until now, Peter had allowed himself to believe that the dangerous Nazi would be far away from Miller's Creek or that he'd been captured. But what if he was wrong? What if Otto had never left? If he was still out there? Hadn't he promised a campaign of terror against the Americans he so deeply despised? Wouldn't arson be a way to obtain his vengeance?

Suddenly, there was a knock on the kitchen door.

"That's probably Huck," John explained. "He said he was going to stop by on his way home."

But when Olivia opened it, she stiffened.

248

As soon as Peter saw the man, noticed the way he smiled at Olivia, the way he tried to look past her and inside, he knew who it was.

This was the man engaged to the woman he was falling in love with.

Olivia stood at the kitchen door and stared out in surprise. Billy grinned up at her, acting as if there was nothing strange about his being there, as if he was showing up as invited. But that wasn't the case. After her lunch with Grace, Olivia had spent the rest of the day thinking about her two relationships; the unexpected, newly passionate one she'd begun with Peter, as well as the muddled mess of her own making with Billy. Eventually, she'd come to a decision.

She needed to break off her engagement to Billy.

To that end, Olivia had phoned him from the hardware store. She'd told Billy that they needed to talk and they had agreed to meet the following afternoon. Still, he must have heard the disquiet in her voice; she'd had to fend off plenty of questions. She'd wanted some time to figure out just what to say.

Clearly, Billy hadn't wanted to wait.

"What . . . what are you doing here?" she

asked a bit more brusquely than she had intended. "I thought we agreed to meet tomorrow at lunchtime."

"Sorry," he answered. "I didn't think you'd mind. I can leave . . ."

"No, no . . . come in . . ." Olivia answered, her heart beating faster knowing that Peter was just behind her.

When she moved away from the door, Billy stepped inside. His eyes immediately found Peter, his smile faltering for a second before he looked away, his attention turning to her father. "I hope I'm not interrupting anything."

"Of course not," the sheriff replied. "I've been expecting you."

"You have?" Billy asked.

John nodded. "Back in my day, it was customary for a young man to ask a girl's father for permission before he proposed . . ."

"I'm . . . I'm sorry, sir . . ." he stammered. "It wasn't my intention. Your blessing is important to me, but with training coming and all I have to get settled at the bank, not to mention trying to figure out when to —"

"It's all right, son," John interrupted with a tired smile. "I'm just giving you a hard time. Heaven knows you've got plenty on your plate. Besides, if you had asked, I hope you know by now that my permission would've been granted."

Olivia quietly stewed; she couldn't help but feel as if they were discussing her future as if she wasn't even in the room. She knew her father had always liked Billy, but she also remembered the conversation they'd had just after she'd accepted the proposal. Her father knew she had her doubts; wouldn't he understand if she ended the engagement?

Out of the corner of her eye, Olivia noticed Peter's reaction to the conversation. He appeared uncomfortable. He kept looking Billy over, as if he were measuring the man; she wondered if he found her fiancé lacking. She'd hoped to spend some time with him that night, to hear what he wanted to say and to steal a few more kisses, but with Billy here, all of that was out the window.

What Olivia didn't want was trouble. Billy had always been self-conscious about his looks; being thin and gangly had gotten him plenty of teasing when they'd been children. Now, looking at him as he stood near Peter, the difference between the two men was striking; Peter's broad, muscular physique and handsome, almost movie-star good looks stood in stark contrast to Billy. Olivia hoped that Billy wouldn't feel jealous or threatened. She recalled the things he'd said about Peter, how dismissive he'd been, wondering and worrying about the stranger who'd suddenly entered her life.

If only she could keep them apart . . .

"You must be Peter," Billy said, ruining her plan as he extended his hand. "I'm Billy Tate." He paused for a moment before adding, "Olivia's fiancé."

Peter took the offered greeting. "Nice to meet you."

"I suppose I owe you my thanks. From the way everyone in town is talking, if it wasn't for you, I wouldn't be about to get married. You're a hero."

"You don't owe me anything. I just did what had to be done."

"I'll give you my gratitude all the same," Billy insisted.

By now, their handshake had gone on far longer than would have been considered polite. Olivia felt the tension in the room rising. But then Peter glanced at her, holding her eyes for an instant before releasing his grip; Billy smiled triumphantly, as if he had won something. Olivia hoped that that would be all to pass between them, but before she could suggest to Billy that they go outside and talk, he again spoke to Peter.

"So what is it that brings you to Miller's Creek?" he asked. "I hope you don't mind my curiosity, but with all of the war's travel restrictions, it's been a long time since we've had much in the way of visitors."

Watching him, Olivia could see that Billy was out of sorts. As he spoke, he puffed himself up, trying to be bigger than he really was, both in stature and in voice. On the other hand, Peter appeared calm; she couldn't help but wonder if it had anything to do with the fact that it was his lips that had touched hers last.

"I'm not really at liberty to say," Peter answered. "What I do for a living is important to the war effort. I have an occupational deferment."

"Really?" Billy answered, clearly skeptical. "And this . . . important job . . . somehow brought you here, to this small town in Wisconsin?"

Peter glanced at Olivia, her eyes lingering. "In my life, the one thing I've learned is that you go where the road takes you."

Unfortunately, Billy had noticed the look they shared; the shocked expression on his face when he stared at Olivia had transformed into a glare by the time his attention returned to Peter.

"What branch of the service do you work

253

for?" he asked.

"I can't tell you that," Peter answered.

"Do you spend your time out traveling the countryside or do you have an office you work from? Superior officers?"

"I told you, I can't —"

"Then what *can* you tell me?" Billy interrupted. Smiling mischievously, he stepped closer to his rival for Olivia's affection. "Am I the only one of us who finds it strange that so much of this man's life is a secret? The only thing we have to go on is his word. For all we know, everything he's said is a lie."

"Billy!" Olivia hissed, shocked by his rudeness.

"Now, hold on there, son," John added.

Ignoring them, Billy looked Peter up and down with an expression of disdain. "Would you like to know what I think?" he asked.

Peter didn't react.

"I think that you're a coward."

Olivia gasped. Billy had gone too far; an insult like that should have been enough to rile Peter, maybe even make him take a swing at the other man.

Instead, he stayed still and silent.

Encouraged, Billy kept going. "My guess is that you're so afraid of going off to fight for your country that you're on the run, hid-

ing, and taking advantage of whoever is foolish enough to take you at your word. You happened to stumble across Olivia, saw your chance, and took it."

"How dare you say such a thing," Olivia snapped. She looked at her father; she'd been wondering why he hadn't jumped in and put a stop to all of Billy's spiteful claims; it made her wonder if it was because he was tired, or if he'd maybe had some of the same doubts. Either way, he remained silent.

"It's all right," Peter said; from the calm expression on his face, it would've been hard to tell that he'd just been insulted.

"No, it isn't!"

"It's nothing I haven't heard before." Turning to Billy, Peter said, "You speak like you can't wait to go and fight."

"It can't come soon enough," the other man said proudly.

"Then you're a fool."

"What?!" Billy snapped.

"I may not know what war is firsthand, but from what I do know, no man should thirst for the battlefield. More often than not, when soldiers come home they aren't the same as when they left, *if* they return at all."

"Not me! I'll be even —"

"He's right," John interrupted. "I've told both of you before, but it's my hope that neither of you have to find out what war is *really* like."

Olivia noticed the way her father looked at Peter; it was as if he was seeing him in a new light, which she supposed he had.

It was clear that Billy was still angry. For a moment, Olivia thought that he was going to argue some more, but he managed to hold his tongue; she supposed that it was one thing to spar with Peter, but another to openly disagree with her father. His hands, which had bunched into fists when Peter had called him a fool, trembled at his sides. His face was flushed a deep red.

"Let's go, Olivia," he said, and headed for the door.

She turned to look at Peter. He still appeared calm, though she wondered what he was thinking; after all, she was about to leave with another man.

"We'll talk tomorrow," he said.

Olivia nodded.

"Are you coming?" Billy asked, holding the door open.

Taking a deep breath, she followed him outside.

CHAPTER FIFTEEN

When the kitchen door clicked shut behind them, Billy grabbed Olivia's hand; his touch was too tight, sweaty, and charged with either nerves or excitement, she couldn't tell which. Without hesitation, he started toward the backyard.

"Come on," he said, smiling expectantly.

Olivia held her ground, pulling them both to a stop. "Not tonight, Billy," she said. "I'd rather we just go for a walk instead."

"But I thought that we could . . ." He didn't finish the thought, although Olivia knew exactly how it ended; he was hoping that, if they were once again sitting beneath the evergreen, they'd resume kissing, something that Olivia didn't want. Though she was still unhappy with how Billy had treated Peter, making baseless accusations, she knew that there was little point in discussing it further; he'd just plead ignorance of his jealousy. Besides, there was a far more pressing matter that they needed to discuss.

"It's a nice night," she offered.

Billy hesitated, torn between his own desires and hers. "All right," he finally agreed, his disappointment as obvious as the moon in the sky above.

For the first couple of blocks, they walked in silence. Since his big plans had been dashed, Billy had soon let go of her hand, for which Olivia was grateful. The night was pleasant so she tried to lose herself in its details; a dog's bark, lights shining in the houses they passed, a faraway car horn. When they passed Geraldine Tubbs's house, a snippet of Benny Goodman drifted out an open window, a serenade that lasted only a couple of steps. But try as she might, Olivia couldn't keep from thinking about what she needed to do.

I'm going to break my best friend's heart . . .

While Olivia had agreed with Grace and Peter about the need to be honest with Billy, she still didn't have a clue what to say. All she knew was that by revealing the truth, by being honest with him, she would hurt him, a prospect that saddened her deeply. Try as she might, she'd yet to be able to find the words. But even though Billy had shown up unexpectedly, she doubted that an extra night to consider her options would have helped.

As they walked, Olivia glanced at Billy. They were passing beneath a streetlight, and just then, for an instant, it felt like it used to before he'd proposed, before they'd kissed, back to a time when there weren't any troubles between them. But Olivia wasn't a fool; she knew that no matter how hard she wished otherwise, there was no going back. There was only forward, which meant somehow finding the words . . .

But then, suddenly, it was Billy who broke the silence. "I hope you don't mind my stopping by like that."

"No . . . no, it was fine . . ."

"Are you sure? If not, I can take you back home."

"It's okay."

"I'm glad to hear that," Billy answered. He stopped walking and Olivia did the same. "It's just that, well, I know we agreed to meet for lunch tomorrow, but after we hung up the telephone, I got to thinking." He paused, his brow furrowed, as if he was weighing what to say. "There are some things we've never talked about, that maybe we've been avoiding . . . important things . . ."

For an instant, a flame of hope flickered

to life in Olivia. The thought suddenly struck her that Billy might be suffering from some of the same doubts and worries that plagued her. Was it possible that he was reconsidering his proposal? For the first time, she allowed herself to believe that breaking their engagement might be easier than she'd expected.

"I agree," she said. "We do need to talk."

"Great!" he answered enthusiastically. "So, I know this might not be what you want to hear," he said, leaving Olivia almost breathless with anticipation, "but I think we should get married next week."

Olivia was stunned speechless; the fantasy she'd constructed had been shattered into a million tiny pieces. "What . . ." she finally managed.

"Just hear me out," he said. "My father met with Maurice Hendricks, pulled a few strings, called in a couple of favors, and managed to rent out the Wiltshire Hotel ballroom for a reception!" Billy explained, the words tumbling out of his mouth faster than a rabbit in spring. "He had to snatch it up quickly. Turns out that it's leased for some traveling war bond fund-raiser in a couple of weeks. If he'd waited, there was a chance it could've —"

But by then, Olivia was no longer listening. Much to her amazement, things were even worse than she'd assumed. Billy was like her mother, making plans for her life without even bothering to ask what she thought or wanted. All of the frustration and helplessness she'd been feeling suddenly boiled over.

"Stop it, Billy!" she snapped angrily, holding up her hands, cutting him off in midsentence. "Just stop!"

"What . . . what is it?" he asked, his eyes wide, confused by her sudden outburst. "Is there something wrong with the Wiltshire? If you don't like it, I can try to talk to my father, see if we can change it, but he won't be happy . . ."

Listening to him, all the anger drained from Olivia and was replaced by a sadness so great that it brought tears to her eyes. Billy was clueless. She didn't know if it was honest, or if he was even aware that he was deluding himself, but he behaved as if he had no idea that she was considering breaking their engagement. Fighting her emotions, she struggled to go through with what she knew needed to be done.

"It's not about the hotel . . ." she began. "It's more than that. It's something that's been on my mind ever since you asked me to marry you . . ." Again and again, silence

261

threatened to descend on Olivia, to over-whelm her and make her swallow the words she knew would cause so much pain. But she refused to let it happen; not just for her sake, but for Billy's, too. "I . . . I can't do this," Olivia finally admitted, tears cascading down her cheeks. "I can't be your wife . . ."

Billy stared at her, dumbstruck, his face twisting from one reaction to the next; disbelief became incomprehension before making an odd turn into a stifled chuckle, as if she'd told a joke that wasn't particularly funny. Olivia imagined that his expression was much like hers had been when he'd proposed, with neither of them able to comprehend what they were hearing.

"I . . . I don't understand . . ." he managed, although she imagined that some-where, deep down, he knew exactly what was happening.

"I'm sorry," Olivia said truthfully, trying to apply a bandage to his wounds before she'd even inflicted them. "I know you don't want to hear this, but I made a mistake, Billy. When you proposed, I should've been honest, I should have turned you down, but I didn't." Before her eyes, Billy began to show the effects of her words; his shoulders slumped and his face hardened, but still she pressed on. "It should never have gotten this far, but now that it has, it has to stop, for both of our sakes." Purposefully, Olivia slipped the engagement ring off her finger and then placed it in Billy's hand; she pressed his fingers around it out of fear that, in his current state, he would drop it.

For longer than Olivia might have expected, Billy remained silent. She wouldn't have blamed him for shouting at her, for letting his temper rage at the thought that she had deceived him. She also wouldn't have thought any less of him had he surrendered to his sadness and disappointment. But instead he just stared. When he finally did speak, his voice was little more than a whisper.

"Don't . . . don't you love me . . . ?"

Olivia swallowed a sob. "Of course I do," she answered. "I always will, no matter what, but not in the way that I should if I'm to be your wife. You deserve better than that."

"But you said 'yes,' " Billy argued. "You accepted . . ."

"I know, but I shouldn't have."

"So you lied to me?" he asked accusingly, the first flare of anger in his voice.

"It . . . it wasn't a lie . . ." Olivia struggled.

"Then what was it?"

"You leave for the Navy in little more than a month," Olivia explained. "You'll be thousands of miles from home, fighting in a war. You could be . . . killed . . ." she said, uncomfortable saying the word. "I couldn't bear the thought of you doing all that with a broken heart. If something happened to you, if I thought for a minute it was because I'd rejected you, it'd be more than I could bear. So I said 'yes,' " she added, feeling sick to her stomach, "to keep from hurting you."

"Looks like that didn't work like you planned," Billy said sarcastically.

Olivia didn't answer.

"What about that night in your backyard?" he asked. "Did you kiss me because you wanted to or was it out of pity?"

His accusation stung. "That's not why it happened, not at all," Olivia answered. "Sitting there, watching my parents, things got carried away. What we did . . . it wasn't us. We aren't supposed to be like that. In my heart, I know that we're friends, not lovers."

Billy stared hard at her. "Do you remember what you said to me the night of my mother's funeral?"

"Of course I do," Olivia answered.

How could she ever forget? She'd come over to his house after the funeral, watching from across the room as Billy stood next to his father, shaking hands and accepting condolences from everyone in Miller's Creek. But then, just after the first guests had begun to leave, she'd caught Billy's eye; he'd been so distraught that he was almost trembling, the look on his face imploring her to take him far away from all the pain and misery he felt. Without a word, Olivia had walked over and grabbed Billy by the hand. The two of them had gone down to the creek and sat beneath the same drooping tree under which they'd first met. For hours, until long after the sun had set and the night sky had filled with stars, she had held him as he sobbed, letting out all the grief he'd been holding inside. She'd kissed his forehead, wiped away his tears, and tried her best to soothe him, whispering the same words into his ear, over and over again.

"I'll never leave you," she'd said, trying to reassure him. "Even when we're old, I'll always be there for you, as sure as the sun will rise in the morning."

And she'd meant it, just not in the way Billy apparently had.

Looking at his face now, nearly ten years later, she saw much of the same grief and desperation she had then.

"Olivia, please," he said. "This isn't the

way it was supposed to be. You promised that you'd always be there, that we'd be together."

"But I don't love you *that way,*" she explained.

Billy shook his head. "But you could! I know it," he declared, almost begging her to understand. "The kiss we shared proves it! It can be the beginning. Once we're married and I come back from the Navy, we can make it work. All it will take is time. You'll see. You just have to give it a chance. Give *me* a chance!"

Immediately, Olivia thought of Peter. From the moment they had met, she'd felt a spark between them. It was so strong she couldn't deny it. To back down now, to give in for fear of hurting Billy any further, meant that she would never again feel his embrace or kiss his lips. As Billy's wife, she would spend the rest of her days wondering if she'd turned her back on her only chance at love.

And for that reason, she couldn't waver.

"I can't marry you," she said, determined to hold her ground.

Billy's face darkened. His hands bunched into fists, his jaw tightened. He looked so angry, so unlike himself, that Olivia took a step back.

"This is all that bastard's fault" he growled.

"Wh-who . . . ?" Olivia blurted, taken aback by his outburst.

"That lying coward who's afraid to fight!" Billy shouted. "Nothing's been the same since he came to town. I don't give a damn if he saved your life. He's ruined everything!"

Olivia knew that Billy was grasping at straws, blaming anything and everything for her not wanting to marry him, but she couldn't help but wonder if there was something she'd said or done to give herself away. Had someone other than Grace seen them kiss? Had Billy heard a rumor?

"This isn't because of him," she said, believing it to be true; even if Peter Baird had never entered her life, Olivia had no doubt that marrying Billy would have been a mistake.

Billy didn't seem at all convinced. "You're lying!" Angrily, he reached out and grabbed her arm. His fury had control of him, making him do things Olivia knew he wouldn't have if he'd been of the right mind, but that didn't keep her from crying out in pain, his grip too tight.

"Stop it!" she shouted. "You're hurting me!"

But Billy wasn't listening. "What all have you shared with him?" he demanded. "Was it a kiss? A promise you have no intention of keeping? What sweet words have you whispered in his ear beneath the evergreen tree?"

Olivia didn't know what to say. No matter what, not now certainly, she wouldn't admit to Billy that he was partly right, that she *had* kissed Peter and that it had played a role in her breaking off their engagement. She could spare him that much, at least. But with every passing second, Billy's grip continued to tighten. Olivia looked around, sure that someone had heard them arguing, that they would shout and bring Billy back to his senses, but nothing stirred in the darkness, no doors opened, and no lights were switched on.

"Why do you want that coward?" Billy hollered as he shook her; though he was thin of build, not nearly as muscular as Peter, he was still far stronger than her. "What does he have that I don't? Tell me. Can he offer you a future? A life like I could give you? What will your mother —"

When Olivia slapped Billy hard across his face, whatever else it was he had wanted to say remained unspoken. In the quiet of the night, the blow sounded loud, like the crack of a gun. Olivia gasped, her hand retreating to cover her mouth as tears raced down her cheeks.

Being struck changed Billy. Gone was the raging, out-of-control bully who had badgered her with questions and accusations; in his place was the young man who'd always stood by her side, her friend. Shock and shame were written on his face. He still had hold of her arm. Billy looked at his hand, as shocked to find it there as Olivia. He slowly released his grip, like the jaws of a bear trap being pulled back; the moment Olivia could break free, she did, rubbing at the red marks on her skin.

"Oh, Olivia," Billy said. "I'm so sorry . . ."

That was all he got to say before Olivia turned and ran. Sobs shook her body but she kept going through a storm of tears. From behind her, she heard footfalls, then shouts.

"Olivia, wait!" Billy yelled. "Please wait!"

But she ignored him. She kept expecting him to catch up to her, to again grab her arm and shower her with explanations and apologies, anything he could think of to make things right between them. But by the end of the street, when she turned toward home, running as fast as she could, there was only silence chasing her.

■ ■ ■ ■

Billy watched Olivia run off into the night, soon disappearing from sight. He knew that he could have caught her if he'd wanted to, but as upset as she was, he doubted she would've listened to anything he had to say. He'd made a mess of things, maybe botched them so badly that they could never be repaired. If there was to be a chance to fix his mistake, he had to give her some time and space. Maybe tomorrow or the day after, Olivia would be ready to listen to reason.

"Damn it all," he muttered to himself.

This wasn't the way it was supposed to be. Sure, when he'd proposed to Olivia, he'd heard the doubt in her voice, seen it in her eyes. He had even tried taking the offer back, wanting to end it on his own rather than be forced to listen to her reject him. But then she'd said "yes." Still, even though he'd known that it all hung by a thread, he'd clung to the belief that he and Olivia would be husband and wife.

But now it was all ruined.

Somewhere down deep in his gut, Billy knew this had something to do with the stranger. He had always been jealous of any man who got too close to Olivia, who made her smile. Even when they were kids, when someone wormed his way into their lives, he'd struggle to pretend that nothing was the matter, but he had seethed inside. He knew that it was irrational, but right now, with what he'd just lost, he had to wonder . . .

Until Peter Baird showed up, everything had been going as Billy had hoped. So who was this man who'd swooped in and destroyed all he'd wanted? Was this man, this *lying coward,* willing to fight for Olivia's hand?

We'll just have to find out.

CHAPTER SIXTEEN

Peter stood behind the closed door to his room and listened. Late-morning sunlight streamed through the window, fell across the floor, and reached toward him to warm his skin, but he paid it no mind. He'd gotten up hours ago, dressing in the murky darkness of dawn, and waited patiently. Before long, the Marstens had woken but he stayed where he was. Peter knew that he could have opened the door, gone to the kitchen, and shared breakfast with the family, as he'd done for days, but he hadn't wanted to be asked any questions, especially any about his plans. He hadn't wanted to lie; he'd already done too much of that.

But he also didn't want anyone to know where he was going.

Long after Olivia left with her fiancé, Peter had been troubled by the fire John had spent the afternoon fighting. All he could think about was Otto and the promise the man had made to continue to wage war against America. Peter wondered if the Nazi was responsible for the blazes. He had to know if his earlier assumption was wrong; he had to find out whether Otto had left Miller's Creek or if he was still lurking about.

But Otto wasn't the only thing on his mind.

Peter had waited patiently for Olivia to return. He'd meant what he had said to her after dinner, that he'd wanted to talk, to maybe find the words to admit who he really was. But when she'd come home, there hadn't been time. He'd heard her mumble something to her mother, followed by her feet hurrying up the stairs, and finally her bedroom door had slammed shut. Since then, nothing. He hadn't even heard her come down for breakfast. As far as he knew, she was still in her room.

For a moment, Peter considered going upstairs and knocking on her door, but then he decided against it. Clearly, something had happened between her and Billy. Maybe she had ended their engagement. Whatever it was, she would tell him when she was ready. Until then, he'd give her the time and space she needed.

Slowly, Peter opened the guest room door.

He listened closely, but heard nothing. Silently, not so quick as to attract attention, Peter slipped out the front door and was on his way.

It was time to find some answers.

Walking away from town, Peter turned north and headed back in the direction of the cabin where he and Otto had first taken shelter. It was the only place he could think of where he might find answers to what happened to the man. Maybe something had been left behind, some clue.

Every step Peter took seemed to lead him further toward the conclusion that Otto was responsible for the fires. One fire in a place like Miller's Creek was an accident. Another blaze on the very next day? That was suspicious. What were the odds? He'd noticed the way John had reacted; the sheriff had tried to mask his thoughts, but Peter had seen the look that crossed his face, as if he found his own words false. No, something sinister was at play.

He was just about to cross the bridge that spanned the creek when he was startled by the sound of a car's horn behind him. Peter spun around to find John waving at him from his police car. Just as when he'd been talking with Ruth Pollack, the Marstens' blind neighbor, Peter's first assumption was that the sheriff was coming for him, that his deception had been uncovered and he was to be arrested. Still, he stamped down his worries as John pulled up beside him, leaned across the front seat, and spoke out the passenger's side window.

"Morning," John greeted him. "Out for a walk?"

"I thought I'd take a bit of air," Peter answered. "Maybe head up in the hills, see a different lay of the land."

The sheriff nodded. "Sounds good. A man stays cooped up inside for too long, he goes a little stir crazy. Besides," he added, "I reckon a nice walk is easier on the constitution than rescuing horses from a burning barn."

Peter chuckled. "It is at that."

"You sure you don't want a lift? I could take you a ways out of town and let you walk back. There's a place you might like a couple miles down the creek, a pond set back a bit from the road with so many fish they practically fight for a place in the water."

"No, thanks," Peter replied as good-naturedly as he could. "I've got my heart set on climbing the hills."

"Some other time, then." But just as Peter

thought the sheriff would head on his way, he said, "There's something that I'd like to talk to you about. I meant to mention it to you yesterday, but I was so out on my feet from the fire that it slipped my mind."

"Oh, yeah?" Peter said as the bottom of his stomach dropped out.

"Hell, it'd be just as easy to show you rather than try to explain it," John said. "You have any plans for later in the day? Say around two o'clock?"

Peter shook his head. "I should be back from my walk by then."

"Great. How about meeting me out in front of the diner? What I have to show you won't take long."

"All right," he agreed. *What choice do I have?*

Watching Olivia's father drive off, Peter struggled against his feelings of dread. Did John suspect? Was there something he'd said or done to give away his real identity? He couldn't know for certain, but since there wasn't anything he could do about it now, Peter resigned himself to wait and confront it when the time came. Until then, he had plenty else to keep him busy.

He turned back toward the hills and resumed walking.

■ ■ ■ ■

Wiping sweat from his brow, Peter knelt behind a bush and stared at the cabin. Unlike his first trip down the hill to Miller's Creek, he hadn't met anyone on the long climb back up. Still, that didn't mean he was alone. He watched patiently. Minutes crawled slowly past as the sun inched its way across the sky, but Peter didn't move. Now wasn't the time to be careless.

When he'd first decided to go looking for Otto, Peter had thought that, if he found the man, he would approach him. But the more he considered what had happened, the more he knew that that course of action was dangerous. If Otto was still around, it was possible he had discovered that Peter had been staying at the sheriff's house, which would undoubtedly make the man suspicious. He would think that Peter had been compromised.

On the other hand, Peter couldn't talk about it with John, either. Until he knew for certain that Otto was still around, that he'd been behind the two blazes, he would stay silent. Besides, there was still the matter of revealing himself to Olivia. When the time was right, he would tell her, then her father.

But first, he had to learn what had happened to Otto.

Finally satisfied that he was alone, Peter entered the cabin. Everything was as he remembered it. Drawers were open, their contents strewn across the floor. The containers from his meager meal still lay on the kitchen counter. Regardless, Peter searched the cabin from top to bottom, re-examined every cupboard, rechecked each closet, and again sorted through every musty-smelling drawer. But when he'd finished looking, he had found nothing that could be tied to Otto.

Back outside, Peter went to the work shed where he had broken free of his handcuffs. At first glance, it looked like the rest of the cabin, unchanged from when he'd been there last. But then the sun glinted off something, drawing his attention. There, on the rickety workbench, was the head of the axe Otto had broken in his desperate bid to gain his freedom. It was wedged into a crack between two boards. Peering closer, Peter noticed that the metal was stained with blood that had dried a dark red; more splotches dotted the wood. Kneeling, Peter searched the ground and found a broken link of chain. There was only one conclusion to draw.

Otto had gotten free of his restraints.

As his mind swam with what that meant, Peter tried to remain calm. Even if Otto had gotten loose he might still have hopped on a train and could now be hundreds of miles away. It didn't necessarily mean he was still in Miller's Creek.

But it sure makes it more likely . . .

Peter's thoughts were interrupted by the sound of a stick breaking near the cabin. He froze, his heart pounding hard and fast. He'd been careful, had waited until he felt sure he was alone, but what if he hadn't been cautious enough? Was it Otto? If it was, what would happen if the Nazi discovered him?

Desperately, Peter looked around the shed, searching for a weapon, something he could use to defend himself. There, lying on the ground, was the axe's broken handle. He snatched it up; it would have to do.

He waited, his eyes searching, his ears straining to hear a sound. There it was again, another snap of a twig or branch. This time, the noise sounded like it was coming from the far corner of the cabin. Without any hesitation, Peter took off running, racing for the edge of the building. Out in the open, he felt vulnerable, as if each second took a minute to pass, as if he would be seen at any moment. But when he pressed his back up against the cabin's wall, trying to quiet his fevered breathing, there was no shout, no gunshot, nothing that would indicate he'd been noticed.

Cautiously, he edged his way to the cabin's corner, steadied himself, and peeked around. Nothing. Thinking that whoever it was who'd made the noises was moving in the opposite direction, Peter hurried forward; if he was quick and bold enough, maybe he could get the drop on him from behind. At the next corner, he stopped and listened.

It was then that Peter heard something that made his heart stop. Two more sticks were broken in quick succession, but this time, the sounds were coming *toward* him; Peter couldn't have said for certain, but from the nearness of them, whoever it was stood only a couple feet away. Had he made too much noise? Had Otto seen him approach and lured him into a trap? Either way, it was too late to run. Gripping the axe handle tightly, Peter stepped around the corner, determined to fight his way free.

Only it wasn't Otto. There, standing ten feet away, nibbling on a patch of early spring grass, was a deer.

The buck raised its head sharply, its

antlers splayed toward the sunny sky, when it noticed Peter watching. For a moment, neither of them moved, but then the animal bounded away, frightened, its white tail disappearing in a clump of bushes. Once again, he was alone.

My nerves are going to be the death of me . . .

Eventually, Peter's heart began to slow. Dropping the axe handle, he went over to the ridge and looked down at the town. Miller's Creek appeared much as it had that first day he'd seen it, but Peter knew that one thing was different. Somewhere down there, whether still in her bedroom, working at the hardware store, or out walking the streets, was the woman he was falling in love with. In his heart, Peter was more certain than ever that Otto was responsible for the fires. That meant he was a danger to Olivia. No matter what it took, Peter knew that the brutal Nazi had to be stopped.

But that meant he had to find him first.

Otto looked down on the quiet town with a frown. Though he had reason to be satisfied, he wasn't happy. Not one bit. After the success of the first fire he'd lit, the very next day had presented him with another opportunity, one he'd seized with a vengeance.

The home had been one among many, nestled in a neighborhood, not as isolated as the barn. It had been a risk to approach it in daylight, but his compulsion had been too great. Filling an empty bottle with kerosene, he'd stuffed a soaked rag down its neck, lit it on fire, and tossed it through one of the home's basement windows. He'd been half a mile away before the first black smoke had billowed into the sky. A few blocks later, sirens had cried out. He'd thought that the house was empty, but Otto wondered if he'd been wrong. Maybe there'd been a housewife with a couple of mewling kids, or a gnarled old crone too sick to get up, confined to bed, and they'd all burned in the blaze.

He hoped they had.

For all that and much more, Otto knew that he should've been feeling good, satisfied with the destruction he'd wrought for the glory of his Führer, but he wasn't. Something was missing. Unless he managed to burn the whole damn town to the ground, lighting fires wasn't big and bold enough. If he was to make these Amerikaners know fear, then he needed to give them a better reason.

Kicking a rock, Otto sent the stone skittering down the hillside. He stood to the south of town, opposite the cabin where he and Peter Becker had first sought refuge. Not for the first time, he wondered what had become of his fellow soldier. Surely, he'd been captured. Becker was weak; if it hadn't been for the fact that they'd been shackled together, Otto would never have taken the man with him after the train wreck. Right now, Becker was sitting in a cell or on another prison transport, his use to Germany ended. Otto hoped that he was faithful enough to his country to have kept his mouth shut, allowing Otto to do as he pleased.

Walking over to the rough lean-to he'd built out of fallen tree limbs for shelter from the cold spring nights, Otto rummaged through the items he'd managed to steal: a few dented cans of food, a smelly old blanket, some ill-fitting clothes, a browned newspaper that he couldn't read yet knew to be full of lies, and a rusted lamp containing a thimble of oil. Just as his frustration began to grow, he found what he was looking for.

In the third place he'd ransacked, Otto had found a knife lying forgotten on a shelf. Holding it up, he pulled the three-inch blade free from its scabbard; the afternoon sun glinted off the still-sharp blade. While it wasn't as useful as a gun would've been, it was better than having to rely on his fists. Turning it over in his hand, he measured its weight, and then slashed it through the air; a blow like that would gut a man. After all, he'd done it before. Returning the blade to its sheath, Otto stuffed the knife into the back of his pants, piled some scrub around the shelter to make it less noticeable, and headed off.

Picking his way through the woods, Otto followed a deer trail leading back toward town. While reconnoitering, he'd noticed a lawman driving around in his car, smiling and waving to everyone he passed, trying to convince his pathetic countrymen that he was keeping them safe. Surely this man had a family, someone he cared for, a wife and children. If Otto could find him and follow the man home, then he'd have his victim. If these people's protector was murdered, cut down in cold blood, *that* would frighten them. Then maybe he'd be satisfied.

In the Führer's name, he was going to kill someone.

Chapter Seventeen

"You did *what*?!"

Olivia stepped back as her mother rose from where she'd been working in her garden. Elizabeth had a dirty trowel clutched tightly in her hand and her apron was stained at the knees with grass and mud. A few stray strands of her long hair drifted lazily in the afternoon breeze, a slip in appearance that Elizabeth wouldn't tolerate for long; even when working in the yard, Olivia's mother had a reputation to protect. But right now, at that instant, Elizabeth wasn't at all worried about what she looked like, or even what the neighbors might think.

She was far too angry for that.

When Olivia had finally left her room, it had been nearly eleven o'clock. After what had happened the night before, she hadn't been able to sleep, the memory of slapping Billy playing over and over again in her mind. She'd tossed and turned restlessly on her bed for hours, finally slipping into a fitful slumber in the hours just before sunrise. Waking from a dream with a start, she'd been thankful that this wasn't a day she was supposed to work at the hardware store. As quietly as a mouse, she'd made her way down the stairs, pausing to look in Peter's room. His door stood open, his bed made, but he was nowhere to be seen. Olivia thought this was probably for the best; even if she'd done the right thing in breaking off her engagement to Billy, she wasn't ready to face Peter, at least not yet.

Standing in the kitchen, she'd spied her mother working in the garden. Once again, feelings of hope welled inside her, a belief that Elizabeth might understand her predicament. *Isn't that what mothers are supposed to do?* Right then and there, Olivia made a decision to tell her mother about Billy; after all, it wasn't as if she could keep it a secret forever.

Olivia went to the garden. Before she could say a word, her mother began to chastise her for staying in bed so late. Apologizing, she wiped sweat from her brow; standing beneath the blazing sun made her feel as if she was being accused of something. Finally, just as she'd done when telling her mother about Billy's proposal, she blurted it out. Elizabeth's reaction was swift and furious.

"I ended my engagement to Billy last night," she repeated.

"Why?" Elizabeth snapped. "Why would you do such a thing?"

"Because I don't love him," Olivia shot back, her mother's indignation causing her own anger to flare. "He's my best friend, but nothing more. I couldn't become his wife knowing that. It wouldn't be fair to either of us."

"Don't be a fool!" Elizabeth sneered disdainfully. "You can't possibly be so naïve! What do you think, that every marriage is like that slop they make in Hollywood? That it's all wine and roses? Far from it!" Her mother's eyes narrowed. "Take your father and me, for example . . ."

"What . . . what are you talking about . . . ?" Olivia stammered.

"Do I love your father now?" Elizabeth asked. "Of course I do. But if you would've asked me that same question the day we were married, you might have heard a different answer." Olivia was so stunned she could have been knocked over with a feather. "What I saw in John was a man destined for great things," her mother continued. "Someone people would look up to, who would command their respect. To me, he was a means to a greater end, and that's exactly what William should be to you. The love will come later."

"I'm not like you," Olivia said defensively.

"You most definitely are not," her mother agreed.

"I won't marry Billy just because he and his family have money. Not even if it means I end up living in a hovel and struggling to make ends meet. I won't disrespect him like that. I'll marry someone I truly love!"

"Stop being such a romantic! Besides, I didn't say that you would *never* come to love him. Just that it will take time." Her mother paused, thinking. "A marriage is a lot like a hand-me-down piece of clothing from your older sister," she explained. "It's something that you have to grow into."

"By your way of thinking, it's also something I'll grow out of."

Elizabeth frowned. "You always have an excuse."

"I've made my decision."

"Don't be ridiculous!" her mother answered. "You've already changed your mind once, you can do it again. All you have to do is go over to the Tates' and apologize. Better yet, go right to the bank. You may have to play it up a bit, explain that you've got a case of the jitters, something that can happen to any bride-to-be. Make sure to lay it on thick. Cry if you have to. As head-over-heels in love with you as William is, I'm sure he'll take you back in the end."

Elizabeth's manipulative suggestions, that a relationship was simply something that could be bartered for a better life, made Olivia feel sick. "You're not listening to me. There's nothing for me to apologize for other than having accepted his proposal in the first place. I don't want him to take me back. I don't want to be his wife. All I want is for things between us to go back to the way they were. I want us to be friends."

"It's too late for that," her mother said with a derisive laugh. "Ever since he proposed, all you've done is make mistakes! You should have set a date for the wedding just as soon as he asked. Instead, all you did was spend time with that man who pushed you out of the way of Sylvester's truck . . ." Olivia watched as a revelation struck Elizabeth; her eyes grew as big as saucers before narrowing to the smallest of slits. "This is because of *him,* isn't it?" she asked, her voice rising. "*He's* the reason you did this!"

Olivia's composure faltered and her mother noticed; even if she wanted to lie, she knew that Elizabeth would never believe her now. Her mother's accusation was both right *and* wrong; while her decision to break off her engagement to Billy was largely because she'd never had any romantic feelings for him, there was no point in denying that her relationship with Peter had played a role. He brought out things in her that she'd never felt before. Kissing him had opened the door to her heart further. Now she wanted to see where it led.

But how could she admit as much to her mother?

Elizabeth had always been obsessed with standing and appearances, measuring her own life by how others saw it. Through that prism, there was no way Peter could ever hope to equal Billy. Though Peter had been lauded around Miller's Creek for keeping Olivia from harm, it wouldn't be enough. His smarts, charm, and good looks didn't count, either. The only thing that truly mattered was what he had in his bank account; in that way, he was a much poorer man than Billy, so in her mother's eyes he would never be good enough for her daughter. Olivia chose to disagree.

"I made this decision on my own," she answered, neither confirming nor refuting her mother's claim.

"I doubt that," her mother said. "Young

ladies like you, the ones who don't have a shred of common sense in their heads, are easily swayed. Slick talkers come along and promise the moon and stars above but they never deliver. Who knows what sort of nonsense he's filled your head with? I wouldn't be surprised if everything he's told you has been a lie!"

"You're being paranoid."

"Am I?" Elizabeth asked. "How would you know? There's no way of checking. Where he's from, his family, what he does for a living, even his name, all of it made up off the top of his head in order to get what he really wants!" She paused, looking closely at Olivia. "You haven't slept with him, have you?"

"Mother!" she shouted, unable to believe what she was hearing.

"I'm just asking."

"I haven't!"

"Thank Heavens for that. You know," she added. "I wouldn't even be surprised if he's lying about the Army."

"What could possibly make you think that?"

"Look at him!" her mother answered. "I don't care what he says he does, no army I've ever heard of wouldn't want a man his size in uniform. William at least has the excuse of his heart, but your dear Peter looks as fit as an ox. He's practically a ringer for the soldier on the recruiting posters!"

Olivia's head spun. She remembered what Billy had told her, the claims he had made; it had been much the same. But whenever she thought of the things Peter had told her about his life, the way he'd smiled at her from across the room, and especially the way she had felt when they kissed, she couldn't bring herself to doubt him. What reason could he have for not telling the truth?

Deep in thought, Olivia was startled when her mother grabbed her by the arm and began to pull her toward the house. "We're going inside and I'm going to call your father," she said. "Maybe he can talk some sense into you. I can't remember the last time you listened to anything *I* had to say!"

Olivia jerked her arm free. "That's because what I want doesn't matter to you! I tried to tell you that I had my doubts about marrying Billy, but you didn't hear a word I said. As long as you don't end up looking bad, you couldn't care less if I'm happy." Without waiting for her mother's reply, she turned and walked away.

"Where do you think you're going?" Elizabeth shouted. "We're not done talking about this! Get back here this instant!"

But Olivia didn't listen. Her mother kept hollering, but she didn't follow; there was too great a chance that someone might see her. The sound of her voice dwindled the farther Olivia walked until, finally, it was gone.

For the second time, confiding in her mother had been a disaster.

Peter stood beneath the diner's awning and looked out into the street. The afternoon sun beat down hard and steady, too warm to stand in for long. Townspeople occasionally passed him on the sidewalk; though most of them seemed friendly enough, smiling or saying a word or two, Peter felt conspicuous, as if he stood out. Though he'd been in Miller's Creek for almost a week, he wondered if he would ever feel comfortable. All around him, there were reminders that he was far from home. Red, white, and blue flags fluttered in the breeze. Posters were taped to windows and pinned to telephone poles, calling for support for the war effort. Walking back to town from the cabin, he'd heard shopkeepers behind their counters, friends in the middle of conversations, even voices calling out from radios, all of them speaking English; the words still sounded foreign to his ear, even when he was the one speaking them. That he was standing where he was, an escaped German prisoner of war, waiting to meet the town's sheriff, the father of the woman he was falling in love with, seemed stranger than fiction.

Growing nervous, Peter glanced at the clock above the bank. It was a quarter past two. John was late.

Suddenly, he was startled by the sound of a car's horn; he looked to see John waving as he drove past and pulled into a parking spot across the street. Peter crossed to meet him.

"Sorry I'm late," the sheriff said as he got out. "Turns out I had more work to do than I'd expected."

"On account of yesterday's fire?" Peter asked.

Olivia's father nodded. "Lots of loose ends to tie up. My phone's been ringing off the hook. I have to watch Huck or he takes his out of the cradle and lays it on his desk," he added with a smile. "Now, come on. There's something I want to show you."

Peter followed as John led the way down the street. Just like when they'd eaten at the diner, everyone they passed shared a word with the sheriff.

"Doesn't that ever get tiresome?" Peter asked.

"Talking with people? Naw, not one bit," John explained. "The way I see things, it's more than just a part of my job. Rather, it's what makes this community so great. In a town like this, everyone knows each other. Most folks are friendly enough to want to talk, no matter for how long. Especially with the country at war, that bond makes us all feel like we're in it together." Looking over at Peter, he added, "Stick around long enough, you'll be doing it like all the rest."

John waved to everyone inside the barbershop, rounded the corner, and then began to climb the wooden stairs mounted to the outside of the building. Peter followed. At the top of the steps was a door. The sheriff fished a key out of his pocket, opened it, and stepped inside.

It was an apartment. The largest room faced toward the street; a picture window gave a view onto the post office and a furniture store. Toward the rear, there was a small kitchen and a bathroom. Down a short hallway, Peter saw a bedroom beyond. The furnishings weren't much, a couple of chairs, a table in the kitchen that leaned to one side, a mattress on the bedroom floor, and an old phonograph player in the corner near the window.

"It may not be the Ritz Carlton," John said with a chuckle. "But it sure beats sleeping in a train car."

Peter flinched; John couldn't have known how close to the mark his joke had come. Still, he was confused. "I don't understand."

"This is for you," the sheriff explained. "I made a few phone calls, cashed in a favor or two, and rented it out for you. It's yours for as long as it takes to get your feet back under you and on your way."

Stunned, his head spinning, Peter stammered, "It . . . it might take me a while to repay you."

"No need. I wouldn't accept it anyway."

"Why . . . why would you do this for me . . . ?"

John smiled. "On account of what you did for my daughter, for one thing," he replied. "But also because I know you're a good man. I saw what you did out at the fire. You risked your life to help folks you'd never met. You did what was right, and that's a quality I hold in no shortage of regard. If this," he added, waving a hand around the apartment, "helps you in some small way, I reckon that's the least I can do."

Peter was speechless; he was also conflicted. On one hand, he was proud to know that John thought so highly of him. He'd always strived to do what was right, to help those in need, just as his parents had taught him. But on the other hand, Peter knew that he'd been lying to the sheriff and his family since the moment he'd met them. It made him feel unworthy of the gift he was being given.

"I don't know what to say," he said.

"How about that you'll take it?" John chuckled as he tossed the key to Peter, who reflexively caught it.

"Thank you," Peter answered.

"You're welcome. Although I reckon that I'm going to be completely honest, there's another reason for this."

"What's that?"

"My wife," he replied a bit sheepishly. "You see, Elizabeth is the sort of woman who worries about what others say. Ever since you arrived, she thinks that everyone in town is talking about the stranger staying in her house. She thinks it's some sort of scandal. It keeps her awake most nights, clenching the sheets so tight you'd think she was trying to strangle them. Now me, I don't mind tongues wagging. Heck, I've heard more than enough gossip to last me the rest of my days. I've never paid it much mind, but Elizabeth . . ."

"I get it," Peter said. "The last thing I want is to cause you and your family any trouble."

"You haven't, no matter what my wife might imagine. Still, I appreciate your understanding all the same." With a chuckle, he added, "Besides, with the way she's been carrying on, I was starting to lose some sleep of my own."

"You were?"

John nodded. "I was wondering when those strangling hands of hers were going to make their way from the sheets to my neck!"

They both laughed heartily at the joke. But then the sheriff's smile faded and his expression grew serious.

"You know, I've been thinking about what you said last night," he explained. "When we were all in the kitchen . . ."

"Yes, sir," Peter answered.

"Your words were wise beyond your years. It was the sort of thing I've only ever heard from men who've served, who know first-hand what war is really like."

Peter's mind raced. John was right; the reason he could talk that way was that he knew exactly how brutal war was. He'd seen men die, suffer from their wounds, starve, freeze in the middle of an unforgiving winter, and face every calamity that combat brought. He'd also seen the lives of civilians ruined, German and otherwise, with everything they'd built gone in an instant. But he could never tell this to Olivia's father. John was a veteran of the First World War, a man who hated Germans. If Peter told him the truth, the sheriff's smile would disappear for good.

And then he'd never see Olivia again.

"I have friends who've fought," Peter replied. "I saw how it changed them, made them into different men than they'd been when they left. So while I believe that war is necessary in order to rid the world of evil, it's not something I'll be rushing into with blinders on. I'll face it for what it is."

John nodded. "Billy was out of line," he said.

"He just doesn't know what he's talking about. I, for one, hope that he never finds out how wrong he is."

"Amen to that," Olivia's father agreed, clapping him on the shoulder. "Now how about we get something to eat. I'm starving!"

As John headed down the stairs, Peter took one last look into his new apartment. Part of the reason he'd been given it was the lies he'd spun, an intricate web that threatened to trap him and all those he'd

begun to care for. No matter what, he
vowed to find a way to cut them all free.

CHAPTER EIGHTEEN

By the time Olivia returned home, the sun had nearly set behind a wall of dark clouds to the west. She'd walked for hours, from one side of Miller's Creek to the other, meandering as she went. She'd passed children playing stickball in the street, waved at Clyde Kirby as he peeked out from beneath the hood of his automobile, and even helped Eunice Martin raise her flag up its pole. With every block she traveled, she kept expecting to see Billy round the corner ahead of her, or hear the honk of her father's horn as he idled up behind her in his police car, but on and on she'd walked, alone. Now, she was back where she'd started. Surprisingly, even though she was tired and her feet ached, she was still restless.

Her head churned. All day, she'd thought about Billy and his proposal, her mother's unrealistic expectations and demands, and even the strange, wonderful way Peter made her feel. She'd turned the past week around and around, looking at it from every angle, but she still couldn't find a way to make everyone she loved happy. And that included herself. No matter what decision she made, someone would end up being hurt.

Inside her house, lights were on in the dining room and kitchen. Her father's car sat in the drive. Right now, all of them, including Peter, were probably sitting down to dinner and wondering where she was; Olivia could hardly guess what excuse her mother had come up with to explain her absence. She knew that she should go inside, stop running away from her problems, but a combination of pride and fear wouldn't let her.

"You can't stand out here forever," she muttered.

While trying to figure out what to do, Olivia heard a door open. She turned to see Ruth Pollack step onto her porch and slowly make her way to her favorite chair; even though the older woman was blind, she'd traversed the path so often that she knew just where to go. Seeing her made Olivia think that she could put off confronting her family a little while longer.

As carefully and quietly as she could,

Olivia started up Ruth's walk toward the porch. Ever since she and Grace had been little, they'd often come to speak with their neighbor, for conversation as well as lemonade and a candy or two. Whenever they went for a visit, they tried to be as quiet as mice, sneaking up not out of childish mischievousness or because they wanted to scare Ruth, but because they'd never made it closer than a few feet before being caught. This time, Olivia didn't even make it to the second step.

"Just because I'm blind doesn't mean that I'm deaf," Ruth suddenly said. "You might as well have called out to me from the sidewalk."

"How could you possibly have known I was coming?" Olivia asked in amazement; she thought she hadn't made a peep.

"Clearly, I did, though," she answered with a bright smile. "Though I have to admit that I wasn't sure if it was you or your sister until just now. Come, sit for a while and talk with an old woman."

Olivia grabbed another chair and pulled it over next to Ruth's. Just as soon as she'd sat down, the blind woman said, "So tell me what's the matter."

"What makes you think that something's bothering me?"

"Probably the fact that its suppertime and your whole family is sitting down to eat, while you're over here with me."

"You don't miss much, do you?"

"When your whole world is black, you learn to pay awfully close attention to it. It's the only way to keep from falling on your face."

Olivia laughed easily and then sighed. "My life's become something of a mess," she explained. "Even with the war and all the changes it brought, my days didn't have many surprises. One wasn't all that different from the next, and that was all right with me. Then, all of a sudden, it got all jumbled up, like a puzzle that's been knocked to the floor."

"And you're having trouble putting it back together?"

"And then some."

"It has to do with love, doesn't it?"

Olivia nodded her head for a moment before realizing that Ruth couldn't see her. "Yes," she said instead.

"And your engagement to Billy Tate?"

She was about to ask the older woman how she knew about that, but stopped; there was no doubt in Olivia's mind that word of her relationship with Billy had raced around town like wildfire; she could only guess how long it would take for news of their breakup to spread. For someone like Ruth, a woman who paid close attention to the world around her, it wasn't much of a surprise that she knew.

"I ended it yesterday," Olivia answered, seeing no point in holding back the truth. She told Ruth all about what had happened; her shock when he'd asked her to become his wife, how she'd accepted out of the fear of breaking his heart right before he left for the service, and about how that decision had weighed on her like a stone ever since. "I love Billy so much, I always have, but as a friend, not as a husband. In the end, I just couldn't go through with it."

"You did the right thing, my dear," Ruth soothed; tentatively, she reached out and placed her wrinkled hand into Olivia's, giving it a gentle squeeze. "Marriage isn't the sort of thing to enter into lightly. Sure, it's normal to have doubts, butterflies in your stomach, that sort of thing. I know I did. But those are nerves of excitement, the thrill of facing the unknown with someone you love completely, with all of your heart. Billy's a good man, but he's not the one for you."

"That's not what my mother thinks," Olivia said sourly. "The only thing she cares

305

about is the money Billy stands to earn. The fact that his family is both wealthy and connected is more than enough reason for her."

"She's only trying to look out for your best interests."

"She told me I'm making a mistake."

"That's because she doesn't want you to struggle," Ruth explained. "Elizabeth may not say it the right way, but deep down in her heart, she's doing what any good mother would. She's trying to protect you. She sees Billy as a way for you to make your way through life easier than she did. No parent wants to see their child suffer. Unfortunately, she's forgotten to take your happiness into consideration."

"Marrying Billy *wouldn't* make me happy. I'm sure of it."

"And you're starting to think that being with the other man would?" the blind woman asked. "That maybe Peter is the one you've been waiting for?"

Olivia looked at Ruth, dumbstruck. The older woman stared forward, her expression expectant, as if she was waiting for an answer. "How . . . how do you know about him . . . ?"

"I spoke with him a couple days ago," she answered matter-of-factly.

"You did?"

Ruth nodded. "He came over and we shared a few words," she said. "I didn't get to talk to him for very long, but he seemed like a good young man. Strong, although it seemed like something was weighing on him. A burden, perhaps."

"What makes you say that?"

"Call it a blind woman's intuition. A hunch. I've spent so many years unable to see the look that crosses people's faces that I have to interpret the sound of their voices. His sounded strained. He has a lot on his mind, that one."

Olivia thought about the times she'd spent with Peter. On a number of occasions, when he was still lying in bed, recuperating from his injuries, she'd noticed him staring out the window, lost in thought. It made her wonder if Ruth wasn't right, that maybe something was troubling him, some problem he was trying to figure out.

"Are you in love with him?" Ruth asked and then shook her head. "Goodness sakes, I shouldn't be asking you that. It's really none of my business."

"It's all right," Olivia reassured her; after all, the blind woman's question was one she'd been asking herself for a while. "The thing is, I've never been in love before so I'm not exactly sure what it is I'm supposed to feel. All I know is that Peter is unlike any man I've ever known. Just thinking about him causes something inside of me to change. So if I haven't fallen in love with Peter already, I'd say that I'm well on my way."

Ruth smiled warmly. "That sounds lovely."

"I'm just not sure what I'm supposed to do now."

"Go to him and tell him the truth. That's usually a good place to start."

"You seem awfully sure of him."

"I am," Ruth admitted.

"Why? You said that you didn't talk with him for very long."

"It doesn't have much to do with me," the blind woman answered. "But I notice the way he makes *you* feel. I pay attention to people's voices, remember? When I listen to you talk about Peter, it's so clear to me that there's something special between the two of you that I imagine I can see it as plain as day."

Tears filled Olivia's eyes. Squeezing Ruth's hand, she said, "Thank you."

"You're quite welcome, my dear."

"I think there's someone I have to have a long talk with."

"There most certainly is."

But then, just as Olivia was rising from

her chair, she suddenly stopped. There, walking down the sidewalk toward her, was Peter. He hadn't noticed her yet as his eyes roamed the streets, peering into the space between houses. He looked concerned, even a bit worried.

"It seems that your opportunity has arrived," Ruth said.

Olivia stared at her. *How could she possibly know?* Then she smiled and headed down the porch steps.

For almost an hour, Peter had walked the darkened streets of Miller's Creek. Earlier, just before sunset, he and John had loaded his meager belongings and taken them to the apartment; other than the clothes Olivia had procured from her father, there'd been almost nothing to pack. When they'd finished, John invited him to continue taking his dinner with the family, an offer Peter had accepted. But when they'd gotten back to the Marstens' home, he'd been surprised to find that Olivia wasn't there. He'd expected her to arrive at any moment, but by the time dinner was ready, she was still missing. When pressed, Elizabeth had been vague, saying that her daughter had gone out and would be back shortly. Still, Peter hadn't felt right about it. All throughout dinner, he'd struggled to pay attention to the conversation, worrying that something had happened to the woman he loved. The thought of Otto watching Olivia made him so uncomfortable that he'd excused himself from the table and gone outside. Once there, he'd paced back and forth, too wound up to remain still. So instead, he had gone to look for her. Up one side of the street and then down the other, he stared into the dark shadows between houses, peered into vehicles as they drove past, and fought the urge to shout her name. He was trying to figure out what he would say to John, how he might convey his worries without giving himself away, when he saw her.

Watching Olivia come down her neighbor's walk made Peter's heart pound; plenty of it was on account of how beautiful he found her to be, but more of it was because he was relieved that she was safe. He struggled to resist the urge to take her in his arms.

"Where have you been?" he asked. "I've been looking everywhere for you."

"I went for a walk," she answered. "I'm sorry. It wasn't my intention to come back so late. I lost track of time, is all."

"I was starting to worry," he admitted.

Before Olivia responded, she looked back

over her shoulder; Peter followed her gaze and saw Ruth staring at them. Without another word, Olivia took his arm and led him away, not stopping until they were standing by the walk that led to her family's porch. Though Peter found it strange that she would be so concerned about a blind woman watching them, he didn't argue, impatient as he was to know where she'd been.

"Didn't my mother tell you what happened between us?" Olivia finally asked, her voice soft, as if she still worried about being overheard.

"No," Peter replied. "All she said was that you'd be back soon."

She frowned. "I suppose I shouldn't be surprised," she said.

"Did something happen between you?"

Olivia nodded. "I made a mistake . . . I told my mother the truth . . ."

"You told her about us?" Though he felt frustrated at having to pull each bit of information out of Olivia, as if he was sifting through a haystack in search of a needle, Peter tried to remain calm; he knew that if he were to seem too anxious, it would only make matters worse.

"Yes . . . no . . ." she struggled. "It . . . it all started because I told her that I broke off my engagement to Billy . . ."

Peter's pulse quickened. "You . . . you ended it . . . ?"

In answer, Olivia held up her hand. Her engagement ring was missing. Peter remembered the way it had pulled at his attention the first time he'd seen it, how Olivia had tried to hide it, the way that it seemed to weigh upon her as if it was an anchor. But now it was gone.

"I told him that I couldn't marry him," she said, her eyes searching his. As she lowered her hand, Peter took it, lightly holding her fingers in his own.

"How did he react?" he asked.

"Badly," Olivia answered. "I hurt him last night. Worse than I ever would've thought possible."

"You didn't have a choice."

"I know. It's just that, seeing him so angry . . ." she said, her voice trailing off into silence.

"My father used to tell me that sometimes, doing the right thing is the hardest of all."

"I never should've accepted his proposal in the first place."

"But you did," Peter explained as gently as he could. "What did he do when you told him you wanted to break it off?"

"At first, he tried to talk me out of it, but

then, when he realized that I wasn't going to change my mind, he grew angry." From her pained expression, Peter understood that she was reliving every horrible moment that had passed between them. "I ended up running away in tears. That was why I went straight to my room when I came home. I know you wanted to see me, but I just couldn't. I needed to be alone for a while."

"It's all right," he reassured her.

"I thought that we could talk this morning, but when I woke up, you were already gone."

"With everything that's happened to me, my accident, and even meeting you, I suppose that I wanted a chance to think things through," Peter explained. "So I went for a walk." He didn't mention where he had gone or his reasons for going there. He hoped that she wouldn't ask; he didn't want to lie anymore, but now wasn't the time to burden her with the truth.

"Did it help?" Olivia asked instead.

"A little," he answered truthfully.

"I wish I could say the same," she admitted. "Everything is such a mess. I don't know where to start trying to put it all back together again."

"Sometimes, time is the only medicine."

"So until then, I guess I'll have to keep

listening to my mother's criticisms," she said, adding a short laugh. "She took great pains to tell me that I'm making a big mistake."

"The only mistake you would've made was to marry someone you didn't love."

"For my mother, that's not much of an obstacle."

"Do you feel that way?"

Slowly, Olivia shook her head. "She's as wrong as she can be. To me," she explained, "it's the only thing that matters."

Gently, Peter squeezed her hand; in return, she clung to him tightly, as if the slightest of touches was to be treasured.

"Not marrying Billy wasn't the only mistake my mother accused me of making," Olivia said softly.

"What was the other one?"

"Getting involved with you." Her eyes watched his closely; he imagined that she was looking for something, for some reaction, but he gave her none.

"Did she give you a reason?" he asked.

"She said that you could be a liar," Olivia explained. "She told me that you might be none of what you claim, that you could be dangerous, the sort of man who'd tell me whatever I wanted to hear, so long as you got what you wanted in the end." She paused before adding, "Me."

Peter's heart thundered louder than the storm that had led him to Olivia. Elizabeth could never have known it, but she was partly right; Peter *wasn't* who he claimed to be. He *had* been lying to Olivia, but not for the reasons she claimed, an important difference.

"Olivia," he answered, raising a hand to gently touch her cheek. "I know that my coming into your life hasn't made things easy. For that, I'm truly sorry. But I swear to you that my intentions are honorable. If there's anything I'm guilty of, it's greed." Olivia looked at him, confused, but he continued. "Ever since the moment we met, all I've wanted was to spend time with you, to share these feelings that threaten to overwhelm me with you. I wasn't just struck by a runaway truck, I was also blindsided by you, and I hope that I *never* recover from those wounds."

Slowly, Peter leaned forward, intent on kissing her. Olivia's eyes closed in anticipation. But then, just before their lips touched, the Marstens' side door opened on squeaky hinges.

It was Grace.

"There you are," she said when she saw her sister. "Is everything all right?"

"Yes . . ." Olivia answered, a bit flustered.

"Mom's getting ready to put a pie on the table. You better get a move on if you want any." With that, she was gone, the door slamming shut with a bang.

"She has a knack for interrupting us, doesn't she?" Olivia said.

Peter smiled. "Seems that way."

Still holding his hand, she tugged him toward the house. Their kiss would have to wait, but Peter didn't mind. He had hopes for what could grow between them, dreams that became larger with every passing day. But something still lay between them and that future, blocking it from sight. The truth.

How am I ever going to tell her who I really am?

CHAPTER NINETEEN

Otto crouched between a pair of bushes and stared at the back of the house. His stomach growled with hunger, but he paid it no mind. Minutes earlier, the sun had set, the shadows stretching across the ground as darkness descended. Just like when he and Becker had watched the cabin, he had to tamp down the urge to act. It was a struggle to remain patient. He slowly ran his fingers along his knife's handle. It was only a matter of waiting for the right time.

Tonight, an Amerikaner is going to die!

He had left his hiding spot in the hills intent on striking a blow for Germany. Keeping to the shadows and away from the most heavily traveled routes, he'd managed to make it into town undetected. He found a trickling tributary to the creek and followed it as it twisted and turned, rose and fell, snaking behind quiet homes. Once, he'd rounded a bend and startled a deer. Later,

317

he'd aroused the interest of a mutt chained to its doghouse; at the sound of barking, he'd frozen in place, waiting until the mongrel lost interest. Finally, he scampered up a muddy incline and was where he wanted to be.

The house was large, in a style Otto had never seen back in Bavaria. Lights were on in the first floor but the upstairs was dark. From where he watched at the rear of the property, past a garden and beneath the limbs of an enormous evergreen tree, Otto hadn't seen anyone other than his prey walk in front of the glass. The man's police car sat quietly in the drive. Still, he imagined that the lawman had a wife and children, people he cared for. At one point, a door opened on the side of the house and he thought he'd heard voices, but from where he hid, he couldn't see clearly. In the end, it hardly mattered.

Everyone in that home was going to die.

Huck Perkins whistled along to Tommy Dorsey as he cleaned his plate from supper and dropped it into a sink filled with warm water. He liked the way the music made him feel, how the notes picked up his spirits after a long, tiring day at work. But most of all, he supposed that he was thankful to the music for providing noise in a house that would have otherwise been silent.

Now inching toward sixty, with more and more gray hair staring back at him in the mirror, Huck doubted that he'd ever find someone to share his life. There weren't too many available women in Miller's Creek, only the occasional war widow, and he doubted whether a younger gal would find what he had to offer all that exciting. He was going to be an old maid, or whatever it was they called a man without prospects. Times like this, when he was feeling a touch maudlin, he thought about Angela Freeman, a woman he'd courted more than a decade before. She'd shown an interest in him, but in the end he'd been too much of a coward to ask the necessary questions. Eventually, she had grown weary of waiting and accepted the advances of another suitor. Nowadays, whenever he saw her around town with her family, he tipped his hat and quickly walked away as a sickening feeling filled his gut. Not for the first time, he wondered if he shouldn't get a pet to cure his loneliness; at least then he wouldn't have to come home to an empty house.

"Maybe a dog," he muttered to himself as Frank Sinatra began to croon from the living room.

At least he had his work. Being an officer of the law had always seemed to fit Huck just right. He was good at it, liked helping folks. People around Miller's Creek treated him with respect; their admiration was something he strived to be worthy of. Most days it was easy, just to the north of boring. He wrote out a ticket or two, hauled drunks like Sylvester Eddings to his familiar cell, and kept gawkers back as the fire department put out a blaze. But every once in a while, things got a bit hairier, like when a blizzard blew in or he had to break up a drunken brawl at the tavern. Huck found those times plenty exciting.

It didn't hurt that he had such a great boss. John Marsten was the best man Huck had ever known, even more so than his own father, a grouch of a farmer who never got over the disappointment of learning that his oldest son hadn't the slightest interest in living off the land. The sheriff was the sort of man Huck would've followed to hell and back. He was strict but fair, a leader who looked after the welfare of others before his own. Why, just that afternoon, he'd ordered Huck to take the next couple of days off on account of how hard they'd worked through the fires. Huck had protested, said that he wasn't tired, when in fact he felt weary all the way to his bones, but John had insisted. Finally, Huck had relented. In the morning, he planned on going fishing, just him, his rusty boat, a rod and reel, and maybe a couple of cold beers for companionship.

Maybe it wasn't such a bad life after all.

Just as Huck plunged his hands into the sink, he glanced up at the window and frowned. For a moment, he thought he'd seen something. It seemed large, bigger than a rabbit. He shook his head. It was probably a deer; they often came up from the brook at the rear of his property in search of food. For all he knew, it was his own reflection, or maybe the light behind him had shone off the glass. He was just exhausted and it was making him jumpy.

I wonder if this is what it's like for old Sylvester, he thought. *Having imaginary things jumping at him out of nowhere.*

But minutes later, as he was drying his plate, Huck stopped again. This time he'd heard something. It hadn't been much, faint over the sounds of swing music coming from his record player, but loud enough for him to notice. It sounded like the squeak of his side door. Setting down the dish, Huck wiped his damp hands on his pants and went to investigate.

Much to his surprise, the door was open a

321

couple of inches. Huck was puzzled. Earlier, he'd gone out to his squad car to retrieve something he'd forgotten, the music drifting out behind him, but he was sure that he'd closed the door when he went back inside. Maybe something was wrong with the latch. Maybe he'd been in a hurry and forgotten. The breeze that stirred the leaves of his elm trees had probably been enough to make the door swing back and forth, causing the noise.

Whatever the reason, he pulled it shut with a click.

Back inside, Huck went to the living room and removed the needle from the record, stopping a horn solo in midnote. An uncomfortable feeling nagged at him, making the hairs on the back of his neck stand on end. Something wasn't right. It was then, just as he was trying to wrap his head around what was bothering him, that he heard another creak; this time it was right behind him, close. He spun around and his heart almost stopped beating.

A man stood there, staring at him. For a moment, it looked as if the intruder was surprised to have been discovered, but the shock quickly left him and a deep scowl settled on his features. He was squat and thickly muscled, his clothes rough and mismatched. Huck had seen his share of men like this over his years as a deputy; mean, with no reservations about inflicting pain. To make matters worse, he had a knife clenched in a tight fist at his waist. Try as he might to recognize him, Huck was certain that he'd never seen the man before.

Silently, Huck cursed himself. He should've trusted his suspicions, the instincts honed by years of being a lawman. But it was too late to listen. Now, he was in trouble. When he'd come home from work, he'd done as always and taken his holster and gun off, placing them on a table near the front door. Now, when he really needed his weapon, it was on the other side of the room. The only chance he had was to talk, play for time, and make his move when the opportunity presented itself.

"All right, buddy," he said calmly, holding up his hands in an attempt to preach for peace. "Let's take a deep breath and talk this through."

But the man didn't seem interested. His eyes narrowed as his hand clenched the knife hard enough to make the thick muscles of his forearm stand out. When he spoke, it was low, guttural. *"Zeit zum Sterben!"* he growled.

Huck stared, dumbstruck. He had enough

trouble speaking English most days, but he would've sworn that the stranger had just spoken German; it sounded an awful lot like the gibberish he'd heard Hitler babble in newsreels over the years.

What the hell is going on?

But before Huck could begin to contemplate the implications of what he'd heard, the man came charging at him. He didn't move like an angry bull, out of control and smashing everything in his path, but more like a deadly predator, a wolf maybe, focused, intent on his prey. Huck's eyes didn't wander far from the knife. He tried not to panic, to stay calm and let his years of experience facing danger, or what passed for it in Miller's Creek, guide him.

His attacker came in low and feinted to his left before suddenly changing direction and coming in from the right. He slashed the knife through the air, missing by only a matter of inches. But then he backed off a bit, cautious, as if he was wary of a man the deputy's size.

"Why don't you put that sticker down," Huck offered. "It ain't too late to find a way out of this."

But the intruder didn't respond.

Seconds later, the man came straight forward, jabbing with the knife as if he meant to skewer his foe. Huck once again barely got out of the way, but as he moved, he threw a punch of his own, clipping his attacker's chin; it wasn't much, but it staggered him, if only for an instant. Blindly, the man lashed out with his knife and this time Huck was too close to avoid it. The blade cut along the back of his forearm, deep, sending a burning ache racing across his flesh. Seconds later, the first drops of blood fell from his fingers to the floor. It hurt, but Huck didn't even bother to look at it; he didn't dare take his eyes off the other man.

I have to get to my gun! It's the only chance I got!

Instead of waiting for the stranger to make the first move, Huck decided to take the initiative. He made a fast first step forward, causing the man to raise his arms in a defensive posture, and it was then that Huck tried to bull his way to the side, willing to take another cut so long as he could get past. In those first two steps, hope flared in his chest. He thought he was going to make it. But instead of slashing at him, the stranger kicked out with his foot, caught Huck at the knee, and sent him stumbling. His momentum carried him forward, but he couldn't maintain his balance and crashed to the floor with a thud, the air rushing from his lungs.

He looked up, sweat running into his eyes, and saw that he was only a couple of feet from the table upon which rested his gun. All he had to do was get to his knees, draw the pistol from its holster, and then he could turn and fill this son-of-a-bitch full of lead. It was just a matter of —

But before Huck could even leverage himself up to his elbows, the man pounced on him. He felt the knife plunge into his back, the pain tremendous, overwhelming, searing hot, like a blacksmith's poker on bare flesh. Over and over, the stranger pulled the blade out before sticking it back in. Strangely, the pain began to fade; the heat became almost comforting. It didn't take long for Huck to feel nothing but a quiet peace. His eyes fluttered as the blackness closed in, enveloping him like a blanket.

Otto felt triumphant. Everything had gone just as he'd hoped, if not entirely as planned. Stealing into the house had been easy, but when the lawman heard his footfall, the creak of a floorboard giving him away, and turned around, Otto had been momentarily surprised, a strange turn of events. But his resolve had hardened; his burning hatred for the enemy had given him the strength to act, to kill the bastard with his own hand.

Once the man was dead, Otto had searched the house, looking for someone else, a wife or child hiding from the carnage. But it had been empty. The fool had lived alone. So he'd ransacked through cupboards and drawers for things he could use, slipping them into a knapsack he'd found in a closet. Finally, he'd taken the man's gun; with it tucked in the waistband of his pants, Otto felt more powerful than he had in a long time, certainly since his unit had been captured in France.

Now, he was more dangerous than ever.

For a moment, he'd considered burning the man's house to the ground, as the destruction would have hidden the corpse, but in the end had decided against it. He wanted the lawman's friends and coworkers to wonder what had happened to him, wanted their curiosity to finally get the better of them, and for them to make a gruesome discovery. Otto could almost taste their fear. By then, he would've moved on to something else, another act to strike them where it hurt most.

Leaving the scene of the crime, Otto drifted toward the center of town. Usually, he had no interest in seeing the place, but tonight, still riding high from what he had done, he was drawn to it, like a moth to a flame. Night had fallen and he no longer needed to hide himself, at least not as cautiously as he did during the day. He peered into houses, avoided the few streetlights that were lit, and soon found himself on the main street. American flags fluttered lazily in the night breeze, proudly displayed on most of the buildings he passed. The sight of them caused his anger to flare; it made him want to cut the fabric into pieces and jam them down the throats of these damn people, to choke them with their pride.

Suddenly, Otto heard the sound of approaching footsteps. So far, he hadn't seen anyone since he'd left the dead man's house. Cautiously, he stepped into the black shadows of an alley and waited. The footfalls grew louder until he saw a man coming his way on the opposite side of the street. He didn't look to be in a hurry; maybe he was out for a bit of fresh air. Otto was considering following him, possibly killing him, when the stranger passed beneath a light and glanced in Otto's direction.

It was Peter Becker.

Otto couldn't believe what he was seeing. It defied all reason. At first, he thought it was a trick of the light, a tease of the imagination, an illusion. But the more he looked, the more he knew he was right. It was in the man's gait, his build, and the few features he could make out.

What in the hell is going on?

His first instinct was to say something, to shout out to Becker and get his attention, but he quickly squelched that urge. Something had happened, some turn of events that he couldn't see just yet. Here was a German soldier, escaped from a wrecked prison train, walking down an American street as surely as if he'd spent his whole life there. It didn't add up.

Otto's second thought was to kill him in cold blood. All he had to do was follow him, wait for the right moment, and then bury his knife in the man's guts. This was an act of betrayal. Becker had turned his back on him, on his nation, on his Führer, and had surrendered. Now, he was working for the Amerikaners. What other explanation could there be for why he was free? Though it was difficult, Otto tamped down his craving for revenge. Instead, he followed the man.

Moving from shadow to shadow, he tailed Becker as he walked leisurely down the street. Otto was cautious, afraid to take too noticeable a step, suddenly fearful that his former ally was the bait, trying to lure him into a trap. But on and on Becker went, acting oblivious to being followed. Eventually, he mounted a flight of stairs affixed to the side of a barbershop, unlocked a door at the top, and went inside. Seconds later, a light was turned on.

Otto was dumbstruck.

Anger filled him. Becker was a traitor. He deserved something *worse* than death. Right then and there, Otto decided that he'd keep a close eye on his countryman, try to figure out what had happened; then he would inflict punishment. Becker would suffer along with all the rest, just like the enemy he was.

He swore it.

Chapter Twenty

Peter was uncomfortable. He shifted in his seat in Goslee's Diner, feeling as if every eye in the room was on him. Olivia sat across from him. The night before, as he was getting ready to leave the Marstens' for his new apartment, they'd agreed to meet the next day for lunch. At first, he'd been excited; any reason to spend time with her was a good one. But the more he thought about it, the more ill at ease he was about being seen in public. Though he'd been among the people of Miller's Creek for a while now, he felt vulnerable, as if his lie was about to crumble at any moment.

Olivia didn't seem to notice. She talked animatedly about her day at the hardware store; he had wondered if she'd be self-conscious about being with him, especially when most people in town knew about her relationship with Billy, but if she was at all worried, it didn't show. To Peter, she was more beautiful than ever. Afternoon sunlight streamed in through the restaurant's large windows, making her blond hair shine a brilliant gold. When she smiled, the room seemed to grow even brighter. She was like an angel. Peter knew that if their situation were different, if they'd met some other way, without any lies between them, he would have felt a tremendous sense of pride that a woman as wonderful and attractive as her would want to spend her time with him.

Instead, all he felt was nervous.

"He thinks highly of you."

Peter startled. "What was that?" he asked; he was embarrassed to realize that he hadn't been paying attention.

"I said that my father must think highly of you to have arranged for that apartment," she repeated.

"I still feel guilty for having accepted. It's too much."

"Don't feel that way," Olivia said. "That's just the kind of person he is. He goes out of his way to do things for people he holds in high regard. When I was a little girl, there was a man my father occasionally brought home for dinner. On holidays, that sort of thing," she explained. "I can't remember his real name, but everyone called him 'Bones' because he was so thin and frail.

Later, I discovered that he was a veteran, that he'd fought in the Spanish-American War, and that he didn't have any family left. My father thought he was a good man and that he shouldn't have to be alone, so he brought him into our family. In a way, I suppose you're a lot like Bones was to him; a good person without anyone else."

Peter knew that Olivia's words were meant to warm him to the idea of accepting her father's charity, but they did the exact opposite. John had helped the old veteran because of his honorable service to his country. While the sheriff had a reason for helping *him*, his keeping his daughter from being badly hurt and rescuing the horses from the barn fire, it was still built upon mistruths. If Olivia's father knew who Peter really was, he never would have helped him; he would've drawn his gun and led him straight to the nearest jail cell.

He was nothing but a fraud.

And he felt like it was so obvious that everyone else knew it, too.

Try as he might to suppress it, Peter was acutely aware of the diner's other customers. Any glance his way felt as if it was a long stare, full of questions and accusations. A few of the looks from older women had a smile attached, as if they got some happiness from seeing a young couple sitting together. Others held frowns; he couldn't help but wonder if those people were friends of Billy or his family. Still other were quizzical; Peter assumed they were wondering who he was or why he wasn't in uniform.

Which was what drew him to the man sitting at the far end of the counter. He was young, right around Peter's age, and fit. He smiled as he dug into his plate, having a friendly conversation with the older man beside him. He was also a soldier, the first Peter had seen since he and Otto had escaped the wrecked prison train. His olive dress uniform was crisp and clean, the buttons shining as bright as Olivia's hair; Peter recognized it as the dress of the United States Army. Once, the soldier looked up and noticed Peter staring at him; he didn't seem to take any offense, nodding a greeting before returning his attention to his food.

What rattled Peter was that this man, in many ways, was his enemy. He knew that the odds were surely impossible, but he could have fought against that very soldier on the snowy battlefields of France. How many Americans had Peter fired his rifle at? How many had he wounded or even killed? The war disgusted him, but he'd fought in it nevertheless. He believed that if there was anyone in the diner who was capable of knowing the truth about him, it was the soldier.

When he turned his attention away from the man, he found Olivia looking at him. She glanced over at the soldier, then back.

"It must be hard for you," she said.

"What is?" he asked.

"Seeing other men in their uniforms," she said. "I've noticed some of the glances you've gotten. People questioning why a man your age isn't dressed like he should be. I just imagined that it'd be hard, especially since you're a part of the service, just not in the same public way."

Right there, on the tip of Peter's tongue, was an answer.

There are plenty of times when I get to wear a uniform that looks an awful lot like that one.

It wasn't the truth, but it would work all the same. Peter took another look at the soldier. Right then and there, even though he was sitting in the middle of a crowded diner, he'd had enough. He was done lying, done pretending to be somebody he wasn't. He wouldn't, he *couldn't,* deceive Olivia any longer.

"Olivia," he said. "I've tried to tell you —"

"I know, I know," she interrupted. "I'm not supposed to ask about what it is that you do. It's all a big secret. I'm sorry. I didn't mean to pry."

"That's not it," Peter replied, angry at himself. "I'm not talking about that." Here he paused, steadying his nerves, trying to steel himself for whatever reaction she would give him. "Ever since we met," he began, "there's something that I've wanted to tell you . . . something about me that might be hard for you to hear . . ."

Olivia's eyes narrowed. "What do you mean?"

"When I saw you, I told you that I'd come to town in order to speak with the sheriff . . . with your father . . ."

She nodded. "That's right."

"It's . . . it's just that my reason . . . it wasn't the —"

But then, just as Peter was about to tell her that he'd come to Miller's Creek because he was an escaped German prisoner who wanted to give himself up, there arose such a commotion in the diner that it was impossible for him to continue.

"Quiet! Everyone quiet down!" a gruff voice shouted.

Peter looked and saw a man in a grease-speckled apron standing in the kitchen, waving one hand up and down to his customers while the other turned a knob on his radio. Silence fell across the diner as everyone strained to listen.

"*. . . effective this afternoon,*" a man's voice explained through the slight hiss of static. "*Word from Washington is that President Truman has accepted. I repeat, the war in Europe has ended. Germany has unconditionally surrendered to the Allies and control of the nation will —*"

Whatever else the newsman had to say was drowned out by the deafening shouts and cheers of everyone in the diner. People jumped out of their seats. A couple of women burst into tears, crying for joy. A couple of men slapped the soldier hard on the back, congratulating him as if he himself had been the one to make Hitler and his Nazis quit. For his part, Peter was speechless, unable to comprehend what he'd just heard.

The nation of his birth had surrendered.

The war was over. But he still had a battle to fight.

Olivia was breathless as she listened to the words coming from the radio. After Sam Goslee's shout, the diner had grown so quiet that she could have heard a pin drop.

Now, the only sound was the newsman's voice. Though she heard what he said, it was so unbelievable that it took a moment for the words to sink in. But then, all at once, at exactly the same time as it happened to everyone around her, she understood.

The war was over!

The Germans had surrendered!

After more than five long years, the fighting in Europe had ended!

Half a heartbeat later, Olivia was up out of her seat, shouting at the top of her lungs, overcome with elation, relief, and many other emotions, more than she could count. The inside of the diner was chaotic, a scene of pandemonium. Everyone acted as if it was the happiest moment of their lives, which, for many, it probably was. Olivia had just turned around for a look, to try to take it all in, when she was embraced by Clyde Harrington, a blacksmith she'd known all her life; two of Clyde's sons had spent the last few years in Europe, chasing Hitler's army back toward Germany, so his joy was especially personal. The moment he let her go, Olivia fell into the arms of Marjorie Ennis, her old schoolteacher. Then it was someone else, all of them celebrating. Shouts rang out around the diner.

"I can't believe it's over!"

"— always said we was gonna show them Nazis a thing or two!"

"My son will be coming home! Oh, thank the Lord!"

Olivia felt relief of her own. For more than three years, her life had been turned on its head, sent down a path she never could have anticipated. Working at the hardware store. Dragging her wagon across town as she gathered material for the war effort. Planting the victory garden with her mother. Making do with less as one item after another was rationed.

But the hardest thing of all had been to watch the young men of Miller's Creek go off to fight. Jay Garrick had died in Italy, Herman McKinnley in France. When their bodies had come home to their devastated families, all of town had turned out for their funerals. Now, even though the war with Japan would rage on, Olivia felt that the clouds that had darkened all of their lives had finally begun to clear. Most relieving of all was that it might mean Billy remained safe. He'd struggled so long to join the military, to get past his rejections on account of his bad heart, that he would probably be disappointed he hadn't gotten a chance to fight. Olivia didn't care. Even if she had ended their engagement, she still wanted him to be safe.

And then there was Peter . . .

Olivia turned to look for him in the crowd, but was surprised to find him sitting in his seat. He was shaking hands with Lew Martin, a farmer whose grin showed a significant lack of teeth. Peter looked stunned, his eyes wide, his jaw hanging slack as his hand was furiously pumped up and down; he was probably just as shocked as everyone else. While she had no idea what it was he did for the military, Olivia was overjoyed that it would be coming to an end. It meant that he might not have to leave. It meant that he might be able to stay with her . . .

"It's over," she said to him, beaming broadly.

"I . . . I can't believe it . . ." he answered; her smile must have been infectious, because one slowly spread across his face.

Even as the diner continued to celebrate, Olivia found herself wanting more. Reaching down, she grabbed Peter by the hand.

"Come on," she exclaimed. "Let's go!"

Together they weaved their way through the crowd, receiving more congratulations. The uniformed soldier clapped Peter on the shoulder as they went by; Peter seemed startled by the man's touch, even a bit uncomfortable, but he recovered to say something Olivia couldn't hear over the din. Eventually, they made it to the door and stepped outside, basking in the sun and the moment.

The rest of Miller's Creek was as jubilant as the diner had been. Men and women spilled out into the streets. Most people were shouting or hugging. Several stood alone and stared up into the sky, smiling. To Olivia, it was like Christmas, the Fourth of July, and everyone's birthday, all rolled into one. She imagined that in every city and town in America, no matter how big or small, the very same thing was happening at that moment. She looked at the flags, their stars and stripes shining in the sun. She noticed the posters that expressed the resolve and might of her nation. From somewhere, either inside a shop or down a side street, she heard a lone voice singing "The Star Spangled Banner." They had all worked and struggled together, doing whatever they could to keep the country going as they supported the troops fighting overseas. All of them had overcome tyranny, freeing the peoples of Europe from Hitler and his Nazis. Olivia remembered how she had felt those many years before, sitting beside her mother at the movies, watching as German soldiers marched menacingly across the screen. They had seemed so frightening, so fierce, that they had even invaded her dreams. But now those bogeymen were defeated, their leaders on the run, the people who brought them to power no longer the victors they supposed themselves to be. Today, the future could truly begin, born out of a day brighter than the one that had come before.

Olivia turned to try to tell all of this to Peter, to convey to him how she felt; when she did, he pulled her to him. At first, she assumed that it was like the diner; he wanted to celebrate the war's end. But this was more than that. Where minutes earlier, Peter had appeared stunned, his face was now serious. His eyes roamed hers as he held her tight; he gripped her as if he didn't want to let go, as if he would fight any attempt she made to escape, though there was nowhere else she wanted to be. Neither of them said a word. Slowly, intently, Peter pulled her even closer, their bodies pressed together tightly in the warm spring sun, the townspeople of Miller's Creek all around them as the revelry continued unabated. Olivia closed her eyes and let herself go, not caring if anyone saw. She welcomed his kiss and all that came with it.

■ ■ ■ ■

Billy hurried down the crowded sidewalk, dodging a pair of women hugging each other and then an overly enthusiastic man who shouted as he jumped up and down. Ever since news of the war's end in Europe had reached the bank, he'd had one overpowering urge; to see Olivia. Even with all that had happened between them, with the hurt that came with the unexpected end to their engagement, Billy knew that a momentous occasion like this wouldn't be the same if he couldn't share it with her, the woman he loved.

Though the bank was only a couple of short blocks from Pickford Hardware, it felt as if it took him forever to reach it. Every few feet, there was someone who wanted to share in the good news. With his family's standing in town, it would have been thought rude for him to ignore the well-wishers, so he'd had to start and stop, over and over.

"Isn't it just the happiest of days!" one well-wisher rejoiced.

But was it?

Billy had to admit that while he was glad the Germans had surrendered, there was a

343

small part of him that felt disappointed, even cheated. He'd fought for so long to join the struggle against the Axis that now, when he was so close to doing that very thing, it seemed almost cruel for it to be yanked away from him. Sure, the war against the Japanese raged on, but everyone knew the end was coming. Maybe he would be one of the first to fight their way into Tokyo, to take the battle right to the emperor. But maybe not . . . He'd wanted a chance to prove himself, to show that he was as much of a man as the next guy. Now, he was about to be denied that opportunity.

When he finally reached the hardware store, Billy was surprised to find that Olivia wasn't there. In fact, no one was; they must've been out celebrating. Craning his neck, he couldn't see her among the dozens of people who'd emptied out into the street, the celebration growing by the minute. He had just made up his mind to walk from one end of Main Street to the other, when he saw her. She was on the opposite side of the street, looking away from him, beaming brighter than the sun. Billy was just about to call out to her when he noticed that she wasn't alone.

Peter Baird was with her.

The words died in Billy's throat, unspoken. Somewhere in the most desperate part of his mind, he tried to play it off as nothing, a coincidence that the two of them were here, together. He thought about walking over to them, acting as if nothing were the matter, being the bigger man. But he just couldn't do it. Instead, he retreated, stepping back into the shadows of the mercantile's awning, mingling with the customers.

Billy watched with cold eyes. He saw the ease with which Olivia enjoyed the other man's company. He noticed the smile on her face when she turned toward him. His stomach clenched when the stranger who'd ruined everything grabbed hold of Olivia and pulled her to him. He watched in horror as the bastard leaned down and kissed her; Olivia did nothing to fight off his advances, but rather closed her eyes and met it with passion of her own. It was just as Billy had always imagined it would look, exactly as he had dreamed. The problem was that she was doing it with another man.

He kept staring, unable to look away, as his guts were twisted into knots. Slowly, the truth dawned on Billy. If he was going to have any chance of making Olivia his, of the two of them becoming husband and wife, something was going to have to be done about Peter Baird. Something drastic.

And he was going to have to be the one to do it.

CHAPTER TWENTY-ONE

Peter walked around in a daze. Ever since he had learned of Germany's surrender, he'd felt as if time was standing still. Even kissing Olivia had done nothing to shake the cobwebs from his thoughts; if anything, it had complicated things further. Now, walking beside her in the coming dark of dusk, he still couldn't completely grasp what had happened.

When their kiss had finally ended, Olivia, giddy with romance and the historic events of the day, had wanted to share it all with her family, and had rushed off to find her father. John was just about to drive away from the jail when they arrived. The sheriff had tried to raise Huck on the telephone, wanting to talk with his good friend and deputy, but the man hadn't answered; John guessed that Huck had gone fishing and that it might be another day before he found out. From there, Peter and Olivia had gone to the Marstens' home, rushing up the front steps at the same time as Grace; the young girl was happy about the end of the war in Europe, but she was equally pleased that school had been let out for the rest of the day.

But while Olivia and her family talked animatedly about Germany's defeat, Peter remained quiet. His thoughts raged like a storm; at one moment he was confused, at another hopeful, and then even a bit frightened. Try as he might, struggling to make sense of it all, he couldn't decide what it meant for him. Was he still considered a prisoner? If he turned himself in, would the charge of escape be held against him? Could he keep living the lie he'd built for himself? Could he hide the truth from Olivia forever, ignore his past and who he really was?

And then there was Otto.

Peter wondered if the Nazi knew what had happened. If he was still lurking around, and Peter believed that he was, it wouldn't take long. But how would a man as brutal as Otto react to learning that his beloved Führer had surrendered, that he had lost his dream of a thousand-year Reich? Would learning of Germany's defeat cause Otto to turn himself in? Or would it fan the fires of vengeance and sadism smoldering in his heart, making him even more dangerous?

"I still can't believe that it's over," Olivia said to him.

"Me, either," he admitted. "It's like a dream."

"If it is, I don't ever want to wake up."

Hours earlier, they had left Olivia's home to walk the streets, reveling in the moment. All around them, the townspeople of Miller's Creek celebrated. Even now, as the evening grew dark and colder, a chill in the air that said the calendar had yet to officially turn to summer, people were out. They congregated on porches, gathered on sidewalks and street corners, everyone smiling, rejoicing. Hails and other greetings were shouted across lawns and streets and over fences. Cars honked as they drove past, an arm raised out of an open window. Radios sounded from inside houses, through open doors and windows, providing the latest details of events in Europe, back in the only home Peter had ever known. Though his feelings were mixed with concern about his mother, to say nothing of his own fate, Peter shared in the townspeople's joy that the war had ended, lamenting that it had ever started in the first place.

"I suppose you'll need to call your superiors," Olivia suggested. "Surely, things will have changed."

"I reckon so," he replied, telling her yet another lie.

"Do you think you'll have to leave?"

Peter heard the worry in her voice, saw it in the quick glance she gave him. "I don't know," he muttered, twisting himself deeper into the web of falsehoods he'd woven. "I'll just have to wait and see."

For a while, neither of them spoke; the only sound other than the neighborhood festivities was the clickety-clack of Olivia's shoes on the sidewalk. Eventually, she broke the silence. "I'm so thankful," she explained. "I prayed for this day, that men like you and Billy wouldn't have to go off and fight. As the years went by, I wondered if it would ever come, but somehow, here it is."

She stopped walking and Peter did the same. Tenderly, he reached out and took her by the hand. He didn't know what to say, so he said nothing.

"I don't want to go back home."

Olivia's words surprised him. They'd been walking for more than an hour, aimlessly going from one side of town to the other and then back again. The darkness of night would soon be upon them. Peter's intention had been to slowly make their way back to her home.

"We can walk a while longer if you'd like," he offered.

"That's not what I'm talking about."

Peter was about to ask what she meant, when the truth struck him; she was asking if they could be alone. The fire inside him, the part that marveled at her beauty, that wanted to feel her touch, her breath upon his face, grew higher, hotter. Though Peter was still unsettled about many things, there was one thing about which he had the utmost certainty: his feelings for Olivia. Standing there, the stars just now visible in the fading sky above them, he searched her face, looking for something that might tell him he was wrong, that he was misconstruing her intentions, but her gaze never wavered; her eyes told him all he needed to know.

"Come with me," he said.

And she did.

Following Peter up the stairs to his apartment, Olivia's heart raced. The whole way there, she'd thought about her boldness, understanding all too well what she had said to him, what she'd insinuated when she'd told him that she didn't want to go home. But the truth was, she'd meant it. Though she didn't have much experience with love, or any of the other romantic things men and women did together, that didn't mean she had never longed for them. Since Peter had come into her life, she'd thought about it often. Kissing him had been wonderful, but the idea that Peter wanted more, just as she did, was tantalizing.

"It's not much, but here it is," Peter said, holding open the door.

Olivia stepped inside and found that she couldn't disagree. The rooms were mostly unfurnished, with only a few cobbled-together pieces. Peter turned on a bare bulb in the small kitchen and the scant light only served to make the place seem more empty.

"It's . . . nice . . ." she said, hoping he would believe her, but from the way he laughed at her attempt to be polite, it was clear that he didn't.

Olivia stepped over to look out the apartment's large picture window. Down below, people still milled about on Main Street. Here and there, she noticed those who'd clearly been drinking; they stumbled about, their voices occasionally turning to shouts, but all in a good-natured sort of way.

Suddenly, Peter slid up behind her, ran his hand along her hip, and lightly kissed her neck, his breath warm against her skin. Olivia shut her eyes, enjoying his touch.

Unused to such attention, she felt a bit nervous, anxious about where the night was headed, but she did her best to ignore such distractions and instead concentrated on how Peter was making her feel.

"That's nice," she said, her voice faint, a little breathless.

Her encouragement brought Peter's hand up the length of her arm and over her shoulder. His fingertips pushed away a few wayward strands of hair before wandering down her cheek, his thumb tracing along her jaw. Olivia sucked in a breath, holding it. But then, just as she was about to turn toward him, to make some advances of her own, they were both startled by an unexpected explosion just outside the window. She was amazed to see a brilliant cluster of green bloom like a flower in the dark sky, twinkling among the stars before fading from sight.

"Fireworks," Peter said softly in her ear.

With his arms wrapped around her, they watched as another rocket raced upward, a faint whistle signaling its ascent. It suddenly burst, erupting into another constellation of sparks, this time red. The boom of the explosion reverberated off the window. Three more came in quick succession, the night lit up in a kaleidoscope of colors.

Finally, it was silent save for a few hearty cheers from the street.

"Someone must've been saving them for this very occasion," Olivia said, turning to face Peter. "Waiting for a night to celebrate."

"No better time than now."

When Peter leaned down to kiss her, Olivia was ready and willing. Their passion soared. His touch felt insistent, almost needy, far more so than any of the other times they had kissed. She rose to him, meeting his intensity as they tried to make fireworks of their own. Her hand strayed to his chest, her fingers searching, roaming across his muscular body. Lightly, she pushed against him, trying to tell him that she was ready for more, that she could be his.

But then Peter stopped.

He looked down at her through the gloom that filled the room, the light at his back making it hard for her to see his face. "Olivia . . ." he began tentatively. "Before we go any further, there's something I've been trying to tell you, something that you deserve to know, that you *need* to know if —"

"Peter, no . . ." Olivia interrupted.

"Please, you have to listen to what I have —"

"Not now," she insisted, pressing her fingers against his lips, silencing him. "This isn't the time for talk. Whatever it is, it can wait a little longer."

Slowly, Peter nodded; he didn't say a word as he took her hand and led her through the kitchen and down a short hallway to the bedroom. It was sparse like the rest of the apartment, with only an old mattress and a shadeless lamp for furnishings. Faint starlight streamed through the window above the makeshift bed. Peter still hadn't said a word when his fingers began to undo the buttons of her blouse. Olivia's pulse quickened. Immediately, she started to do the same to Peter's shirt; both of them moved fast, each wanting the other to be undressed.

Within seconds, their shirts, pants, shoes, and undergarments were all on the floor. Olivia stood before him naked, without shame, her skin lit from outside. When Peter lowered himself onto the mattress, he held out his hand for her to join him and she took it.

Peter's hands fell on her skin, which caused Olivia to suck in a breath through tightly clenched teeth. He traced her collarbone, an almost tickling touch, before sliding downward. The back of his fingertips drifted sideways, circling the underside of her breasts. His hand turned, cupping her, holding her heft as he gently squeezed, feeling her as no one else ever had before. When his thumb began to turn counterclockwise over her raised nipple, she shivered with pleasure.

Olivia's hands returned his advances. She marveled at the thick muscles beneath his skin; her fingers lingered on the cords of his forearm, the sharp rise of his bicep, the peaks of his shoulder, and the breadth of his chest. The way her attention roamed, it was as if she was addicted to him, as if she couldn't possibly get enough.

"Peter," she said breathlessly between kisses.

Their passion grew even more intense when his hand left her breast, descended across her ribs to her belly, then curved across her hip before dipping to her inner thigh. Moments later, as his fingers slipped between her legs, touching Olivia's womanhood, seeing for himself how their love had made her feel, she was nearly beside herself with pleasure. Her head thrashed about on the mattress and her back arched as her fingers dug deep into Peter's arm, so hard that she feared hurting him.

Desperately wanting him to share what she was experiencing, Olivia groped below his waist. When her fingers found what she was looking for, wrapping around him, sliding up and down the length of his taut skin, Peter took several quick breaths, followed by a gasp.

"O . . . Olivia . . ." he managed, too overwhelmed to kiss her. Empowered by how she was making him feel, Olivia began to move faster, almost greedily, wanting more and more. Suddenly, he stopped her, grabbing her tightly by the wrist, his breathing ragged.

"That . . . that was almost too much . . ." he explained.

When Peter raised himself above her, Olivia spread her legs to accommodate him. She stared up into his face, her eyes adjusted to the darkness, drinking him in. While he maneuvered himself into position, he never once looked away. When he first touched her, preparing to enter her, Olivia flinched, not out of discomfort or fear, but out of surprise at how sensitive she was. Finally, Peter was ready. Slowly, he eased himself forward. Olivia felt her body being opened, followed by a momentary jolt of pain, forcing her to bite down on her lower lip. Peter went deeper and deeper, until finally their bodies were pressed closely together, the meeting of their flesh complete. For a long moment, they were content to stay still and silent. When Peter finally spoke, what he said sent shockwaves racing through her.

"I love you, Olivia," he said.

Tears filled her eyes. *This* was the man she had waited her whole life for. *These* were the emotions she'd always wanted to experience. *This* was the beginning of the future she had always dreamed of.

Unable to find words to answer, Olivia kissed him instead; Peter met her advances as if he'd heard her speak. As his tongue encircled hers, he slowly began to move his hips, almost imperceptibly at first, sliding in and out of her. Olivia felt some discomfort, but her love for Peter was so great that it was hardly worth noticing.

Pleasure crashed over Olivia as Peter began to move faster. Soon, they had developed a rhythm, each moving in the opposite direction, sliding apart before coming back together. Beads of sweat dotted their skin, their fluids mixing, a hint of salt on Olivia's lips as she kissed his face. The sounds of their lovemaking echoed off the walls of the small room.

"I love you, Peter!" Olivia declared, finally finding her voice, burying her face into the crook of his neck. "I love you so much!"

This time, it was Peter's turn to let his actions stand in place of words. He began to kiss her, devouring her lips, his body pistoning against hers, their ecstasy growing to a fevered pitch.

In the midst of all this, Olivia thought about how meeting Peter Baird had changed her life. Even before he'd pulled her out of the way of Sylvester Eddings's truck, she'd felt something pass between them. But the more she'd gotten to know him, to learn who he really was inside, the more she knew that Peter was the man she'd been destined to be with. Though it had meant hurting her best friend, breaking off their ill-advised engagement, Olivia had done what she had to in order to finally have *this*.

On and on, their bodies kept moving. Olivia moaned, her pleasure growing nearly unbearable, making her feel as if she was on the peak of a wave, hanging in air. But then, suddenly, the wave broke; she barely stifled a shout before spasming with pleasure. Peter reached a crescendo of his own, his fevered movements coming to a halt, his muscles tightening, as he spilled his warm seed inside her. For a moment, neither of them moved as their ragged breathing slowly steadied. Then Peter lowered himself to lie by her side. Olivia placed her hand on his cheek. A smile slowly spread across both their faces. Gently, she kissed him. Neither of them said a word, but they didn't have to.

They both knew that this was love.

Peter stared up at the ceiling as he absently rubbed his thumb across Olivia's bare shoulder; she lay against him, one arm draped across his chest, dozing softly. Though tired, he couldn't sleep. His mind churned as it considered everything that had happened. Making love to Olivia had been even greater than he'd imagined, amazing, like a dream. When she had told him that she loved him, it had freed his heart, had made him give himself over to her completely, in body and mind.

But with that had come a revelation.

When Peter first heard about the end of the war, he'd considered never telling Olivia who he really was, about where he had come from or what had befallen him before they'd first met. He had debated whether Peter Becker shouldn't disappear forever, replaced by Peter Baird, a man who had nothing to hide. But now, in the wake of what they'd just shared, Peter knew he could no longer lie to Olivia. It was time for the truth, even if revealing it cost him everything, including his freedom and the woman he loved.

"Mmmm," Olivia purred as she woke, pushing away her blond hair to look up at him. "I'm sorry," she said. "I didn't mean to fall asleep."

When she leaned up, intending to kiss him, Peter turned away.

"What's wrong?" she asked, confused.

Peter stared at her. So many times now, he'd meant to come clean, to tell Olivia everything, but something always seemed to get in the way: the loss of his nerve, bad timing, or some other interruption, including the end of the war. Even tonight, when they'd first arrived at the apartment and he had wanted to unburden himself, she'd cut him off and he'd allowed her to, giving in to his urges, wanting to make love to her.

But now it was time.

"Olivia . . ." he began. "From the moment I first saw you, there's something I've wanted to tell you . . . something that you need to know, but . . ."

She leaned up on her elbow and smiled at him, encouraging, completely unaware of what was about to be said. "You can tell me anything."

For what felt like the hundredth time, Peter thought about swallowing the truth forever, but looking into her eyes, seeing the love and trust that gazed back at him, he knew that to continue to lie to her meant the damning of his soul. So he plunged forward, right into the fire.

"My family name isn't Baird. It's Becker. And I'm not an American, not completely. I'm German. I'm an escaped prisoner of war."

CHAPTER TWENTY-TWO

Olivia's first thought was that she had misheard Peter. Her second was that he was telling a joke, though one she didn't find the least bit funny. But the longer she waited, watching his face, expecting there to be some sign, something to give him away, the more she began to realize that he was telling the truth.

"What . . . what are you saying . . . ?" she stammered.

"I know this is going to be hard for you to hear, but you need to listen," he answered, his face conflicted, almost pained. "I was born and raised in Germany, but my father was an American, a soldier just like John. He stayed in Europe after the war and soon after met and fell in love with my mother. That's why I speak English the way I do. My father taught me."

Disbelief and shock began to overwhelm Olivia. Try as she might, she couldn't wrap her head around what Peter was saying. It was incredible, unbelievable. She leaned up, dragging the bedsheet with her, suddenly self-conscious enough to want to cover herself. Slowly, she began to shake her head.

"This isn't possible," she said.

"I never wanted to be a soldier," Peter continued; now that he had finally started to talk, the words kept coming. "I hate Hitler and all that he and his Nazis stand for, but I didn't have a choice. After I was conscripted, I could have run away, but my mother would've been the one to suffer. Her health was bad and I was afraid of what could happen to her if I was considered to be a traitor."

By now, Olivia was on her feet, backing away. Her thoughts reeled. Inch by inch, she moved farther from him, the man she thought she'd known, whom she'd come to love. In her head, she was transported back to the time when the war in Europe had just begun. She saw the newsreels, with the jackbooted soldiers marching across the screen; she'd been terrified. The idea that Peter was one of those men, that it had been *him* who'd entered her dreams, waking her from sleep, was more than she could bear.

"You're . . . you're the enemy?" Olivia asked.

"No, I'm not," Peter answered emphatically. "I'm just a man who did what he had to in order to survive. Every day I fought, I prayed for the war to end. When my unit was captured in France, all I felt was relief."

"If you were caught, then how are you here?"

"It was an accident. I was with hundreds of other prisoners, put on a boat and sent across the ocean, here, to America. But then the train I was riding on had an accident in a storm. It crashed. The man whom I was chained to and I escaped into the woods during the confusion. I shouldn't have followed him, but I did."

Olivia was conflicted. On the one hand, she wanted to hear what Peter had to say, to try to understand who he was. But another voice screamed at her to run as fast and far away as she could. In the end, she found a compromise; she gathered up her clothes and began to dress as she listened.

"I don't know how far we traveled or even how many days we rode on trains, trying to stay out of sight, but in the end we found ourselves here, in Miller's Creek. Eventually, I got free of my restraints, then scrounged up some clothes and something to eat. When I walked into town, I had every intention of surrendering."

Olivia paused while buttoning her blouse. "That was why you were asking for my father, wasn't it?"

Peter nodded. "But that changed the moment I met you."

The more Olivia considered Peter's story, the more it made sense. His admission explained why he hadn't had any clothes or other belongings with him when they'd met. Why he had no money or identification. She thought about how evasive he had been, even when they'd first talked, the vague way he spoke of family back in Pennsylvania. She recalled how when the subject of his military service had been raised, he'd claimed that what he did was a secret; in that, Peter *hadn't* lied.

What made it all so much worse was that she'd been warned. Olivia thought about what Billy had said beneath the evergreen tree. He'd told her that she really knew nothing about Peter, that he could be dangerous, that everything he'd told her could be lies. She'd laughed it off, defending Peter, already starting to fall for his charms. Then there was her mother; Elizabeth had argued much the same thing, that her daughter only knew the side of Peter he'd chosen to show her. Olivia doubted her mother had considered the possibility that Peter was an escaped German soldier! If she only knew that she'd harbored such a man in her home.

Olivia had been taken for a fool, her and her whole family.

"You . . . you lied to me . . ." she said, her hands shaking with anger.

Peter stared at her, a faint look of shame in his eyes. "I did," he admitted. "But I couldn't have told you the truth. Not at first. You wouldn't have understood."

"You said it yourself!" Olivia shouted. "You're a German soldier!"

"But that doesn't mean that I'm a monster!" Peter insisted. "I told you, I despise Hitler and all he and his Nazis stand for." He sighed, trying to control his emotions; his piercing blue eyes held Olivia in place. "I am as you see me," he said. "I'm the man you fell in love with, who loves you back with all his heart. The only thing truly different between who I am and who I pretended to be is my family name. You've got to believe me . . . you just have to . . ."

There was a part of Olivia that wanted to do just that. She loved him; there was no point in denying it. Peter had always been kind to her, funny, and intelligent. His touch sent her heart racing. Even now, standing before him, not an hour since she'd given herself to him, Olivia had no regrets. Maybe things could be fixed. Maybe he could better explain himself. All it would take was to fall back into his arms . . .

But there was another part of her that couldn't let it go. Just like how Billy had kept his love secret from her, Peter, too, had chosen to hide something; a truth that he knew would change everything between them. How could she be with him now? He was a German soldier! Tears welled in Olivia's eyes, spilling over to tumble down her cheeks.

"I . . . I can't!" she cried, running for the door.

After breaking off her engagement to Billy, Olivia had thought her life couldn't possibly get any more complicated.

She had been wrong.

"Olivia, wait!"

But she didn't. As the door slammed shut behind her, Peter swore under his breath. Only a few moments earlier, she'd been lying asleep beside him. An hour before that, they had made love for the first time. He could still hear her voice as she said that she loved him. But now, because he'd finally revealed the truth about himself, she was gone.

Peter couldn't blame her. He'd known the risk.

He'd seen the disbelief in her eyes. What a shock it must've been. He remembered the way she'd spoken about Germans, saying that they deserved everything they were getting; to learn that *he* was one of those Germans must have been a bitter pill to swallow.

What could he do but let her go? Surely she would run and tell her father what had happened; it'd only be a matter of time before John showed up at his door with his gun and handcuffs.

Go after her!

The thought raced through Peter as if it was electricity. He stared at the door. His reasons were selfish. It wasn't because he was having second thoughts about being locked up; escaping from the wrecked train with Otto had been a mistake for which he knew he should pay. The real reason Peter wanted to stop Olivia was that he loved her. No matter what, he couldn't let her hate him. He had lied to her, hurt her. But maybe he could still make it right between them. Maybe he could convince her that he wasn't the enemy. Maybe he could taste her lips, tell her that he loved her, just one more time . . .

Peter reached for his clothes.

Olivia ran as fast as she could. Once she'd hurried down the stairs from Peter's apartment, she'd had only one destination in mind.

She had to get home.

Even as she dashed past the post office, the hardware store, and then the bank, its clock showing that it was nearly midnight, Olivia wondered how she could possibly tell her family what had happened. What would her father say? Would he feel as betrayed as she did? John Marsten had gone out of his way to help Peter, letting him stay in his home while he recovered from his injuries, and then finding him an apartment. If word got out about Peter, if the people of Miller's Creek learned that he was German, her father's reputation as sheriff would be left in tatters. Olivia could only imagine what her mother would say. Would Elizabeth crow about being right to doubt Peter? To this day, Olivia's mother still held on to the tiniest of slights, to instances in which she knew she was right; would Olivia have to hear about her mistake for the rest of her life?

And what about Billy? How would he react? Would what remained of their friendship survive this revelation?

But worst of all was the struggle Olivia knew she would have to face alone. The man she loved, who had unexpectedly come into her life and then stolen her heart, was an enemy of her nation. *It wasn't possible!* He had lied to her, betrayed her trust, and deceived her. She had allowed herself to believe in him, in their growing relation-ship, to think that she had finally found the man she loved, the person she might spend the rest of her life with. Then, when Peter had revealed the truth of who he was, it was ruined in an instant.

But even now, as tears flowed down her cheeks, sobbing as she ran, Olivia couldn't bring herself to hate Peter. All she wanted was to rewind time, to go back to a week earlier, a day, even an hour, back to when she believed him to be as American as she was, to a moment when their future together seemed bright and limitless.

Stop dreaming! It's too late for that . . .

Olivia ran on. Fortunately, the earlier celebration had died down and she only saw a couple of people at a distance. The ragged sound of her breathing filled her ears and her legs burned, but she never slowed. But then, just as she rounded the corner that would lead her home, Olivia heard the fevered pounding of footsteps behind her.

Glancing back, she saw a man racing toward her; it was Peter.

"Olivia, wait!" he shouted. "Just wait!"

She shook her head and tears flew from her eyes. Though she continued to run as hard as she could, Peter was too fast; little more than a block from her house, he caught up, reached out, and grabbed her by the arm. Desperately, Olivia tried to break free, but he held her tight.

"Let me go!" she insisted.

"Not until you hear me out!"

"What more is there to say?! You lied to me! You're the enemy!"

"If that's so, then why would I tell you?" Peter demanded. "Why would I admit to who I really am? If my intention was to do you or anyone else harm, I would've shut my mouth and done it! No one would ever have been the wiser! But by telling you the truth, I put myself at your mercy! My life is in your hands!"

Olivia opened her mouth but found herself speechless. Peter was right.

"When we first met, I'd come to town to turn myself in," he continued. "I knew that it was wrong to have run away from the wrecked train. I was willing to surrender. But then I met you." Peter paused, his eyes searching hers. "I pulled you out of the way of that truck and got hurt. When I woke up, when I saw you again, when I heard the sound of your voice and got to know the beautiful woman it belonged to, I found myself unable to tell you the truth. Not then. Not when I was starting to fall in love with you."

"Peter . . ." she managed, her heart racing.

"My coming here might have been an accident. A twist of fate. But now it's too late. I've found you and I don't want to give you up." Abruptly, Peter let go of Olivia's arm. "What I'm telling you is the truth. If that isn't enough or if you still don't believe me, then go ahead. Run and tell your father. I won't try to stop you and I won't escape. Whatever happens now is up to you."

Only a few moments before, Olivia had been running as fast as she could, desperately trying to get home. Now, she found herself unable to move. Time stretched slowly forward, her heart thundered, as her future with Peter hung in the balance. She thought about everything he had told her, as unbelievable as it was, how he'd laid himself bare, leaving it up to her what happened next. She could go to her father, tell him all she knew, and the authorities would decide Peter's fate. Deep down, she knew that that would be the end, that she would never see him again. Just the thought of their separation, of never feeling his touch or hearing his voice, made her weak in the knees. But what choice did she have? She loved Peter with all her heart, but could she keep his secret? Should she?

But then, just as she was about to admit to how conflicted she was, a figure burst from the bushes beside them and threw itself at Peter, filling the night with punches and curses.

Olivia was too terrified scream.

Billy felt like a fool. It was growing late; the moon shone down on him as he paced back and forth a block from Olivia's home. It was colder than he'd expected, especially for early spring, so he stamped his feet and rubbed his arms for warmth. Every minute or so, his eyes rose to look at the Marsten house, but it never changed; only a lone light shone in an upstairs window. He had no idea where Olivia was.

His disbelief at seeing Olivia kiss Peter Baird had become anger and disappointment as the day wore on. Billy had gone back to the bank and stewed in his office, alone as the rest of the employees took the remainder of the day off to celebrate the end of the war in Europe. Finally, around suppertime, he'd screwed up enough courage to confront Olivia, to demand an explanation for what he'd seen. He'd marched across town, hoping that he wouldn't lose his nerve the second he saw her.

But she hadn't been home.

Olivia's mother had quickly ushered him inside, offered him a bite to eat, and apologized for her daughter's decision to break their engagement. Elizabeth had argued that it was only cold feet, that Olivia would eventually come around if he'd just be patient; but then, she hadn't watched Olivia kiss another man in the middle of the street. When John had come home, he'd seemed sympathetic, shaking Billy's hand in a sort of commiseration, but only to a point. Grace had watched silently from across the room. When Elizabeth asked Billy if he wanted to stay for dinner, his discomfort had become so great that he'd turned down the invitation.

Instead, he had decided to wait around outside.

Billy glanced down at his watch; it was too dark for him to see it clearly, but he knew that hours had passed. For a while, the streets had been filled with those celebrating Germany's surrender. Earlier, he thought that he'd seen someone heading toward the house from the opposite direction, but he hadn't gotten a good look and no lights had come on in the house, so he figured that he'd been mistaken.

"Where is she?" he muttered to himself.

The more time that passed, the more frustrated Billy became. Earlier, he had considered giving up and going home, but his stubbornness kept him there, watching and waiting. Deep in his gut, he knew that with every passing moment, Olivia was slipping further away.

Is she still with him? *She has to be . . . What are they doing?*

The answer to that last question made Billy's stomach churn, so he quickly tried to put it out of his head, though he wasn't having much luck.

But then, Billy heard the unmistakable sound of footfalls.

Peering into the darkness, he saw her. It was Olivia . . . and it looked like she was running from something . . .

Or someone . . .

Right behind Olivia was Peter. Incredibly after what Billy had seen that afternoon, she didn't seem to want to be with him. It looked like she was crying. When Peter reached her, he grabbed her arm and refused to let go no matter how much she protested. Olivia was shouting, but she was faced away from Billy and he couldn't make out what she was saying.

Seeing her, his lifelong friend and the woman he'd loved for as long as he could remember, suffer, infuriated him. He felt the overwhelming urge to come to her aid, to protect her, to make her see how much she meant to him.

Staying to the shadows, he started to move closer. His eyes never left them. Billy's mind concocted all sorts of explanations for their behavior; he finally decided that Peter had made unwanted advances toward Olivia, that he was trying to take her against her will. Billy's hands clenched into fists. At any moment, he expected them to see him coming, but neither seemed to notice.

Billy sprang out from the darkness; his weight slammed into Peter hard enough to knock the man down. He threw a blind punch that connected and made his hand throb with pain. Through it all, he didn't say a word, determined to protect Olivia. Silently, Billy swore to himself that he would make this man pay for the trouble he had caused, not only for trying to steal Olivia's honor, but also for what he'd done to Billy's hopes and dreams, for leaving them in tatters.

CHAPTER TWENTY-THREE

Peter never saw the attack coming. He had been so intent on Olivia, wondering what decision she was going to make, that he was completely unaware when a figure came roaring out of the darkness and crashed into him. The blow was enough to knock him down; he landed awkwardly on the sidewalk. Somewhere in there, a punch clipped his jaw; it wasn't solid, but it still stung.

What in the hell . . . ?

His first thought was that it was Otto. Even with all that had happened the last couple of days, from his trip to the cabin, Germany's surrender, as well as making love with Olivia, he'd never stopped thinking about his fellow prisoner. If the brutal Nazi had been watching from the shadows, it was certainly possible, maybe even likely, that he had noticed his former cuffmate. Maybe he'd come for revenge on Peter for abandoning him.

But through the blizzard of wild, ineffectual punches, he soon understood that his assumption was wrong. It wasn't Otto but Billy Tate; Olivia's former fiancé had every reason to hate him and now seemed hell-bent on making his rival pay for stealing away his bride-to-be.

"Stay away from her!" Billy shouted, his eyes narrow and determined. "I won't let you hurt her any more than you have."

Straddling Peter, Billy kept raining down punches, determined to hurt his opponent, but it was obvious that he'd never been in a fight before. It was more like he was throwing a fit, as if he was a child having a tantrum. It didn't help that he was so thin, almost gangly, and therefore had little weight behind his blows. Reaching out, Peter grabbed one of the other man's wrists and yanked him to the side; Billy fell off and both men scrambled to their feet.

"Billy, stop it!" Olivia shouted.

But her old friend wasn't listening. "I saw him forcing himself on you," he answered. "He wouldn't let you go!"

Before Olivia could respond, Billy was back on the attack. One after the other, Peter swatted away his punches, but never fought back. The sad truth was that he pitied the man. Even if Olivia had accepted

Billy's proposal in error, that didn't mean that his pain wasn't genuine; no one, man or woman, wanted his or her love to be rejected. Knowing how much Olivia still cared for Billy, the last thing Peter wanted was to hurt him.

Billy was doing enough of that on his own.

Olivia could not believe what she was seeing. Moments before, she'd been struggling to decide what to do about the revelation that Peter was an escaped German prisoner of war. The love she felt for him was beginning to overwhelm her sense of duty to tell her father, but just as she was about to admit to her doubts, Billy had rushed out of the darkness and begun attacking Peter. No matter how much she yelled at him to stop, he seemed intent on a fight.

But Peter had no such interest.

Every time Billy threw a punch, Peter pushed it away. He kept moving backward and to the side, trying to stay out of range. Olivia could see that it wasn't cowardice, but rather a conscious choice not to fight back. Even when Billy landed a lucky punch, the blow striking high on Peter's chest, he didn't react as might have been expected. He didn't sneer or spit out a curse. His hands never balled into fists.

381

Though Olivia knew that Peter could have easily bested Billy, he chose not to; instead, he kept looking over at her, his eyes imploring.

It was up to her to stop this.

"Billy!" she shouted, stepping forward. "Stop this! Stop!"

Olivia grabbed Billy's shoulder, but he was so intent on gaining his revenge that he didn't notice her. When he reared back to throw yet another ineffectual punch, his elbow struck her arm. Olivia wobbled and was certain that she was going to fall. But then, just as she began to tip over, a pair of hands grabbed her, and held her up. Only when she'd regained her balance did Olivia realize that *both* Peter and Billy had come to her rescue.

"Let go of her," Billy demanded of Peter, looking as if he meant for the one-sided brawl to start again.

But Olivia was having none of it. Pulling herself free from both men's grasp, she stepped between them, her attention focused on Billy. "What were you thinking? You don't just start hitting someone like that!" she snapped, a finger rising in rebuke; with each word, she kept coming forward, forcing Billy to retreat. "Have you completely lost your senses?!"

"But . . . but he was hurting you . . ." Billy stammered. "I saw you running from him, heard you shouting . . . I wanted to protect you . . ."

"We were having a disagreement, that's all," Olivia explained, though she knew that the truth was much more complicated.

Quickly, she glanced at Peter; from the look on his face, she understood that he expected her to tell Billy who he really was. Olivia knew it would be easy to do just that. Still, she didn't reveal his secret. It made her wonder if she hadn't already made her decision.

"That's not what it looked like to me," Billy argued, a little defensively. "I thought that you were trying to get away and that he wouldn't let you go."

The sincerity in her friend's voice, how badly he wanted to protect her, made Olivia feel terrible. She couldn't help but think about all the pain she'd caused him. The worst part was knowing that there was more; she had chosen to make love, for the first time in her life, to another man.

"Billy . . ." she soothed, wanting to calm him, to take away his anger. "I wasn't in any danger. Peter would never hurt me."

"You don't know that," he corrected her. "Like I told you before, you don't know anything about him." Billy stared daggers at Peter, his words full of accusation. "Why is everything about him so secretive? I doubt that he's anything like who he claims to be."

You have no idea how right you are . . .

But then, just as Olivia was trying to figure out how to respond, not wanting to lie but unsure what else she could do, Peter suddenly shouted, "Dear God!"

She was shocked to find that he wasn't even looking at her and Billy, but staring past them. Turning around, Olivia screamed.

Her house was on fire.

Otto heard the woman's scream and smiled in the darkness. He had been watching Peter Becker and the two people with him for a few moments, pausing as he retreated from the now-burning home. He wondered if his old compatriot understood how much danger he was in, that his death was coming, a moment as inevitable as the train crash that had bought them both their freedom.

Behind him, flames began to consume the home. They licked hungrily, their colors shifting with the intensity of their heat, climbing higher, their desire for consumption nearly unquenchable. Thick, black smoke began to billow up into the night sky, blotting out the moon and stars, carried away on the wind.

To Otto, it was beautiful.

Ever since he had discovered Becker living among the Amerikaners, pretending that he was one of them, Otto had kept a close eye on the man. It had been risky to move about in broad daylight, but he was determined to make the traitor pay. At the same time, he hadn't wanted to neglect his duty to his Führer; to do so would've made him no better than the deserter he was pursuing. In the end, he'd decided to do both.

But it hadn't been without some confusion.

That afternoon, having followed Becker from where he was staying to a restaurant, he'd been surprised when people began to rush out into the street, shouting, clapping, and even singing. Clearly, it was a celebration. Deep down, Otto knew what it must mean; the Japanese had surrendered. *Mischling* bastards! Those weak, yellow vermin had ridden far on Germany's coattails, but Otto had always known it was a matter of time before their mongrel cowardice made them surrender. Still, with them out of the war, that meant that the Amerikaners could focus entirely upon the conflict in Europe;

Otto vowed to redouble his efforts to hurt them here at home.

Becker had come outside to revel with the Amerikaners. He'd been with a woman, a pretty young thing who must have caught the traitor's fancy. At the edges of the celebrating townspeople, Otto had had to be cautious not to be seen too clearly, so his attention had drifted back and forth to Becker and the woman. Therefore, when he'd happened upon them kissing passionately in the middle of the street, it had been a surprise. But even to a man as jaded as Otto, the sight had brought a smile to his face. It was a revelation.

He'd found the means to his vengeance.

Otto had followed them from a distance when they left the center of town. Arriving at a residence, they'd gone inside; Otto knew that it had to be the woman's home. He hadn't waited around for long. He'd known just what to do.

Under the cover of night, he had returned with a large canister of gasoline he'd stolen. He'd waited in the bushes, anxious to act but still patient, watching as each light in the house went out one by one. Then, Otto had walked around the perimeter of the house and splashed the flammable liquid everywhere. He coated the walls and pooled it on the porch. He poured it on the doors that led to the cellar. He used every last drop.

The only surprise had been to discover *another* police car in the drive. Becker must have gone straight to the authorities when he'd come into town. Why else would he be consorting with the law? Otto could feel the pistol in his waistband, the weapon he had stolen from the Amerikaner he'd murdered. If he succeeded in killing another lawman, surely that would mean there weren't many more left to oppose him.

Finally, Otto had lit a match and dropped it into the puddle of gasoline at his feet. He watched as the flame raced forward as if it were a living thing, like a wolf running after its prey. It practically leaped at the house. Within seconds, the fire had already spread to the point where he knew it couldn't be extinguished.

Now, as he watched Becker, Otto felt a pang of disappointment to see that the woman was with him; he'd wanted her to burn. Her death would've hurt his fellow soldier, something he greatly desired. The traitor had to suffer. Still, it pleased him that she would have to stand by and watch helplessly as her family went up in flames.

"Heil Hitler," Otto hissed before hurrying

away into the dark night.

Peter was amazed by how fast the fire spread. As he watched, flames raced up the outside of the Marstens' home, rising higher and higher with every passing second. The blaze grew so quickly that he wondered if it wouldn't soon burn out, like a match; but a match had only a stick to consume, while this conflagration had an entire house. In the black of midnight, the fire was painfully bright. But he knew that it was anything but beautiful; it was deadly.

Suddenly, like a lightning bolt, Peter knew what had happened.

It was Otto! It had to be!

Peter spun around, looking for the Nazi. He peered into the dark shadows, but there was nothing, no one there. Still, he had no doubts.

But why had he chosen the Marstens?

A sickening feeling filled Peter's stomach. Otto had seen him. He'd noticed him with Olivia and was striking at her and her family to get to him.

"No!" Olivia screamed. "Mom! Dad! No!"

Without a moment's hesitation, she was off, running frantically for the house. Peter followed, his mind reeling. Faintly, he heard the sound of Billy's footfalls behind him, their brawl forgotten.

Before they had even reached the Marstens' property, Peter felt a wall of heat wash over them. Smoke burned his eyes and lungs. He heard the sound of a window breaking. The American flag that flew from the post near the door vanished before their eyes. Shielding his face with his arm, he kept expecting to see someone come out of the house, to see John struggle outside with his wife and younger daughter, all of them covered in sweat and coughing, but nothing stirred. His hopes quickly began to fade.

"Let's go!" Olivia shouted, her voice hysterical with fear. "We have to save them!" But when she started to run for the house, Peter grabbed her arm. "What are you doing?" she screamed. "They'll die if we don't do something!"

"If we go inside, there's a good chance that we'll be the ones who don't make it out!" he argued.

"I don't care!" Olivia shouted, and he knew that she meant it.

Looking into her eyes, Peter made a decision. He had already risked so much in order to share in her life, had come to love her more than he ever would've thought possible, that he realized he couldn't refuse her. When he'd pulled Olivia out of the way of the runaway truck, the Marstens had taken him in and nursed him back to health. Even though much of what they knew of him was a lie, how could he refuse to help them now, when they needed him the most?

Turning around, Peter found Billy staring dumbly at the fire. The gangly young man looked to be in a state of shock. He had to shout Billy's name twice to get his attention.

"Go to the neighbors and call for help," he commanded. "Someone may have already contacted the fire department, but assume they haven't." Billy nodded absently but he still stood transfixed. "Now!" Peter shouted.

Billy frowned, making Peter wonder if he was about to disagree with him; if it happened, he swore that *this* time, he wouldn't hold back his fist. But finally, Billy did as he was told and started off for Ruth Pollack's house.

Peter still had hold of Olivia's arm; as distraught as she was, he'd been afraid to let her go even for an instant, fearful that she would try to run into the burning house. When he looked at her, her eyes were filled with tears.

"I'll go get them," he said.

"I'm coming with you," she insisted.

Peter shook his head. "Someone needs to be here when they come out. They may be hurt or in shock. Besides, I know what to expect inside," he explained, thinking about the burning barn.

"I . . . I can't . . . I can't lose . . ." Olivia began but couldn't finish.

"I'll bring your family back to you," he promised.

Or die trying . . .

Looking up at the burning house, Peter wondered how he was going to get inside. Flames surrounded the side door near the kitchen, making that a difficult point of entry. Running around to the front of the home, he took a few tentative steps up onto the porch; the fire was there, too, but it wasn't as bad. He was considering smashing out a window when he was startled by movement inside the house. Rushing to the front door, Peter pulled out the hem of his shirt, wrapped his hand for protection against the hot metal of the knob, and opened the door. Instantly, a wall of heat slammed into him. But that wasn't all.

Elizabeth Marsten stumbled into his arms.

Olivia's mother was a mess. Sweat plastered her usually immaculately coifed hair to her forehead. Streaks of dark soot and grime were smeared across her cheeks. Her eyes were narrow and bloodshot. Huge coughs heaved up and out of her chest from all of the smoke she had inhaled.

"Mother!" Olivia shouted as she ran to help Elizabeth down the porch steps. Gently, they eased her onto the dewy grass.

"Where are the others?" Peter asked insistently; if the situation were different, he would have been more patient with Elizabeth, more caring, but time was against them and he needed answers.

"Where are Dad and Grace?" Olivia echoed.

But her mother couldn't stop coughing long enough to answer.

"Are they still in the house?" Olivia prodded, her voice growing more and more frantic. "Tell me!"

"Your . . . your father . . ." Elizabeth began, her voice a wheeze. "He sent me . . . me down . . . down the stairs . . . while he went to . . . to get . . ." But that was as far as she got before another fit of coughing overwhelmed her.

"He went to get Grace," Olivia finished.

She and Peter turned back to the burning house. Even in the short time since Elizabeth had exited, the blaze had gotten worse; flames rose all the way to the roof. The sound of a beam cracking cut through the fire's cacophony of sounds, another indication that the house was weakening, slowly giving way to the fire that was consuming it. Peter knew that if Olivia's father and sister were still alive, they wouldn't be for much longer.

Peter looked at Olivia. In her face, he could see panic, but also a flicker of hope, a belief that it wasn't already too late. He wanted to take her in his arms, to gently kiss her and tell her that he loved her, one last time. But he didn't. Instead, as he ran up the porch steps, shielding his face from the oppressive heat, through the front door and into the burning building, he could only hope that she knew how he felt, that even if he were to die tonight, he wouldn't have regretted a thing.

It had all been worth it to share his heart with her.

CHAPTER TWENTY-FOUR

The burning barn had been different. It had been angry, violent, and destructive, but it had been easier for Peter to see and move around. He had worked his way down the long, wide corridors, opening stalls and shooing the horses to safety. Here, inside the inferno that engulfed the Marstens' home, the space was smaller, more cramped, a warren of rooms. The choking black smoke burned his eyes and made it almost impossible to see more than a few feet. The other difference was the heat. At the barn, he'd doused himself with water from a duck pond before entering. It hadn't offered much protection, but it had been enough to keep the worst of the heat at bay, at least for a while. Now, it attacked him mercilessly. He could feel it reddening his skin and crawling into his lungs.

It was a living hell.

Keep calm. Use your head and don't panic.

Remember what served you well on the battle-field.

Peter went to the stairs. Given the late hour when the fire had begun, everyone would've been asleep in their rooms. If John and Grace were still alive, he felt certain he would find them there. Every step was a struggle. The sound of breaking glass, cracking wood, and the steady roar of the blaze filled his ears.

Halfway up, he paused. There, on the small landing where the stairs turned at a ninety-degree angle, Peter peered through the smoke, hoping to see Olivia's family coming toward him. But there was nothing. Even as a pinprick of fear needled its way into his thoughts, warning him that he was heading for a certain death, Peter swallowed it down and kept going.

He was soon rewarded for his perseverance.

From the head of the stairs, a long hallway ran the length of the house; there was so much smoke that Peter couldn't see the window at the opposite end. Fortunately, he didn't have to. There, a couple feet away, was John.

Olivia's father was on his hands and knees, half of his body sticking out into the hallway, the rest inside one of the bedrooms.

As Peter watched, John strained, as if he was trying to get to his feet, his arms trembling, before he suddenly collapsed onto his chest. He lay motionless.

"John!" Peter shouted, straining to be heard over the fire.

But there was no response.

Worst of all, Grace was nowhere to be seen.

Olivia couldn't take her eyes off the front door. Only a couple of minutes had passed since Peter had disappeared inside, but she kept expecting him to reappear at any moment, bringing her father and sister to safety; the anticipation was so great that she found herself holding her breath. But with every second that ticked past, her fear grew that she was about to lose the people she loved most.

Come on! Where are you, Peter?!

Her mother still lay on the wet grass beside her. Elizabeth's coughs had subsided enough for her to sit up. She, too, stared at the house.

"How . . . how could this have happened . . . ?" she asked.

Olivia didn't respond; she had no answer to give.

In the distance, the shrill sound of a siren

rose into the night. Moments later, Olivia heard the sound of someone approaching. Tearing her gaze from the burning house, she saw Billy running toward them.

"The fire truck will be here soon," he said breathlessly. Looking at Elizabeth, he began to ask, "Where is —" but stopped, realizing how insensitive his question might sound. For a long moment, he was silent. Finally, he said, "Did Peter go in there after them?"

Olivia nodded.

Without another word, Billy knelt and began to tend to Elizabeth; her mother looked grateful for the attention and began talking about the ordeal she had faced inside the burning house. Olivia didn't hear a word she said; at that moment, she suddenly understood one of the many differences between the two men in her life. Billy was caring and dependable, even in the worst of situations. He was thoughtful and safe. Peter was different. Even with everything she had learned about his origins, about the secrets he'd been keeping, she still felt that she *knew* him, who he really was as a man; in the end, what mattered wasn't his nationality, but rather who he was on the inside. No matter what danger he faced, whether it was on a battlefield or when he ran into a raging inferno, Peter

Becker never shrank from his responsibilities, from doing what was right. That Billy wouldn't follow Peter, that he wouldn't take the same risks, didn't necessarily speak ill of her friend; few would have done what Peter had. But Olivia couldn't deny that it made Peter the man she wanted, the one she loved. Because of that, she couldn't allow him to act alone.

"I'm going inside," she suddenly declared.

"What?" Billy exclaimed. "Olivia, what are you saying? You can't go in there! It's too dangerous!"

A part of Olivia knew that he was right; one look at the way the fire was slowly but steadily consuming the house would have been enough to convince almost anyone of the foolhardiness of going inside, but she wasn't to be deterred. Calmly, she turned to look at Billy. "I won't sit here and do nothing," she explained. "I can't play it safe. Not when the people I love need me the most."

"Peter will bring them out," her former fiancé replied, offering an argument she knew had to be difficult for him to make; either he believed what he was saying or he was grasping at straws, desperate to keep her from harm.

"He needs me," Olivia answered. She had

made up her mind; there was nothing anyone could have said to change it.

Still, that didn't stop her mother from trying.

"Olivia, no! It's too dangerous!" Elizabeth shouted; her daughter was surprised to see worry written so plainly in her face. "Stay here and pray that they come out." Turning to Billy, she added, "Talk some sense into her, William!"

Olivia had no idea if he tried.

She was already running for the burning house.

Peter hurried to where John lay motionless. He dropped to a knee beside him, put a hand on the lawman's back, and shook him. Nothing. Smoke burned his eyes and tried its best to crawl down into his lungs. The heat was like a slap to his face. Peering into the room that Olivia's father had been leaving, he saw that the fire was growing stronger. Flames climbed up the walls. As he watched, the lace doilies on the dresser caught; the fire ate them so quickly that it seemed as if one moment they were there, the next they were gone. Peter knew they were running out of time to get out alive.

"John!" Peter shouted to be heard over the inferno. "Can you hear me?"

The sheriff didn't answer.

"Where's Grace?" he prodded. "Where's your daughter?"

This time, Olivia's father stirred. He mumbled something, but it was spoken so faintly that Peter couldn't make any of it out.

Peter assumed that John had been looking for his younger daughter when he'd been overcome by the smoke. Grace wasn't with him, which meant that he'd yet to find her. Since Peter hadn't met her as he'd gone up the stairs and she hadn't come outside with Elizabeth, she was still in the house. But where?

"Grace!" Peter yelled as loud as he could, hoping that he could be heard down the long hallway. "Grace! Are you there?"

But even if Olivia's sister screamed in answer, Peter doubted he would've been able to hear her; the fire was so loud that it wouldn't have mattered whether she was ten feet away or a hundred. Unless she stepped out where he could see her, he'd never know where she was.

That left him with a difficult choice to make.

John was in a bad way. He couldn't leave the man lying there, half-unconscious, while he went to look for Grace. But if he took

John outside, odds were that he wouldn't have time to come back; with the way the fire was gaining strength, it'd be too late. He could either save John or try to find Grace. He didn't have time to rescue them both.

But then, as Peter struggled to decide which path to take, something tugged on his shirtsleeve, startling him. He spun around.

It was Olivia.

"What are you doing here?" he shouted. "I told you to wait outside!"

Peter was angry, yet happy to see her. He was mad because she'd disobeyed him, had run headlong into a dangerous situation, putting her life in jeopardy. But maybe it might provide an answer to his dilemma . . .

Olivia didn't respond. Tenderly, she placed a hand on her father's back. "Is he . . . is he . . . ?" she asked, unable to say the one remaining word.

"No," Peter told her. "He just inhaled too much smoke. But we need to get him out of here."

"Where's Grace?

Peter shook his head. "I don't know."

"We have to find her," Olivia said, her voice panicked, as she began to rise to her feet. As he'd done earlier, Peter grabbed her by the arm, stopping her.

"I told you that I'd find her and I meant it," he said. "But I need you to take your father outside. He can't make it on his own."

Each of them grabbed John under an arm and lifted; with no small effort, they managed to get him to his feet. He wasn't steady, but with help, Peter felt certain he could make it down the stairs.

"Get him out of here," he told Olivia.

She looked at him, her eyes wet from both smoke and fear. "Be safe."

Peter nodded and turned away.

Right now, he was the only thing between Grace and certain death.

Peter made his way down the hallway, checking each room he passed. He was hunched over, his arm pressed against his face, his eyes burning; the smoke had gotten worse, thicker, as it tried to drag him down. The heat was brutal; sweat beaded his forehead and slicked his skin. He tried to push down the persistent fear that he was about to die, and instead tried to focus on finding Grace.

Don't give in . . . keep going . . .

With every room that Peter checked, he felt a twinge of hope flare in his chest, a belief that he was about to find Olivia's sister. But with each door he opened, he was disappointed. There was no Grace, only more fire, the flames consuming everything, deadly.

"Grace!" he shouted again and again. But there was never any answer.

Finally, he arrived at the last room.

Unlike the others, this door was shut tight; carefully, Peter turned the knob, pushed it open, and stepped inside. There, cowering behind a bed, her face a hysterical mask of tears, was Grace. When she saw him, her eyes grew wider and she scurried farther away; she was so frightened that she didn't see his arrival as a means to her rescue, but rather as another threat.

Though the urge to grab Grace and carry her to safety was strong, Peter knew it could mean both of their deaths; panicked, she might struggle or try to run away from him, even as the burning house crumbled down around their heads. He needed to calm her, to reassure her that coming with him of her own free will was the only way to live.

"Grace," he soothed as he knelt a few feet away; all around them, the fire swirled, relentless. "You need to come with me. You need to take my hand."

The teenager whimpered, but Peter was relieved that she hadn't tried to move farther away.

"Trust me," he continued. "We don't have much time."

"My . . . my folks . . ." she managed, her voice catching.

"They're safe. They're outside with Olivia," he explained, inching closer. "Everyone is waiting for us."

"I'm . . . I'm so scared . . ."

"I know. I am, too. But together, we can make it. I need you just as much as you need me."

Slowly, his heart in his throat, Peter watched as Grace worked herself free of the fear that paralyzed her. With trembling fingers, she reached for his hand.

"We're . . . we're going to be . . . all right . . . ?" she asked.

"I promise," Peter answered, determined to make good on it.

When Grace's hand finally found his, she fell into his arms. Peter felt the girl's heart pound against his chest. Gently, he pried her away and looked into her eyes.

"Follow me," he told her. "Whatever you do, don't let go."

But then, just as they turned to leave, there was a sudden, earsplitting crack. Right in front of their eyes, the doorway crumbled, collapsing in a heap of burning wood, blocking their escape.

Beside him, Grace screamed.

They were trapped.

Olivia struggled to help her father down the stairs. He leaned heavily against her, forcing her to take the steps slowly. Heavy coughs heaved their way out of his chest. Only a few steps down, his foot slipped and he lurched forward; it was all Olivia could do to keep him upright.

"Take your time," she told him, even though every instinct screamed at her to run out of the burning building as fast as she could.

Soon, the house she'd spent her whole life in would be destroyed. Flames devoured everything in sight, faster by the minute. The smoke was thick, the stench burning her nose. The heat was worse, utterly inescapable; she felt as if she was being smothered by it. At any moment, she expected the whole place to come crashing down. But as bad as Olivia felt physically, her head was even more of a mess; knowing that Peter and her sister were somewhere above, even further from safety than she and her father were, made it hard to think straight. Trying to navigate the burning stairwell would've been a chore under the best of circumstances; to be distracted meant courting certain death.

Concentrate! Do what Peter told you and get out alive!

Suddenly, just as Olivia and her father reached the landing, an ominous snap split through the cacophonous sound of the fire; there was barely time to think before part of the ceiling came raining down. Olivia jumped out of the way, pushed against her father, and sent them both tumbling down the remaining steps. Debris crashed all around them. Olivia's head and side ached from bumps she'd taken during the fall, but she pushed the pain away. Scrambling backward on her rear, she fought to escape. In horror, she realized that the hem of her skirt had caught fire and she swatted it out with her bare hands. Unwittingly, she sucked in a deep breath of smoke and began to gag. Her eyes watered. Panicked, she looked around for her father, but couldn't see him.

"Dad!" she tried to shout, but what came out sounded more like a wheeze.

Olivia grew more frightened. She strained to hear some sound, a sign that her father was nearby, but she couldn't make out anything over the fire. The smoke was so thick that she wasn't even certain what direction she faced.

She was so beside herself with worry that when a pair of hands grabbed her by the shoulders, she screamed.

Spinning around, she was shocked to find her mother kneeling beside her. Elizabeth's face was still streaked with sweat and grime, but there was something else there, too, an expression that Olivia had trouble recognizing; it was a look of genuine relief.

"We need to get out of here," her mother insisted.

"But . . . but Dad . . ." Olivia struggled to explain. "I don't know where he —"

"He's safe," Elizabeth cut her off. "Now, come on."

Taking her mother's hand, Olivia followed as Elizabeth led the way out of the burning house. As she ducked through the front doorway, the flames felt so close that she feared her hair would catch fire. They stumbled down the steps and onto the grass. Almost immediately, blankets were wrapped around her; Olivia looked up to see a few of their neighbors, woken from their slumber, each face wearing a look of sympathy. Down the darkened street, the fire truck rounded a corner and raced toward the house, its siren screaming high and loud.

Though Olivia knew she should've felt

some relief, there was none.

"We have to help Dad . . ." she insisted, trying to rise, but her mother placed a hand on her chest and held her down.

"I told you he's fine," Elizabeth answered.

Olivia followed her mother's eyes and saw her father lying on the grass. He was rolled over on his side, hacking and coughing, his whole body shaking. His nightclothes were filthy, his whole body soaked through with sweat. Billy knelt beside him. Suddenly, she understood; he must've grown worried and entered the house with her mother. Fortunately, they had stumbled upon her and her father when they needed them most. Billy must have carried John to safety.

When their eyes met, Olivia's filled with tears. In that moment, she couldn't have told Billy how sorry she was for hurting him the way that she had, nor could she have expressed how thankful she was for what he'd done. Because of their lifelong friendship, she hoped that he already knew.

But while Olivia was happy and relieved to know that her father had been carried to safety, fear still held her tight. Peter and Grace remained in grave danger. Struggling against her mother, ignoring her protests, Olivia managed to get back to her feet, intent on rushing back into the burning building. Billy did the same; she wondered if he could sense what she was about to do. But before either of them could move, fate intervened.

Before their eyes, the house began to crumble. With a groan, the roof fell in and sent a cloud of smoke and sparks billowing high into the night sky. Like a domino, the roof's collapse caused a wall on the upper floor to give way, tumbling inside to cause another deafening crash, and then yet another. Gasps rose from the gathered crowd.

Olivia was too horrified to scream. This wasn't a bad dream; it was real. No one could have survived what had just happened.

Peter and her sister were dead.

CHAPTER TWENTY-FIVE

Peter struggled to remain calm. Back in the barn, when debris had fallen, blocking the doors, there'd still been space to move around, to search for a way out, but inside Grace's small bedroom, it felt as if the walls were closing in. Broken and burning beams filled the doorway, leaving far too little room to try to squeeze through. Besides, if he were to push against the blockage, it might only cause a bigger collapse. They would need to find another way out.

But first, he needed to tend to Grace.

Ever since they had become trapped, Olivia's sister hadn't stopped screaming. Tears streaked through the dark soot and grime that dirtied her cheeks. She was beside herself with fear.

"Listen to me, Grace," Peter said firmly. He grabbed the girl and pulled her to him. Try as he might to hold her eyes, she kept moving them away, avoiding him. "Hold it together," he told her. "It's the only way we're going to get out of here."

Instead, Grace shivered so badly one might've thought she was freezing cold.

Leaving her, Peter began to search for another exit.

Opposite the impassable doorway was a pair of windows. The intense heat from the fire had cracked one of them; Peter kicked it out. Carefully sticking his head through the broken pane, he looked down. Silently, he cursed. The drop went all the way to the ground. A fall from that height could break both of their necks; he'd take the chance to avoid being burned alive, but only as a last resort.

Come on! There has to be something else!

Looking around the girl's room, he finally found it. There, above Grace's bed, was a smaller, crescent-shaped window. It wasn't big, but he thought that it'd be large enough for them to squeeze through. Peter jumped onto the bed and yanked it open. Pulling himself up, he glanced over the ledge. His heart jumped. There, about ten feet down, was the lower roof of the kitchen. They had a chance; now they had to take it.

Jumping down, Peter went to Grace. Olivia's sister was still sobbing; the look on her face said she'd given up.

"Grace!" he shouted. "Grace! Look at me!"

Reluctantly, the girl did as he said.

"Do you want to live?" he asked. When she didn't answer, he grabbed her by the shoulders and shook her. "Answer me!"

Shakily, Grace nodded.

"Tell me! Say that you want to survive this!"

"I . . . I . . . do . . ." she stuttered through tears.

Satisfied, Peter pulled her up onto the bed and to the window. Understanding what was about to happen, Grace slowed down, fighting against the current, but Peter pushed her on; since she'd come this far, it was too late for second thoughts. He lifted himself up and through the window, found some purchase on the short window frame, and leaned back inside, extending his hand toward Grace, who looked at it, unsure.

"Now!" he shouted.

Grace reacted as if he'd broken a trance and urgently grabbed hold. Effortlessly, he lifted her up and out. His intention had been to pause, get their bearings, and then jump when they were ready. Instead, Grace's wiggling knocked them off balance and before Peter knew it, they were plummeting toward the lower roof. Grace screamed the whole way down. When they landed, Peter hit hard enough to drive the air from his lungs. Beside him, Grace moaned in pain; he was elated that she was still alive.

But then he heard a sound that filled him with dread. It spread low, grumbling to life above them, back where they'd just been. Instantly, Peter understood that the roof was giving way. For all he knew, the whole house was going to collapse. They were still in danger.

Scrambling to his feet, Peter grabbed Grace's arm and yanked her up.

"Hold on tight!" he shouted.

Taking a couple of steps, they jumped off the roof. They hit the ground hard, tumbling in the dewy grass. When Peter finally stopped moving, he looked back at the Marstens' home. The back of the second floor, where Grace's bedroom was, gave way, dropping down onto the lower roof, smashing through and into the house. If they had been either place, they would be dead.

Instead, somehow, they were alive.

Olivia cried. Through a haze of tears, she stared at the wreckage of her family's home, unable to turn away. Everything had been reduced to a pile of still-burning rubble. It was all gone: the way the banister felt beneath her bare hand; the sunlight that streamed through the kitchen windows in the morning; the view from her favorite chair in the parlor. While the memories would remain, they could never be experienced again. New ones would be made.

But what could never be replaced were the lives of those she loved. Hours earlier, she'd made love to Peter, giving him her body and heart. Hearing his bombshell of a confession had muddied things between them, had caused her to run away in fear and confusion. But once he had caught up to her and further explained himself, she'd come to believe that they could find a solution. But now, just like that, he had been taken from her.

Peter and Grace were gone. Forever.

"Olivia." Billy had come to stand behind her. Gently, he placed his hand on her shoulder, but she shrugged herself away.

There was nothing for her to say.

But then, as Olivia started to wonder how she'd ever put the pieces of her life back together again, she saw something. There was a stirring at the edge of the crowd. People parted. Someone shouted.

The next thing Olivia knew, she was running. Weaving between her neighbors, she had to push a few of them out of her way. When she saw what it was that had attracted all of the attention, she could only stop and stare.

It was Peter and Grace.

They looked terrible, covered in sweat and soot. Her sister leaned heavily against Peter; she limped as she walked beside him. When Grace saw Olivia, she smiled weakly.

"I don't believe it!" Olivia shouted. "You're alive!"

Olivia took her sister in her arms. She held Grace close as they both sobbed, thankful to be together again. Eventually, someone pulled them apart; surprisingly, it was their mother. Elizabeth had tears in her eyes when she grabbed her younger daughter, with whom she'd argued more times than Olivia could count.

"Oh, my poor little girl," she soothed, stroking Grace's hair. "I can't begin to tell you how happy I am to see you."

"I . . . I . . . I was so scared . . ." her daughter cried.

"Hush now. It's all over. You're safe."

When Elizabeth led Grace away, Olivia turned to Peter. He stared back. Neither of them said a word. But then, the powerful emotions Olivia had been struggling to hold back burst through and she threw herself at him. Over and over, she kissed him; his mouth, his cheeks, and even the tip of his chin. It didn't matter that people were watching; she no longer cared whether her neighbors or Billy approved, so great was her relief that Peter was alive.

"I thought you were dead," Olivia said through her tears. "When the roof fell in, I thought that you and Grace were still inside . . ."

"You can't get rid of me that easily," he replied with a weary smile. "Besides, I promised you that I'd get them out, and I'm nothing if not a man of my word. Is your father all right?"

She nodded.

"Where is he?"

Olivia felt a growing sense of unease. "He's with Billy . . ."

"I need to talk to him."

She looked up at Peter; from his expression, Olivia could tell what he intended to do.

He was going to tell her father who he really was.

"You can't do that," Olivia said.

"I have to," Peter answered. He paused for a long moment. "This fire wasn't an accident."

416

Olivia gasped. "What?" she blurted. "It . . . it was set on purpose?"

He nodded. "I'm sure of it," Peter explained. "I know who did it. It's the man who escaped with me from the prison train. A man who hates America and everything it stands for. He's out for revenge. I'm certain that he's the one responsible for the other fires, too. He won't stop, not until he's dead. For that reason, I can't just stand by and do nothing. He has to be stopped."

Olivia's mind reeled. "But if you tell my father the truth, you'll be taken away."

"If that's the price I have to pay, then so be it. This is about more than me now. Someone could have died here tonight. If I do nothing, if I stand by and someone is hurt, I won't be able to live with myself."

"And I can't live without you."

Peter stared hard at her; what she'd said had touched him. Olivia knew that her words weren't just talk; they were the truth. Peter might be an escaped German prisoner of war, but he wasn't her enemy. She'd been wrong to assume that all Germans were the same as Hitler, that every soldier was like the ones she'd seen in the newsreels. Peter had risked his life to save her father and sister; if it wasn't for him, odds were high that both of them would now be dead.

"I love you, Olivia," he finally said, "but I can't stay silent. I have to tell your father who I really am."

"I don't want to lose you . . ."

"You won't. Not forever." Peter took her hands in his, quieting their trembling. "No matter what happens, I will find a way back to you. Nothing will stand in my way."

"You . . . you promise . . . ?"

Peter gave her a thin smile. "Trust me."

Olivia knew she didn't have a choice. Though it was hard, in the end she agreed. But she wouldn't let him go alone.

They would tell her father together.

"Is this your idea of a joke?"

John sat wearily on a chair in front of his workbench in the garage. Fortunately, the fire hadn't spread to the detached building; it was now the only thing the Marsten family had left that hadn't been destroyed. Outside the closed double doors, the fire still smoldered.

Olivia's father stared at Peter, while she and Billy stood off to the side, watching; her mother had taken Grace next door to Ruth Pollack's home to try to get some rest. It was an uncomfortable gathering; Olivia had hoped that Billy wouldn't try to tag along, but he had insisted. In the end, she'd

418

relented; soon enough, her former fiancé, as well as everyone else in town, would likely know everything Peter intended to reveal.

And that was just what he'd done.

Peter shook his head. "I know this isn't easy to hear," he said. "That it sounds unbelievable, but I assure you it's the truth."

"But . . . but if you're German . . . how do you speak English . . . ?"

"My father was born and raised in Pennsylvania, just like I told you. He went to fight in France, but unlike you, decided to stay behind. He moved to Germany and soon met my mother. He was the one who taught me."

John turned to look at his daughter. "Did you know?"

"Not until tonight," she admitted.

"I knew it!" Billy suddenly exclaimed, his voice full of anger and disgust. Until that moment, he had been stone silent. Now his face was creased by an angry snarl. "I knew something wasn't right with him, but I never would have guessed that he was a Nazi!"

"No, he isn't!" Olivia shouted.

"He's a German soldier. He's the enemy!"

"Peter just saved my father and my sister's lives! If he was the villain you claim him to be, why would he bother?"

While Olivia and Billy bickered, neither

Peter nor John said a word. The sheriff watched the former prisoner intently. In the short time that they had known each other, a bond had formed between the two men. Olivia's father had always considered himself to be a strong judge of character. Because he'd believed Peter to be a good man, he had gone out of his way to help him, especially with the apartment. He struggled to think that it had been based on a lie.

"This is why you said what you did about the war, isn't it?" John asked. "You weren't in a rush to fight because you already knew what it meant."

"Yes, sir."

John frowned as he rubbed his temples. "If this isn't the damndest problem I've ever faced, I sure as hell don't know what is."

"It was never my intention to hide this from you. When I first came to town, I was on my way to see you, to admit to who I was and what I had done, to surrender," Peter explained. "But then I met Olivia . . ."

"And Sylvester Eddings hit you with his truck," the sheriff finished.

Peter nodded.

"That still doesn't explain why he didn't fess up when he came to," Billy interjected. "What's your excuse for that?"

"He fell in love with me."

Everyone turned to look at Olivia. She had spoken without thinking; maybe she should have been embarrassed to say the truth so bluntly, but she wasn't. Listening to Billy digging at Peter, clinging to the notion that he was their enemy, infuriated her. The result was that she'd hurt him yet again; Billy held her eyes for only an instant before quickly looking away.

"Is that what happened?" John asked.

"It is," Peter answered. "My feelings for Olivia made me behave selfishly. I started to wonder if I couldn't just go on living the lie I'd created. I considered being Peter Baird for the rest of my life." He paused, his jaw tightening. "But now, after all of you nearly dying, I realize that I no longer have a choice. I have to face up to who I am."

"Why? What do the fires have to do with it?"

Peter glanced at Olivia; she took a deep breath. "They were set on purpose," he replied. "And I know who did it."

In detail, Peter explained exactly the sort of man Otto Speer was. He recounted his excesses on the battlefield. He told of how he'd taken pleasure in antagonizing their guards. He spoke of the vengeance the Nazi swore to inflict upon Americans. He even

admitted that he'd thought his fellow escapee had moved on until he'd made the
grim discovery of his broken cuffs up at the
cabin.

"He's behind all of this, I'm sure of it,"
Peter said. "I'll gladly accept whatever
punishment I have coming once Otto is
stopped. But until then, I want to do my
part to help capture him."

Olivia watched her father closely. She
wondered if he would be able to accept
Peter's offer. She thought of his lifelong
hatred of Germans, of the bitterness that
had been forged on the muddy battlefields
of France. Could he overcome decades of
bad feelings? Would he even want to try?
Though Peter had admitted lying to him,
could her father see past that and trust the
man who had saved his life, as well as those
of both of his daughters?

For his part, Billy had already made up
his mind.

"You can't possibly be considering this!"
he argued incredulously. "For all we know,
they're working together. It could be a trap!"

Olivia held her tongue, fearful of what she
might say.

John seemed hesitant. "Do you know
where to find him?"

"Maybe," Peter answered. "I know how

he thinks."

"He'll fight?"

"The only way to stop Otto will be to kill him."

More silence. Finally, John got up out of his chair. "We'll do it your way," he said, raising his hand to silence Billy's coming objection, "but when it's over, you'll have to turn yourself in. I'll have to call the Army. Is that acceptable?"

Peter nodded. Olivia shivered.

"All right then. Let's go find our man."

The wind that whipped through the open passenger's window was cold, but Peter made no move to roll it up; after fighting his way through a second fire, he wondered if he'd ever forget the feel of flame near his skin. John drove quickly through the darkened streets, cutting sharp turns as his hands gripped the steering wheel tightly. It was almost three o'clock in the morning.

After leaving the Marstens' garage, they'd gone to the police station. There, John had tried to call Huck, but he hadn't answered. Frustrated, he'd decided to drive over to the deputy's house, but had asked Olivia and Billy to stay behind. Peter had understood; the sheriff didn't want to let the escaped German prisoner out of his sight, but he also wasn't comfortable with the idea of leaving Peter alone with his daughter.

"Why burn down *my* house?" John asked, turning to follow the creek.

"I suppose it was because your police car was parked outside. Otto would want to strike at whatever authority he could find."

"Like on the battlefield. Take out the head and the body follows."

"Exactly," Peter agreed. "The first two fires he set were a matter of feeling things out, wanting to give people a reason to be afraid. Now that he's started, Otto won't stop until the whole town is nothing but a pile of ashes."

For a while, they drove in silence. Peter stared out the window. The sun wouldn't begin to peek over the horizon for a couple more hours, so darkness prevailed. He couldn't have known exactly where, but Otto was out there somewhere, planning his next attack.

"It bothers me that I can't raise Huck," the sheriff said.

"He's probably just asleep," Peter suggested.

"Maybe," John said without any conviction.

Pulling into Huck's driveway, John parked his police car right behind the deputy's; Peter saw the way the sheriff's jaw tightened at the sight of it. Huck's house was dark and silent, like everyone else's on the block. They got out of the car and went to the side door. John had his hand on the butt of his pistol. He rapped hard on the frame twice, waited, and then knocked again.

Nothing. The hair on the back of Peter's neck stood on end.

Olivia's father turned the knob and pulled the door open on squeaky hinges. Peter followed him inside. Instantly, he knew what had happened.

It smelled like death.

There was a time when Peter wouldn't have known about what happens to a man when he passes on. But then he had gone to war. Civilians and soldiers suffered the same fate. Initially, the smell had nauseated him, but as time passed, he'd slowly grown used to it. Still, it was unforgettable.

John recognized it, too. He turned on a light in Huck's living room and stopped, staring at the unmoving, lifeless form of his friend. Peter backed out of the room, giving the man some privacy.

When John stepped back outside, he'd managed to compose himself.

"I'm sorry," Peter offered, though he knew it wasn't much.

"Not as sorry as that son-of-a-bitch is going to be."

Together, they drove back into the night.

CHAPTER TWENTY-SIX

Well into the afternoon, they continued to search for Otto. After John and Peter had returned to the police station, the sheriff had organized dozens of men from Miller's Creek and the surrounding countryside. They were all older, some wrinkled grandfathers, many with sons fighting overseas. John spread out a map and directed groups on where to search. Peter had described the man they were looking for and what he'd done; when it was announced that he was an escaped Nazi, the men gasped and began to talk angrily. When someone asked about Huck, the sheriff had fallen silent; everyone instantly understood, giving the whole operation a greater sense of urgency.

Together, they had tramped up and down the hills surrounding town, worked their way through narrow gullets, checked behind outcroppings of rock, peered into ditches and drainage pipes, and tramped back and forth across the creek. They walked down the railroad tracks and through the depot, throwing open every rail car. They searched abandoned buildings like the cabin in which Peter and Otto had first sought shelter. On the opposite side of town, high in the hills, a group had come across the remnants of a campfire, but it hadn't been used for days. All morning, they searched high and low, leaving no stone unturned.

But no one saw Otto.

"Do you suppose he's run?" John asked Peter.

"No. He'll stay and do as much damage as he can before we catch up to him. Otto is many things, but he's not a coward. He's not afraid of dying."

With an unseasonably hot sun beating down on them, John gave his volunteers a break for lunch. Some of the men went home while others trudged into Goslee's Diner. Peter went to look for Olivia.

Back at the police station, Peter found some of the men looking over the map, marking off the areas they'd already checked. Olivia was at the stove, pouring cups of coffee. She looked out on her feet; her hair was a tangled mess, her face still streaked with soot, while dark circles hung beneath her eyes. She hadn't slept all night;

none of them had. When she saw him, she managed a weak smile.

"Any luck?" she asked.

"No, not yet. You should go and try to get some sleep."

Olivia shook her head. "There's too much work to be done. I can rest all I want after he's been caught. I can't walk away now, not after what he did to Huck . . ." Her voice faded as she struggled to hold back tears.

Peter took her hand. "We'll catch him."

"It's . . . it's just that . . ."

"Why don't you go over to the apartment and close your eyes for a while. As soon as you're rested, you can come back."

He thought that Olivia was going to disagree, to continue to insist that she was fine, but her shoulders slumped and she nodded wearily.

"Maybe you're right."

"Let me walk you over there and you can —"

"I'll take her."

Peter turned to see Billy push himself up and out of a chair beside the jail cells; he hadn't noticed the man when he came in. Olivia's friend looked as tired as everyone else, but either stubbornness or worry kept him at his former fiancée's side. When he reached Olivia, he put a protective hand on her arm and pulled her away from Peter; her hand slipped from his, too tired to resist.

"Billy . . ." she began.

"I'm not leaving you alone with him," he argued. "Not for a second."

"It's all right," Peter replied, knowing that this was neither the time nor the place for an argument. "I just want you to get some rest."

Olivia nodded and let Billy lead her toward the door. But then, only a few feet away, she pulled her arm free from his grip and returned to Peter. Rising up onto her tiptoes, she kissed him, a gentle touch that lingered for a few dozen fevered beats of his heart. When she pulled away, she smiled at him.

"For luck," she explained.

Watching her leave as Billy frowned, scarcely able to contain his growing jealousy, Peter figured that he just might need it.

Olivia knew that it had been impetuous to kiss Peter, that it would only make Billy more irritable, but she was too tired to care. As they walked silently down the street, she considered everything that had happened over the last twenty-four hours; the war in Europe had ended, she'd made love with

Peter, her family's house had been burned to the ground, and poor Huck had been murdered. Worst of all was the realization that as soon as Otto was apprehended, Peter was going to be taken away from her.

"What is your father thinking?" Billy complained, his hands stuffed down deep into his pockets. "He had that *German* standing up there in front of everyone, acting like he was one of us! They should lock him up and throw away the key."

Olivia sighed; the weight of her friend's criticisms had finally become more than she could bear. She'd had enough. Stopping in the middle of the sidewalk, she turned to face him. "I know that this is hard for you, Billy," she said. "Seeing me fall in love with someone else. But you need to stop being so angry. You need to accept that Peter isn't the villain you want him to be."

"How can you defend him? He's an escaped prisoner!"

"Who saved my life. My father and sister, too."

Billy finally faltered. "Olivia . . ." he muttered, his face pained. What he wanted was for time to rewind itself, to before Peter Becker had become a part of their lives. But that wasn't possible. It had happened whether he liked it or not. "I just don't want to see you hurt."

"I won't be," she reassured him.

"You don't know that. Not for certain."

"Who does?" she asked him. "Sometimes, in order to be happy, you have to take a chance. That's what you did when you asked me to marry you. In the end, because I was too much of a coward to be honest, you paid the price. For Peter and me, the die hasn't been cast. Maybe you're right. Maybe Peter will go to prison or be shipped back to Germany. But if I don't try to make it work, if I don't trust in him now, I'll spend the rest of my life wondering about what might have been."

"That sounds awfully familiar," he said with a frown.

Olivia stepped closer and kissed him softly on the cheek. "I will always love you, Billy Tate," she told him. "You know, I've thought an awful lot about something you said the day you proposed."

"What was that?"

"That you didn't want to do anything to damage our friendship."

"Turns out I was right to be worried. I've ruined it."

"No, you haven't," Olivia disagreed. "Things might never be the same, but that doesn't mean we can't still be there for each

other like always."

"Do you really think so?" Billy asked.

"I do. At the very least, it's worth a try."

Slowly, Billy began to smile.

The rest of the walk to Peter's apartment was better, lighter now that they had unburdened themselves. Tired, Olivia opened the door, ready for some much-needed sleep. The apartment was darker than it was outside so it took her eyes a moment to adjust. When they did, she almost screamed.

There, glaring at her, was a man with a gun.

Olivia had no doubt who was standing before her; it was Otto, the man who had escaped the prison train with Peter, the bastard who'd murdered Huck and burned down her family's house. He was physically intimidating; muscular and menacing, he scowled at her, his eyes narrow. The pistol was gripped tightly in his hand, its barrel pointed right at her. When Billy followed her inside, as unsuspecting as she had been, he froze, just as shocked.

"Rien hier! Mach schnell!" the man barked; Olivia didn't understand a word he'd said, but the meaning was clear. She and Billy raised their hands and shuffled away as Otto came over to them. He quickly looked

outside, then frowned before shutting the door.

"Wo ist Becker? Warum ist er nicht bei euch?" Otto asked. He stepped close to Olivia, the smell of his sweat thick. Leeringly, his eyes roamed up and down her body. *"Bist du ihm schon zuviel geworden, du Hure?"*

"Leave her alone," Billy warned, though there wasn't much steel in his voice.

Otto sneered cruelly, a disturbing sight.

"What are you going to do with us?" Billy continued.

"Halt's Maul, Amerikaner," the Nazi soldier growled menacingly.

Though it was clear that his words were meant to be threatening, Billy didn't take the hint; Olivia could plainly see that he was trying to protect her. "You'll never get away with what you've done," he kept on. "We've already beaten your damned Führer! When they catch you, they'll —"

Faster than Olivia would ever have expected, Otto raised his pistol and whipped the hard steel across Billy's face. Her friend crumpled into a heap, unconscious before he even hit the floor. The only thing that kept Olivia from screaming was the fear Otto inspired in her.

"Richtig so, Hure," he smirked. *"Halt's Maul*

oder dir passiert das Gleiche!"

Olivia shut her eyes and prayed. She'd never been so frightened in all her life. *This* was the nightmare she'd dreamed of all those years before.

How was she ever going to wake up?

"All right then, I want Phil and Walter to go check that shack northwest of Alice Palmer's place. It's small and worn enough that it'd collapse in a stiff breeze, but we're gonna look it over anyway. Mike and Ben, you go to the embankment where Baker's Road meets the highway and snoop around under the bridge. The water's low this time of year, so there shouldn't be . . ."

Peter listened absently as John explained the next steps in the search for Otto. After Olivia and Billy had left, the sheriff had approached him and asked his thoughts about where the Nazi could be. After some brainstorming and a close inspection of the map, those plans were now being put into action. Still, something nagged at Peter's thoughts, as if there was a clue he was missing, just out of reach.

Ever since the fire, he'd been trying to think like Otto, to remember their shared experiences and training. Where would he go? What things would he require in order to stay alive? What risks would he be willing to take? It was like trying to put together a puzzle, only he didn't have all the pieces. Desperation began to gnaw at him; he knew that the longer it took to catch Otto, the greater the risk that someone else would die.

Right this instant . . . where are you . . . ?

When the meeting broke up, the men began to head for the destinations they'd been given. John came over to Peter. "You and I are going to head down to the old flour mill," he explained. "There are a bunch of small caves notched into the rock wall to the south of the creek. It'd be awful hard to get in and out of there, but with this guy, anything seems possible."

On their way to the car, the sheriff added, "You know, I may not like everything you've done, the lies and all, but I'm still glad you're with us."

"I just want him caught," Peter said.

"We'll find him. If anyone knows how this guy thinks, it's you."

The truth hit Peter like a punch to the gut. After the two lawmen in Miller's Creek, *he* was Otto's biggest threat. If the bloodthirsty Nazi was going to inflict the most damage possible, removing his fellow soldier and escapee was the surest means to that end.

It was obvious to Peter that Otto had been around town enough to have identified John and Huck. He'd followed them home, waited for just the right moment, and then struck. Who was to say that Otto hadn't done the same with him? It wasn't as if he'd been trying to hide himself; he thought about his walks with Olivia and eating at the diner with both her and her father. If Otto had seen him, then stayed out of sight to watch his comings and goings, then that likely meant that he knew where he was staying. If he knew where the apartment was . . .

Olivia!

Peter started running. An icy chill raced through him. He was only a couple blocks away. Behind him, John shouted his name and then started to follow; Peter didn't bother to turn around. He pushed himself as hard as he could.

He might have sent the woman he loved straight into the hands of a madman.

Otto stepped closer to Becker's woman, causing her to shrink away. Her discomfort pleased him, so he did it again. Her fearful eyes stole a glance at him, but quickly looked away. She was attractive to him, in a harlot sort of way; he imagined what it would be like to see her as the traitor undoubtedly had, naked and vulnerable. Possibilities filled his thoughts; maybe after he'd slit his former companion's throat from ear to ear, there might be time for him to have a little pleasure.

"You will never forget this day," he told her.

The sound of his voice made her flinch. While the woman didn't understand a word he said, she had no trouble grasping the meaning. Her fear was delicious. Surely she knew that he was the one who had lit the fire that killed her family. His only regret was that he couldn't tell her about it in excruciating detail.

Absently, Otto looked at the man he'd pistol-whipped. Who was he? Probably a Jew. Annoying and weak, both at the same time; if every American man was as pathetic, it'd only be a matter of time before Germany's fortunes turned and the war would be won in the Fatherland's favor. Still, he'd wanted Becker.

"Where is he? Where is your lover?" Otto growled at the trembling woman. "Why are you here without him? Is he meeting you?"

He was growing frustrated. When he'd left

the fire, he had thought about retreating to his hiding spot in the hills outside town. He would plan another attack and execute it the following night. But then he'd had a moment of inspiration. He knew where Becker lived. All he had to do was go there and lie in wait. Eventually, the bastard would return, either alone or with the woman. Murdering them both would have been a pleasure.

"Did he tell you who he was? Did he tell you that he's a traitor?!"

Otto knew that his temper was beginning to get the better of him. He would have to act soon. Maybe he should have his way with the whore now, kill her, and leave her broken body for Becker to find. Then he could —

Suddenly, he heard footsteps racing up the stairs.

Quickly, he grabbed Becker's woman and clamped a hand over her mouth; he couldn't let her shout a warning. Clutching the pistol tightly, he dragged her away from the door. When the knob began to turn, he was excited.

The moment Peter whipped open the door to his apartment, he realized that he'd made a terrible mistake. There, standing ten feet away, was Otto, with a pistol pointed straight at him. Billy lay on the floor to his right, unmoving; Peter wondered if he was still alive. To make matters worse, the brute had Olivia. Taking the steps two at a time, Peter had been so preoccupied about making certain she was safe that he hadn't stopped to consider what to do if she wasn't. Barging in the door, he'd placed himself at Otto's mercy.

His heart pounded and his chest heaved. The sweat that slicked his body grew cold. At any moment, he expected a bullet to tear into him, but much to his surprise, nothing happened. Otto's sneer grew wider.

"Traitor!" he growled.

"Let her go," Peter replied; he had been speaking English for so long that German sounded strangely odd to his ears. "She doesn't have anything to do with this."

"The hell she doesn't! You turned your back on who you are, on your Führer and your nation, all for this slut! You decided that these people, *these Amerikaners,* are more important, and for that, she will pay!"

Peter's mind raced as he desperately searched for a way out that would spare Olivia's life. She stared at him wide-eyed and frightened; any doubts she might have had about the truth to Peter's story had surely vanished the moment he spoke German. Silently, he swore that he wouldn't let anything happen to her, even if it ended up costing him his life.

"Listen to me, Otto," he began calmly. "The war is over. Germany surrendered yesterday. Surely you heard everyone cheering. There's no longer any reason to fight."

His words shook Otto; the man's sneer faltered but the anger quickly returned. "Lies!" he exploded. "That . . . that was the Japanese!"

Peter shook his head. "It's the truth."

But instead of defusing the situation as Peter had hoped, his revelation only enraged Otto further. The murderer trembled with fury and his hand squeezed Olivia so hard that Peter saw the pain in her eyes. The barrel of the man's gun shook but never turned away from Peter's chest.

"This is a trick!" Otto hissed through clenched teeth. "You're trying to make me believe something that isn't real! Hitler would never give up! The German Reich is meant to last for a thousand years! It has to!"

Suddenly, before Peter could say another word to try to calm Otto down, he heard a sound that sent shivers racing up his spine.

There were footsteps outside on the stairs.

Instantly, Peter knew that it was John. It had to be; the sheriff had followed him to the apartment. Indecision filled him. He stood a couple of feet inside the apartment's door, so John wouldn't see him until it was too late. If he yelled out, Otto would know what was happening. It could cost them all their lives. But if he stayed silent, if he didn't try to warn Olivia's father, they were no safer.

No matter what he did, the end was coming.

When Peter had first burst through the door of the apartment, Olivia had experienced a strange mix of both fear and hope. She was going to be rescued! But now, still held in Otto's fierce grip, with the Nazi's rage becoming even more unstable, she wondered if either of them would survive.

But she never would have expected what happened next.

Suddenly, her father stood behind Peter. He looked winded and sweaty, his face colored a bright red. When he saw Olivia, his eyes widened and his hand reached for the gun holstered at his waist. But he was too slow. Otto squeezed the trigger and his pistol fired, bucking slightly in his hand. In the small space, the sound was deafening.

The bullet tore into her father's shoulder, sent him spinning sideways, and forced him to drop his weapon, which fell with a clatter at his feet.

Olivia should have screamed, but didn't. Instead, she saw this as the only chance they were going to get. Pulling back her elbow, she drove it into Otto's stomach as hard as she could. It wasn't much, it felt like she was hitting a brick wall, but it was enough to stagger him; his grip loosened just enough for her to break free.

As soon as she hit Otto, Peter moved, trying to close the gap between them. Startled, the Nazi managed to fire off another round, but his balance had been thrown off and the shot went wild, hitting the wall beside the door. An instant later, Peter's fist slammed into his jaw. Otto reeled backward with Peter right after him. The two men crashed into Olivia, knocking her to the floor.

Otto shouted in German, spittle flying from his mouth.

Peter didn't say a word, his face determined.

Grabbing the wrist that held the pistol, Peter raised it toward the ceiling. Otto strained against him, but Peter held on strongly, the muscles on his arm standing out. Peter forced the other man back, driving him into the wall. In retaliation, the snarling Nazi threw a short punch that connected with the side of Peter's head, stunning him; still, he hung on tight, refusing to let go. In their struggle, another bullet was fired, hitting the ceiling.

While the two men fought, Olivia hurried over to her father. John lay on his back, half in the sunlight, his fingers pressed against his shoulder; blood seeped between them, darkening his shirt. His face was a twisted mask of pain.

"Dad!" Olivia shouted.

"Don't . . . don't worry none about me . . ." John mumbled. "Just go get help . . . it's our only hope . . ."

But Olivia stayed where she was. She couldn't leave Peter, Billy, and her father, not when all of their lives hung in the balance.

The brawl continued, growing in ferocity. Peter barely avoided a punch before bringing his knee up into Otto's ribs, causing the murderer to grunt in pain. Moments later, either in desperation or as a roughhouse tactic, the Nazi drove the crown of his head into Peter's face. Blood spurted from his nose. Peter wobbled, shaken. Otto lashed out and succeeded in knocking him to the floor. With his gun hand finally free, he grinned maliciously as he began to lower the weapon.

Without thinking, Olivia began to run right at him. Otto had been so focused on Peter that he didn't notice her until she was practically on top of him. She crashed into him as hard as she could; though it wasn't enough to topple him, he staggered.

"Hure!" he shouted, cursing her in German.

With his bare hand, he struck Olivia in the face and sent her sprawling. His eyes brimmed with hate as he began to turn the pistol toward her.

But Olivia's desperate act had borne fruit; before the barrel could reach her, Peter was back in the fight. He landed a blow to Otto's stomach, causing him to double over, and then threw another punch to the man's chin. With both hands, Peter again grabbed for the gun. Instead of pointing straight up as it had before, the pistol stayed low, between them. Grunting and groaning, each man struggled for an advantage. The gun fired again, sending pieces of wood flying from the floorboards.

Slowly, the gun's barrel began to rise. Olivia held her breath; Otto and Peter wrestled so violently that she couldn't tell

who it was aimed at. When the pistol dis-
charged, Olivia shrieked in fear. For a long
moment, neither man moved. The smell of
gun smoke filled the kitchen. Then, suddenly, Otto collapsed to his knees. The hand
that had gripped the pistol slowly slipped
off. The other was pressed against his
stomach; when he pulled it away, he stared
disbelievingly at the wet mess of blood that
stained it. Otto slowly looked up at Peter;
his mouth opened but no sound came out.
Then, he tipped over onto his back, dead.

"Peter," Olivia said through her tears,
rushing to him.

He enveloped her in his arms and held
her close. When he saw that he was still
holding the pistol, he threw it away, sending
it skittering across the floor. Peppering her
cheeks with kisses, he tried to speak.

"I . . . I thought that . . . I was afraid that
I might . . ." but the emotion of the moment was too great for him to continue.

"You saved me," she told him.

Suddenly, her father groaned; they ran to
him and Peter checked the wound.

"We need to get the doctor," he said to
John, then looked over to where Billy still
lay on the floor, "for the both of you."

"I'll go," Olivia said.

She was about to take the first step down

446

to the street when she stopped and looked back. Peter's eyes found hers and words passed between them unspoken.

One nightmare might have ended, but another was about to begin.

Olivia went for help.

Three days later, soldiers from the United States Army arrived in Miller's Creek. When they opened the door to the police station, John, Peter, and Olivia were waiting for them. In the aftermath of Otto's rampage, Olivia had hoped that another solution could be found, anything that meant Peter wouldn't be taken away from her. But in the end, it was Peter himself who decided that he should surrender, just as he'd intended weeks earlier.

The two soldiers looked as if they meant business; Olivia wasn't as unsettled by their impassive faces as she was by the sidearms they wore. One of them began to ask John questions. The sheriff had been stitched up and bandaged, yet was still sore and weary. Elizabeth had argued that he should stay in bed, but John had insisted on being there for Peter's sake.

The other soldier walked over to Peter.

"Hold out your hands," he said.

Peter did as he was told and had handcuffs

snapped around both of his wrists. The cinching sound of the metal made Olivia's skin crawl.

"It's all right," Peter tried to reassure her. "I'm leaving town in much the same way I arrived."

Olivia had to look away to keep from breaking down.

Soon, everything was settled. Peter would be going to the same internment camp to which he'd originally been assigned. One of the soldiers grabbed Peter's elbow and started toward the door. They'd only gone a few steps when John stopped them.

"If it's all right with you gentlemen, I'd like to give the two of them a moment together," the sheriff said, nodding toward Peter and Olivia. "Why don't we step out-side and have a smoke. One for the road, and all that."

The two soldiers looked at each other, and then agreed. As Olivia watched them leave, she knew that they didn't have long.

"I keep thinking that this is just a bad dream," she began, a tear sliding down her cheek. "How can this be happening?"

Tenderly, Peter raised his cuffed hands and wiped away her tear with his thumb. "This is the only way."

"But why? The war is over! You shouldn't

be a prisoner anymore!"

"I can't change who I am, where I come from, or what I've done," he explained. "And the truth is, I wouldn't want to. Because I was a soldier, captured on a battlefield, I was brought to America. From there I survived a train crash, escaped into a storm chained to a lunatic, and made my way here. I was a fugitive on the run, the enemy. But if I could do it all over again, I wouldn't change a thing. If I hadn't made those choices, I never would have met you."

"But it's so unfair," Olivia answered, the tears now falling too fast to be wiped away. "I've waited my whole life for you, but now that you're here, now that I've finally found happiness, you're being taken away."

"This isn't forever," Peter said, tilting her head up so that he could look into her eyes, his handcuffs jingling. "I'm coming back. No matter how long it takes, no matter what I have to do, I promise you that we will be together."

With that, he leaned down and kissed her. It began softly, but its passion grew. Olivia felt as if she was pouring out her heart, trying to show him that she, too, was thankful that their lives had intersected, even if for a short time. When it ended, she opened her eyes to find him smiling at her.

"I love you, Olivia Marsten," he said.

"And I love you, Peter Becker," she answered, using his real last name.

There was a knock on the door. "Time's up," one of the soldiers said as he leaned inside.

Peter started for the door but Olivia didn't move; just the thought of watching him being driven away was almost enough to break her heart in two; there was no way she could actually see it happen. Just before he stepped outside, he stopped and turned back to look at her, sunlight streaming through his blond hair.

"I'll be back," he told her.

When the door closed behind him, the only sound in the police station came from Olivia's sobs.

EPILOGUE

January 1946

Olivia stood beside her father inside the train depot. Outside, the cold winter wind raced down the tracks, battered against the building, and shook the doors that led to the platform. Snow swirled into drifts. Frost covered the windows. Their breath clouded in front of their faces. Other than the woman behind the ticket counter absently reading a paperback, they were the only people there.

"What time is it?" Olivia asked.

"About two minutes since the last time you pestered me," John answered.

"I just worry that he'll be late."

"The schedule says 11:18. You've still got ten minutes to go."

With a frown, Olivia went over to the window and looked down the rails, hoping that her father had been mistaken, that the train would be chugging toward her, carry-

451

ing the man she loved.

Today was the day Peter was coming back to her.

Eight months earlier, the moment he had been driven away by the soldiers, Olivia had wondered if she would ever see him again. That first night, she had prayed for his release. Her father had decided to do more than that. In his position as Miller's Creek's sheriff, John had written letters and made telephone calls to anyone he thought could help; congressmen, military personnel, and his fellow law enforcement officials had all been contacted. When one lead resulted in failure, he tried another. In the end, he had enough clout to be heard. Over and over, he explained what Peter had done, not shying away from the man's deceptions, but also detailing how Peter had risked his life by rushing into two raging fires, including one which saved the life of John and his family. He emphasized the role Peter had played in stopping Otto's bloody rampage. Finally, after months of persistence, John had helped to secure Peter's release.

While they had waited, life had gone on.

Huck's funeral had been heartbreaking; even in the celebratory aftermath of the war in Europe's end, the town had been deeply saddened by the loss of their beloved deputy.

When Sylvester Eddings had stood beside Huck's grave and delivered an impromptu eulogy for a man with whom he'd often argued, there hadn't been a dry eye in the crowd. Olivia knew that her father still missed his friend, though John rarely talked about it.

As for the other person who had died that fateful May day, Olivia had no idea what had happened to Otto's body; she hoped that it had been tossed in an unmarked hole in the ground and forgotten.

"What time —"

"Olivia," her father scolded.

It took every ounce of willpower she had not to look out the window again.

Billy had gone to his naval training in Chicago as scheduled. But before he could ship out, the Japanese had surrendered and the war ended; the scene in Miller's Creek that afternoon had been every bit as euphoric as the one in May. Billy returned, disappointed yet safe, and resumed his duties at the bank, though Olivia felt that things between them never truly recovered; just as Billy had feared, their relationship had changed. They still talked, had lunch at Goslee's Diner, but Olivia saw the way he occasionally looked at her, longingly, as if he was about to request she give him one more chance. To his credit, he hadn't. Sadly, his love had come full circle, once again locked behind closed doors. For her part, Olivia never mentioned Peter in Billy's presence, though he was always in her thoughts.

Her father was the first to see the train. "There it is," he said.

Olivia looked up. The engine's light shone through the snowflakes as it dragged its cars to the depot. She'd been so lost in thought that her attention had wandered from the tracks.

Peter!

Olivia's heart pounded. It was hard for her to believe that all of the months she had spent trying not to get her hopes up, preparing herself for a different outcome, were finally coming to an end. That morning, she'd tried on countless outfits, looking for the one that was just right, turning one way and then the other in her mirror, but now she worried that she'd made a poor choice, fearing that he wouldn't find her as beautiful as he once had.

"Well, I'll be," John said, checking his pocket watch. "Looks like they're a couple minutes early. I hope this leaves your mother with enough time to get supper ready. If it doesn't, I reckon I'll get blamed for it," he said with a chuckle.

There was a time Olivia would have agreed with her father, but not now.

After their home had been burned down by Otto, the Marstens had rebuilt. Because of John's position and popularity in town, there had been so many volunteers that help had been turned away. Elizabeth had been right in the thick of things, distributing both lemonade and words of encouragement to friends and neighbors. The experience seemed to have changed her for the better. Though she could still be judgmental and short with her daughters, there was more genuine warmth and affection as well. Nowhere was this more evident than in her relationship with Grace. The fire had changed Olivia's sister; the rambunctious girl had grown up a bit. She still preferred spending her days tromping through mud puddles looking for frogs, but nowadays Grace was always clean and on time when meals were served.

Strangely, chaos had brought order to Olivia's family.

Before the train had shuddered to a stop, clouds of steam hissing as the engine settled, Olivia was already outside. The wind was bitterly cold, making her blond hair swirl around her shoulders, but she paid it no mind. She ran along the platform and peered into windows, hoping for a glimpse. But then, two cars ahead of her, Peter stepped down the stairs. He wore a dark peacoat turned up at the collar and a duffel bag was slung over his shoulder; ironically, Olivia's first thought was that he looked just like a soldier returning from war. He turned toward her; when he saw her, he smiled.

Unable to control her happiness, Olivia hurried to him as tears began to fall down her cheeks. Before she reached him, Peter dropped the bag at his feet, then swooped her into his arms, holding her tight as he swung around in a circle.

"I can't believe it!" she cried into the crook of his neck. "I can't believe that you're here!"

"I made a promise to you," he said, setting her down. "And I've kept it."

Olivia rose up and kissed him. It was sweet, tender in all the right ways, something that had been many long months in coming, and it nearly made her swoon. Everything about him was as she remembered it; how he looked, his smell, the sound of his voice, the way his lips felt pressed against hers.

No, it was *better.*

Once she was certain where Peter was, Olivia had begun to write him letters. Every night, she sat down with paper and pen to tell him about her day and how badly she missed him. Slowly, a few letters had trickled her way in return. He never burdened her with the life he faced in the camp, but instead he asked questions about her family, encouraged her to stay positive, and above all else, told her how much he loved her. Unfortunately, not all of Peter's news had been good.

In November, Peter had learned that his mother had passed away back in Germany. Fortunately, she had died peacefully in her sleep rather than in a bombing raid or some vindictive Nazi act. Peter was sad to have lost her, but saw it as another sign that his life was to have a new beginning.

"Look at you," he said, rubbing the redness that colored Olivia's cheeks. "You must be freezing."

"I'm fine," she replied. "For the first time in far too long, I'm fine."

"You're more beautiful than I remember."

Olivia blushed.

Peter smiled. "So much time has passed since I saw you last that I can't take my eyes off you. I want this moment to go on forever."

"It will," she said, and meant it with all of her heart.

Once Peter's release had been granted, the process had begun to formalize his new citizenship; because his father had been an American and a veteran, they hoped it wouldn't take long to be granted. But Olivia was impatient; she wanted them to be married sooner rather than later. Whenever she thought about their future, of the children she hoped to have and the incredible story she and Peter would someday tell them, Olivia was filled with wonder.

"You look just like I remember," John said warmly as he shook Peter's hand. "Seems like only yesterday you were here."

"It feels a lot longer to me, I'm afraid."

"I reckon it would."

"I want to thank you, sir," Peter said. "For everything that you did."

"Don't worry," Olivia's father replied with a smile. "I might just have a way for you to repay me."

John was still in need of a deputy. After Huck's death, the sheriff had made do with a ragtag group of part-timers, but hadn't hired anyone on a more permanent basis; Olivia suspected that her father held out hope of Peter's someday taking the position. Once his paperwork was finished, they'd just have to see.

While John went to get the car, Olivia

458

stood with Peter inside the depot. Since she'd first thrown herself into his arms, Olivia had yet to let him go. She also hadn't stopped smiling; it was as if she could finally exhale.

"I love you, Olivia."

She looked up to find Peter staring at her; his expression was serious, yet warm, even a bit playful. Olivia thought about all that had happened, about the accident that had brought them together, the adventure that they had shared, and especially the romance that had bloomed from it. She even thought about his deception. "You're not lying to me, are you?" she asked.

Peter grinned. "I may not have always told you the truth about my life," he said, "but I have never lied about my feelings for you, and I never will."

"Do you promise?"

Gently, he kissed her forehead. "With all my heart."

And that was just fine with her.

SPECIAL THANKS

To Ulrike Carlson for all of her help with the German language. It is truly wonderful to have a dear friend who is a native speaker.

ABOUT THE AUTHOR

Dorothy Garlock is one of America's — and the world's — favorite novelists. Her work consistently appears on national best-seller lists, including the *New York Times* list, and there are over fifteen million copies of her books in print translated into eighteen languages. She has won more than twenty writing awards, including an *RT Book Reviews* Reviewers' Choice Award for Best Historical Fiction for *A Week from Sunday,* five Silver Pen Awards from *Affaire de Coeur,* and three Silver Certificate Awards — and in 1998 she was selected as a finalist for the National Writer's Club Best Long Historical Book Awards. Her novel *With Hope* was chosen by Amazon as one of the best romances of the twentieth century.

After retiring as a news reporter and book-keeper in 1978, she began her career as a novelist with the publication of *Love and Cherish.* She lives in Clear Lake, Iowa. You

can visit her website at www.dorothygarlock
.com.

The employees of Thorndike Press hope you have enjoyed this Large Print book. All our Thorndike, Wheeler, and Kennebec Large Print titles are designed for easy reading, and all our books are made to last. Other Thorndike Press Large Print books are available at your library, through selected bookstores, or directly from us.

For information about titles, please call:
(800) 223-1244

or visit our Web site at:
http://gale.cengage.com/thorndike

To share your comments, please write:
Publisher
Thorndike Press
10 Water St., Suite 310
Waterville, ME 04901

CHAPTER TWO

"I done told you I weren't drinkin'!"

Even from where Olivia sat, ten feet from the jail cell that held Sylvester Eddings, she could tell that he was lying; the unmistakable scent of alcohol wafted across the room, strong enough to cut through the aroma of a freshly brewed pot of coffee. Sylvester leaned awkwardly against the cell's steel bars, looking as if he could collapse at any moment. In his midfifties, he appeared older, aged by his love of drinking; white whiskers peppered his bloated cheeks and his eyes were wet and bloodshot. His shirt was stained and wrinkled, likely worn for days.

"I ain't touched the stuff!" he insisted.

"If you haven't been drinking, you mind telling me how your truck ended up hitting that telephone pole?"

Huck Perkins leaned back in his chair, his feet up on his desk, flipping through the forbid, he was killed in action, Olivia would never have been able to forgive herself.

Both fear and guilt had made her accept his proposal. And now, just as with Billy's declaration of love, it was too late for her to take her words back.

It wasn't until Olivia was standing out in front of the hardware store, her head still spinning, that she thought of the one question she should have asked herself when Billy proposed, but hadn't. She was watching Billy head back to the bank, walking down the sidewalk with a spring in his step, talking with every person he passed, thrilled that she'd agreed to become his wife, his ring circling her finger, when it hit her like a punch to the stomach.

Do you love him?

Olivia hated to imagine what Billy would think if he could see her face now.

have a well-off life. In short, Billy was exactly the sort of man most women wanted for a husband. Still, questions filled Olivia's head.

Am I ready to get married?

Do I want to?

No matter what I choose to do, what will my mother and father say?

From the change in Billy's features, Olivia knew that her doubts were obvious. He looked deflated, as if every one of the fears that had plagued him for so many years had suddenly been proven true. His hand slid from hers.

"It's all right, Olivia," he said as he struggled to smile. "It wasn't fair of me to ask you like this. I shouldn't have —"

"Yes," she blurted, the words jumping from her mouth, cutting him off.

"What?" Billy asked as shock raced across his face, a flicker of hope rekindling in his eyes. "What did you say?"

Olivia's heart raced. Her words had surprised even her. "Yes," she repeated, her throat dry. "I'll . . . I'll marry you . . ."

Faster than a jackrabbit, Billy jumped to his feet and pulled Olivia into his arms. But then, just as quickly as he'd grabbed her, he let her go, so excited that he couldn't stand still. He raised his arms toward the rafters

31

high above.

"Yes!" he shouted, beaming brighter than the spring sun. "Oh, Olivia! You've made me the happiest man in the world!"

Olivia returned Billy's smile, but it was a struggle to maintain it. She still couldn't believe what she'd done. She'd always imagined that she would be married someday, that someone would enter her life, sweep her off her feet, and capture her heart, but she had never considered Billy to be that man. Now, unbelievably, she had promised herself to him. Slowly, it began to dawn on her why.

I don't want to hurt him . . .

When she thought back on all the years they'd been friends, of all that they had shared, Olivia knew that Billy had been right to be fearful of admitting his feelings. Once he'd revealed them, they could never be taken back. Things between them could never be the same. It had been a huge risk. So while Olivia had plenty of good reasons to say "no" or to ask for more time to think about it, when she understood how much hurt her rejection would cause him, she couldn't bear to go through with it. To turn him down now, just before he shipped off for training, would have devastated him. If something had happened to Billy, if, God